Sister Eve and the Blue Nun

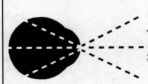

This Large Print Book carries the
Seal of Approval of N.A.V.H.

A DIVINE PRIVATE DETECTIVE AGENCY
MYSTERY, BOOK 3

SISTER EVE AND THE BLUE NUN

LYNNE HINTON

THORNDIKE PRESS

A part of Gale, Cengage Learning

GALE
CENGAGE Learning·

Farmington Hills, Mich • San Francisco • New York • Waterville, Maine
Meriden, Conn • Mason, Ohio • Chicago

GALE
CENGAGE Learning®

Thorndike Press® Large Print Christian Mystery.
The text of this Large Print edition is unabridged.
Other aspects of the book may vary from the original edition.
Set in 16 pt. Plantin.

LIBRARY OF CONGRESS CATALOGING-IN-PUBLICATION DATA

Names: Hinton, Lynne, author.
Title: Sister Eve and the Blue Nun / by Lynne Hinton.
Description: Large print edition. | Waterville, Maine : Thorndike Press, 2016. |
  Series: A Divine Private Detective Agency mystery | Series: Thorndike Press large
  print Christian mystery
Identifiers: LCCN 2016015597| ISBN 9781410491039 (hardcover) | ISBN 141049103X
  (hardcover)
Subjects: LCSH: Nuns—Fiction. | Women private investigators—Fiction. |
  Murder—Investigation—Fiction. | Conceptionists—Fiction. | Large type books. |
  GSAFD: Mystery fiction.
Classification: LCC PS3558.I457 S56 2016b | DDC 813/.54—dc23
LC record available at https://lccn.loc.gov/2016015597

Published in 2016 by arrangement with Thomas Nelson, Inc., a division of HarperCollins Publishing, Inc.

Printed in Mexico
1 2 3 4 5 6 7 20 19 18 17 16

*For Kelly Middlesworth and
my friends at Heartland Hospice.
Thank you for your many
acts of kindness.
I am honored to have worked with you all.*

ONE

The tea had arrived on a simple wooden tray and was left outside Dr. Kelly Middlesworth's room without a note or card but announced by a soft knock. The young woman now stood inside with the answered door held only partially open. She was wearing her nightgown and robe, having changed for the evening, and was hiding behind the door, assuming her night attire would be disconcerting for the monks.

One of the residents at the monastery, after all, was who she expected to see. It would be Father Oliver, she thought, or Brother Gary, who earlier in the week had brought her clean towels and a blanket; the youngest of them could never quite look her in the eye.

More than anybody else, however, Kelly expected, or rather hoped, it would be her sibling, Brother Anthony, who knocked so late. She knew he would still be observing

7

the evening silence, but she hoped he would stop by and at least demonstrate an effort to make amends for the argument they'd had earlier at dinner. She hated that things were left as they were and she knew she was to blame, but she still hoped he would make the first move and come around to offer his forgiveness.

It had been strategy on her part to wait until the last minute to tell him, knowing that after dinner he was required to go to the service of Adoration of the Blessed Sacrament at seven, followed by compline at seven thirty. Once those services in the monastery chapel had been completed, she knew the monks would enter into Grand Silence, which meant he would be unable to speak to anyone until after breakfast, and by that time it would be too late. She would have already made her presentation; she would have already made his discovery public.

The truth was that she had broken her promise not to tell days before, right after he had shown her the discovery, by calling a colleague at the university to tell him of the unusual finding. She had spoken to Professor Peter Pierce five or six times in the last four days, only to find out during the last conversation that he had done some checking and had been given an amount, the real value of the discovered treasure.

When she leaned forward, getting a better look outside the door, she glanced to her right, noticing the tray sitting on the small table that was situated between the two hard-backed chairs in front of the window that looked out onto the parking lot. There was a simple pot and one cup on a saucer, a small spoon, and a little pitcher of honey, the only thing she liked in her tea. There were also two strings with tiny pieces of paper attached at the ends and hanging from the pot, tea bags, green tea or mint, she assumed, two of the favorites that she and Anthony enjoyed together every evening just after dinner when she came to visit him at the monastery. She smiled, understanding that the tea was a way for Anthony to say that everything really was all right between them. It was the perfect peace offering.

The young professor stepped out of her room to pick up the tray, and when she did she saw several additional cars parked in front of the long building that made up the guest quarters where she stayed. She guessed others had arrived for the conference. She knew some of the attendees had gotten to the monastery earlier in the day;

she had even met a few, mostly professorial types, but also a few nonacademics, including Sister Eve, a local nun who came roaring up to the monastery grounds around lunchtime on a motorcycle.

A close friend of Kelly's brother, Eve was a colleague she had met before who had apparently left the community, according to Anthony, and was not wearing the traditional habit when they met. The two women had spoken previously on a number of occasions about their interest in and devotion to Sister Maria de Jesus de Agreda, and Sister Eve had seemed quite excited about the keynote address Dr. Middlesworth was scheduled to make at the early-morning session. She had even expressed her hopefulness that this conference about the venerated nun would finally bring news that progress had been made in Sister Maria's beatification process.

Of course, Kelly knew there was no such actual news of forward progress in the beatification process to share, but she hadn't told the nun. And with the news of Anthony's discovery that she was planning to introduce at her keynote, Dr. Middlesworth was actually just as hopeful that what they all wanted might finally come to pass.

She picked up the tray and turned back to

reenter her room but glanced around once more at the parked cars, wondering if Dr. Pierce had left Austin, if he was somewhere close to New Mexico. In their last conversation he had said that he was taking a late flight out of Texas to Albuquerque, without his wife, Kelly recalled him saying, and was not scheduled to arrive until sometime around midnight. He had promised to meet her first thing the following morning; he would call and then stop by her room, and that way she could show him the pages before she gave her address.

She couldn't help herself and smiled, thinking about her colleague, thinking about how thrilled he was to hear about the papers, how he'd promised to host a great celebration party when they returned to the university, and how he had also shared the news that he was now ready to file for divorce. Kelly couldn't decide what made her happier, the discovery of writings by Sister Maria or that she was finally going to be able to marry the man she loved.

She felt her face flush with excitement as she turned to walk back inside and then stopped just as she entered, sticking out her right foot behind her to close the door. She walked all the way inside the small room and set the tray next to her laptop computer on the desk. When she did so, she pushed aside a stack of books, which consequently slid down, ultimately exposing the thick, unmarked brown envelope that had been placed underneath them.

Kelly looked first at the envelope and then back at the door, thinking about locking it, and then remembered that there were no locks on the doors at the abbey. She sighed, tugged her long, curly brown hair behind her ears, turned back to the desk, and lifted the lid off the teapot to make sure the bags were steeping. As she sat in the chair by the desk, she thought once again about her brother and particularly the argument they'd had in the dining room earlier that evening.

She recalled how Anthony had slammed down his dinner tray when she explained her plan to share the news in her keynote address, how he stormed out after she confessed to him that she had already told someone else. She thought about the awkwardness that remained in the dining room and how she sat alone at the table while the others sitting near her stopped talking and watched until she finally got up from her seat, left the main house, and hurried back to her room. It had been terribly embarrassing, and as she glanced at her watch, realizing it had been several hours since dinner, she could only hope that none of those at the evening meal would bring up what happened at her all-important morning presentation.

She breathed out a long breath, knowing that she needed to make things right with her brother. Even Peter had mentioned that she should try to make amends when she told him earlier about the argument, and she hoped that the tea meant Anthony had forgiven her. She reached for the envelope and pulled out the papers to examine them once again, still in shock that she had such a thing in her possession. It was hard to believe that Anthony had just happened upon something so valuable while visiting the little church south of Albuquerque. His discovery consisted of pages from the 1600s written by Sister Maria de Jesus de Agreda during an event of bilocation with the Jumano Indians. Kelly put the writings down and picked up the pot and poured the tea, still in disbelief that Anthony had kept the historical and religious artifact for her, hid the writings under his robe, and brought them back to the abbey to give to her when she arrived. She took a few sips of her brother's gift, recalling how he'd acted when he handed the pages to her, how clumsy and sweet he was, making her promise that she wouldn't tell anyone, explaining that he had to give the writings to Father Oliver, but because of their bond and her passion, he wanted her to see them first.

When she heard the door open, she jerked up, startled, almost spilling her tea and ruining the pages. She put down the cup, noticing as she did a slight sense of vertigo. When she looked away from the desk and over to the door, she was unable to make out who was coming in. Her vision had become blurred and her heart rate quickened. As the person entered and then closed the door, she assumed it was Anthony, assumed her brother had decided to reunite with her, but with the blurred vision she couldn't tell. She suddenly felt sick to her stomach, nauseous and dizzy as she fought for her next breath.

She watched without speaking as the person who had entered her room took a seat on the twin-sized bed that was situated beside the desk. She tried calling out, thinking that her brother would surely help, thinking that he would do something, but as she spoke his name, he never moved in her direction. Rather, he just sat and watched her as she grabbed her throat, trying to breathe. She pushed aside the tray on the desk, the teapot, cup, and saucer sliding across the tray but not falling off, searching for her phone to make an emergency call as she continued to struggle to breathe.

"It's easier if you just relax," the voice spoke. "It can be like a vision, really." There was a pause. "You know all about those, right?"

The young professor felt her legs weaken as she slid off the chair, dropping to the floor. She never saw the night visitor get up from the bed and move in her direction, but as she lay on the floor, looking up, she thought she saw a cape, a blue one, as she watched the figure standing over her, the face veiled, gloved hands moving across the desk until they stopped at the brown envelope. She tried to cry out as the person placed the pages back inside the envelope and stood over her holding it. She felt her throat tighten and was unable to make even a slight sound as the person knelt down beside her.

"May our Lady in Blue bring you comfort," the voice whispered, and then she was alone.

The door opened, and Kelly thought she felt a brush of clothing lightly touch her on the cheek a second before it closed. Her eyes fell shut just as the darkness covered her, just as she took her final breath.

Two

Eve closed her eyes and clasped her hands with the rosary looped around her fingers. She had not been able to sleep and had walked over to the chapel to pray. It was dark and quiet in the narrow room, the only light coming from the small votive candles burning at the prayer station on the east side and from the large candle burning inside the red glass cylinder next to the altar of repose where the reserve sacrament was kept. The shadows danced across the wall, filling the space around the Benedictine nun standing in front of the second pew.

She pulled out the long wooden kneeler and placed it in front of her before slowly lowering herself onto it. Her head was covered but not with her veil. She was not in her habit. Instead, Eve was wearing what had become her new work attire since leaving the abbey, her private detective uniform: jeans and a long-sleeved flannel shirt, a gray hoodie that supplied the covering for her head, her old cowboy boots, a leather belt, and a jacket. In actuality, since she was still a nun, she could in good faith wear the long tunic and veil. She still had it back at her father's home, but when she was packing for the weekend, it somehow didn't feel right to wear it when she knew she would be at the monastery only for a two-day conference. She had not planned to stay, not yet, anyway. She was still in the period of time dedicated to her discernment. And presently, things were even harder than they had ever been.

Eve had talked to Father Oliver several times since moving back to Madrid, had taken another leave of absence since her father's surgical amputation, and then was given another couple of weeks before a decision had to be made. She was going to have to choose which path she wanted to take: being a private detective with her father, Captain Jackson Divine, or keeping her vows and remaining a Benedictine nun.

However, now that the monastery no longer housed the women, the result of a decree handed down by the New Mexico diocese months prior to this return visit, if she decided to put the habit back on, Eve wouldn't be making a decision just to return to the religious life, she would be making a decision also to leave her beloved home state of New Mexico. This was the reason she was given more time for discernment. If she kept her vows, she would have to transfer to another Benedictine convent. She would not be able to stay in Pecos as a nun even if she wanted to. This decision carried more weight than ever.

"It's no good," she said, shaking her head and rising. "I can't sleep and I can't pray."

Even as she tried to call out the familiar words, her mind kept racing, thinking about the cases she had solved with her father, how much she enjoyed the detective work, and thinking about the other sisters who had left the order, of how lonesome it felt without them there. A couple of the women, Sister Vivian and Sister Jeanne, had left the religious life altogether, angry with the decision that forced their departure. And the rest of the nuns had chosen other convents, moved away, the new housing at the monastery originally built for them now turned into guest quarters.

It was all so confusing and overwhelming. She hadn't been sure she wanted to remain in the religious life as a nun, and now, even before she was prepared to make her decision, she was having to face this terrible fate handed to the sisters in her own community. "Maybe this is the sign I was looking for," she said out loud. "Maybe this is more than enough to let me know that I should revoke my vows."

Eve got up from the kneeling bench and sat on the pew, remembering the meeting Father Oliver had called with members of the monastery, herself included. She recalled his words: "Our great experiment of men and women living together, being in community together, is over. The archbishop has made his ruling; the nuns have to go."

"But it's not just an experiment," one of the women had contested. "This worked. We worked."

Father Oliver had given no response.

"Can't you say something? Can't we fight this?" Eve had demanded.

"They didn't ask for my opinion any more than they asked for yours," he had explained to the monks and the nuns. "We cannot fight. We must only obey. It is in our vows to do so."

Eve leaned back, placing the rosary in the front pocket of her shirt, and looked around the chapel where she had prayed and sung and received Communion for almost all of her adult life. It was the center of community worship at Pecos, just like the dining hall had been the center of community life. It was true, she thought; she missed that part of her vocational life. She missed living in community, missed being with other men and women devoted to the Christian practice, devoted to the Benedictine rule, devoted to living and serving together, but she also realized that she didn't miss it enough to be excited about joining a new convent.

She knew that she wasn't twenty years old any longer, and the thought of starting over, meeting new nuns, working with a new mother superior, none of that was appealing to Sister Evangeline. She knew that it had been hard just getting used to her father again, living with him, and she couldn't imagine starting over with a group of women she didn't know. She also knew that it was going to be very difficult for her to accept the decision of the diocese with devout submission like the others. She had written a letter to the archbishop to complain, and whenever she thought about it, the anger took over. She sighed; it was going to be a long night, she guessed, without sleep and without being able to pray.

Still, even with all that she felt — the sadness, the disappointment — she was glad to be back in Pecos, glad to be able to attend

the conference on Sister Maria de Jesus de
Agreda, one of Eve's favorite nuns, one she
favored for her courage and her willingness
to stand up to those who questioned her
religious gifts, her calling. She hoped there
would be new information about the faithful nun who had demonstrated the gift of
bilocation, showing up in Spain and to the
Jumano Indians in New Mexico at the same
time. And Eve was looking forward to hearing the speakers, especially the young female
professor from Austin, Texas, the sister of
Brother Anthony, one of Eve's closest
friends at the abbey.

Anthony had talked about Dr. Kelly
Middlesworth for years, told Eve about his
little sister: how smart she was when she
started to work on her PhD; how devoted
she was to Sister Maria; how she had traveled to Spain, to Agreda, to write her dis-
sertation from the place where the nun had
served and lived over four hundred years
ago; how close Kelly and Anthony were,
always writing each other, calling. Eve
remembered meeting her when the professor had come to the monastery on previous
occasions, and she had always thought of
her as quiet and studious, much like Anthony. But as she sat in the chapel, thinking
about things, she realized that this time,

having seen her earlier in the day, the young scholar had appeared to be a completely different woman.

Talkative and animated when they ran into each other, the professor had seemed excited about being in Pecos and giving the first speech of the conference. She had even hinted at some exciting news that would she would share in the keynote address, but when Eve had pressed for more, pressed for a story that she hoped might finally convince the Vatican to complete Maria's beatification process, Anthony's sister had only smiled and shrugged, clearly unwilling to say anything until the presentation scheduled for the following morning.

Eve thought about Kelly and how she physically resembled Anthony with the curly brown hair and blue eyes, the freckles; how they even shared some of the same mannerisms, rubbing their chins before they spoke, covering their mouths when they laughed, as if somehow laughter was meant to be hidden; and while thinking about the two, she recalled the disagreement she had witnessed between the siblings earlier that evening at dinner.

She was sitting at a table close by with a couple of monks, and they all noticed the brother and sister arguing. At first it just seemed petty, insignificant, but quickly the volume rose and Eve heard some of the argument in which Anthony accused his sister of being selfish and of breaking a promise she had made. When Kelly tried to calm him down, tried to explain, clearly embarrassed by the situation, it seemed that nothing she could say helped matters, and the confrontation ended only when Anthony stormed out of the dining hall.

Eve had wanted to comfort her friend, wanted to check on Anthony, but Father Oliver had gotten up first, and she was sure he had gone after the monk to offer guidance or comfort. Not long after that departure, Kelly left as well, and neither of them had been seen in any of the public areas since mealtime.

Later, when the service of Adoration of the Blessed Sacrament had started, Anthony was not in the chapel, and he had not attended compline either. Eve had gone searching for him everywhere she thought he might be, including in the library and the monks' quarters, but he was nowhere to be found. Then, just before coming to the chapel, sometime after nine or ten o'clock, she had walked by the guest rooms and noticed that in the first room, the one she knew Kelly was in, the light was on.

Thinking that the professor might still be up, Eve had knocked on the door lightly, hoping to hear that the two siblings had worked things out, but there had been no response. So Eve had come to the chapel to pray and hoped that she would find Anthony before the conference started the following morning and that he would break Grand Silence so she could find out what had happened and perhaps know how to help. She did, after all, know all about conflict with a sibling. Dorisanne, her younger sister, knew how to push every button Eve had.

She slid down a bit on the pew and bowed her head, clasping her hands together, trying once again to do what she had come there to do.

"I pray for Brother Anthony," she said out loud, "and his sister, Kelly."

"It's too late for prayers," was what she heard just as she ended her prayer. And then came a sentence that caused the nun to turn quickly to see who had entered the chapel.

"She's dead," was what came next.

THREE

Sister Eve scrambled from her seat, turning to the chapel doors behind her. Brother Anthony was standing at the last pew. His head was in his hands, and he stumbled forward in the aisle, falling to his knees. Eve ran to him.

"What's happened?" she asked her friend, dropping beside him. "What do you mean, she's dead? Have you called 911?"

The monk leaned into Eve and began to cry. She held him as they both sat on the chapel floor.

"Hail Mary, full of grace —" she began to recite as he sobbed into her shoulder.

"It's too late," he said, interrupting her. "It's too late for that."

"Anthony, what's wrong?" Eve faced her friend, trying to look him in the eye. "What happened to Kelly?"

He held up his face, his eyes filled with tears, and shook his head. "She's dead," he said again.

"How do you know this?" Eve asked. "Did she fall? Was there some accident?" She began trying to think of all the ways the young woman might have died. "Is she sick?" she asked, still not believing that his sister was dead.

Brother Anthony kept shaking his head. "I did it. I've done this," he said, his voice breaking.

"What have you done? You couldn't have killed Kelly," Eve responded. She clasped his chin, stopping him from shaking his head back and forth. "Anthony, look at me; tell me what has happened."

He didn't answer.

"Is she in her room?" Eve asked, prompting her friend. "Did you see her in her room?"

He nodded.

Eve started to stand. "Let's go there," she said. "Maybe she's not dead. Maybe I can help."

Anthony pulled on the sleeve of her jacket, yanking her back down beside him. "No," he answered forcefully. "Not yet. Not until I tell you."

Eve nodded and waited. She had never seen her friend in such distress. She knew she needed to hear what he had to tell her, even though she wanted to run to the guest room to check on the young woman.

The two sat in silence. There were only a few candles still burning at the prayer station, and it had grown darker in the chapel than it had been when Eve first arrived. She was having a difficult time seeing the monk who sat beside her.

"We argued," he said, and Eve nodded in agreement. She had, after all, witnessed the exchange at dinner.

"I . . . I found something."

Eve didn't respond.

"I made her promise that she wouldn't tell anyone. I needed to show it to Father Oliver first, and she promised."

Eve felt him slump a bit. She was leaning against the side of the pew, resting her back but still keeping one arm around him.

He was shaking his head. "Only, she told. I don't know who or how many people she told, but she told, and now someone's killed her."

Eve couldn't believe the news. Not only was his sister dead, the young, beautiful, smart Kelly Middlesworth, but now he was saying that she had been murdered.

"How do you know this?" she asked, her head reeling with the information.

"I just came from there. I was just in her

room. The pages are gone and she's dead."
He slid farther down, dropping his face into
his hands. "It's my fault. I never should have
given them to her. It's all my fault and now
she's dead."

Eve reached over and pulled his hands
away from his face. "Anthony, how do you
know for sure? I need to go to her. I need
to check to see if she's really dead."

He grabbed her hands. "She's dead.
There's no pulse. There's no breath. I
checked. I checked over and over. She's
dead."

Eve looked at her watch as he held on to
her hands. She could tell the time because
the hours on the face of her watch stayed lit
in the dark. It was after midnight. She
pulled her hands away from his and touched
his face, studying his eyes. She didn't ask,
but she wondered where Anthony had been
all evening, wondered why he had gone to
his sister's room so late, wondered how
Kelly had been killed and why, if indeed she
had been murdered. This was all just too
much to believe.

"Tell me what happened," she said. "Tell
me why you went there."

"I wanted to tell her that I forgave her,
that I understood why she did what she did
and that I forgave her."

"Why? What did she do?" Eve wanted to know. "Why did you need to forgive her?"

Anthony shook his head. "I can't tell . . . It's something I found and shouldn't have taken in the first place. I was wrong to take them. I know that now. Father Oliver said not to tell anyone else and that we'd just take them back, and that's what I was going to tell her. I was going to tell her that I needed the pages back and that she was just going to have to wait until we went through the proper channels and that she'd be the first to have access to them later if we got them again, but that we had to take them back."

He was rambling, and Eve was having difficulty following what he was saying. "So, this thing, these pages, Kelly had them in her possession?"

He nodded. "I gave them to her when she first arrived.

"Last week," he added and then smiled. "She was so happy." He looked at Eve. "I really made her happy."

Eve smiled in return. "But she wasn't supposed to tell anyone about them?"

He nodded again. "I just wanted to give her some time with them alone, let her enjoy this revelation all by herself, as one of the first people to know about it." He reached up and pounded his forehead with his fist. "But I was wrong to do it, and Father Oliver said I was and that I needed to get them so that we could take them back. But she had already told people and she was going to tell everybody at the presentation tomorrow." He stopped and looked at Eve. "The conference," he said. "What will we do about the conference? I don't know what to do."

"Anthony . . ."

He was rocking back and forth, both hands now clenched and pushed against his forehead. "What have I done? What have I done?" he kept asking as he continued to rock.

"Anthony." Eve tried to get his attention once again. She pulled at his arms, but he was too strong. "Anthony, listen to me!" she shouted.

"I've killed her . . . I made this happen . . . It's my fault . . . I've killed Kelly," he repeated over and over.

"Anthony, you didn't kill her. Let's go to her room and let me see what has happened. We'll make this right, I promise," Eve said, her hands still on his arms. "Let's just go to her room."

"I can't go back there." He was shaking his head. "I can't go back."

31

"Okay, you stay here," Eve instructed him. "I'll go to her room and see for myself. I'll call an ambulance and the police. I'll help make this right."

He stopped rocking and dropped his hands from his face, looking Eve in the eye. "It's too late. You can't make this right. It's too late."

FOUR

Eve was able to pull herself away from Anthony, who promised he would wait for her in the chapel, and she ran as fast as she could all the way to the guest quarters and to the room where she knew the young professor was staying. She was winded when she arrived at the door, conscious that she wasn't in the greatest shape. She bent down, grabbing her sides, trying to catch her breath.

There was no one around that part of the monastery as far as she could see. It was late, and the New Mexico night sky was dotted with bright stars and a full moon. It was chilly too, even though it had been seasonably mild for the high desert winter. Eve could hear coyotes in the distance, three, maybe four, a pack, she couldn't tell for sure, but the cries were familiar to the nun, and she wondered how far away the animals were from the Pecos abbey.

33

She stood up, breathing normally, and leaned in, placing her ear to the door, trying to hear if there was any noise coming from the small guest room at the end of the quarters that had been built with the intention of being the residence of the nuns — a place away from the monastery proper that Father Oliver had hoped would change the archbishop's mind about making the nuns leave. In the end it didn't sway the leaders of the diocese, and the residences became the guest quarters.

Eve felt her heart rate quicken, knowing that it had nothing to do with her run from the chapel but was because she didn't know what she was about to find in the guest room occupied by the religion professor. There was nothing coming from inside, no sounds of any kind as, slowly, she reached for the doorknob, turned it, and opened the door.

The overhead light was burning inside, and when Eve looked in she immediately saw the young woman lying near the center of room, between the bed and the small wooden desk. She was on her right side, one arm raised above her head, the other resting on her chest; her legs were bent at the knees, one in front of the other. She was wearing a robe, probably her nightgown underneath, Eve assumed, with her pale white feet stuck beneath the chair that was pulled away from the desk as if she had been sitting there at one time. Eve entered the room and then shut the door behind her, aware that she should not touch anything but also knowing that she needed to make sure Kelly was really dead. She had to feel for a pulse, had to make sure the young woman couldn't be helped. Eve walked over and knelt down by the victim, placing her fore and middle fingers on the woman's neck, and waited. She held her breath, trying to listen for a heartbeat, trying to will the young woman back to life. But there was no pulse. Anthony was right. His sister was dead. Quickly, Eve made the sign of the cross over the woman, bowed, closed her eyes, and said a quick prayer for the soul of Kelly Middlesworth.

Eve stood with plans to search for a phone, knowing that she must call the police, but she couldn't help herself. She didn't move, and instead of trying to find a phone, she glanced around, trying to take and keep a mental picture of everything in the room. She had been working with her dad as a private detective for only a few months, but there were some lessons she had learned well.

From wall to wall she studied everything. The narrow bed by the desk was covered with a thick brown comforter that appeared ruffled, not as if someone had slept under it recently, but rather as if someone had been sitting on top of it. There were two pillows, both pushed against the headboard and situated one in front of the other, giving the appearance that they had been placed that way to be leaned against and not slept upon. A blanket was folded and lying across the end of the bed. The room was warm, the heaters still on and working in all the buildings of the monastery for the late winter season. A small crucifix hung on the wall over the bed, and a thin pair of tan curtains were closed over the only window in the room.

On top of the desk next to the bed were five books, hardbacks, religious in nature, she thought, all somehow pertinent to Dr. Middlesworth's studies. Eve recognized the spine of one, a copy of *The Mystical City of God,* the book written by Sister Maria in the 1600s, a book the nun claimed had been given to her word for word by the Virgin Mary. The others appeared to be books about the Spanish sister, even a novel written about the appearance of the nun to the Indians in New Mexico. Eve thought she had read that one, suggested to her by one of the monks after she had first become interested in the woman known as the Lady in Blue.

She noticed the tray, the small teapot, the cup and saucer, and a small pitcher with what looked like honey, all items that she recognized from the kitchen at the monastery. She saw a legal pad with scribbled notes; several manila folders; a computer bag; a thin binder, closed, white; and a small glass with several pens and pencils inside. That was all Eve could see on top of the desk. A long gray sweater hung on the back of the chair, and a trash can stood near the bathroom with several pieces of rumpled paper inside. A lady's navy-blue skirt and jacket, along with a pink silk blouse, hung on the outside of the closet, the hooks of the hangers placed over the top of the door, which was partially open.

Eve looked around slowly as she took notes in her mind of everything she was seeing. Her father, Captain Jackson Divine, had taught her how to pay attention to details when he was in the police force and she was still a young girl. He said that entering a person's house or private room was always an opportunity to learn about that person, that what a person owned and how they kept their personal items spoke volumes about who that person was, which was why he always made Eve and her sister, Doris-anne, keep clean rooms. He demanded neatness and tidiness from his children so that even if these were not traits they actually valued, they would always give the appearance of being that way.

Eve glanced into the bathroom without moving from where she stood at the desk. She could see a towel hanging on the shower curtain rod and toiletries lining the windowsill. A mat lay on the floor next to the tub; the light was on, and everything seemed to be in place, even though she was not able to see the area around the sink, the area just behind the door.

Clearly, Eve thought, there had been no struggle that caused young Kelly Middles-worth to die. The two rooms gave the appearance of an occupant who had showered without incident, sat at the desk, and then lay on the bed to think or more than likely read, and who was planning to dress up the following day in a newly pressed navy-blue business suit. Nowhere in the room that she could see was there evidence of foul play, nothing out of order except, of course, for the dead woman who still lay at her feet.

Eve looked down again at Anthony's

sister. She was pale, like the monk, and her curly hair spilled around her. Her eyes were closed and there was a slight lift to her lips, almost but not quite a smile, as if she had found a measure of contentment before she passed, as if she had died at peace. She took one last glance across the room that the woman had occupied for almost a week before her death, and the first thing that caught her eye this time was the tray and the pot and the cup, still half full.

She took in a breath and made the sign of the cross once again, knowing that she was about to do something she shouldn't really do, then she yanked the sleeve of her hoodie over the fingers of her right hand to prevent leaving prints, leaned forward, and reached for the cup. Slowly, she wrapped her hand around it and brought it to her nose, getting a good whiff of its contents, smelling a slight almond aroma. She was just about to put the cup back where it had been when suddenly the door flew open, startling her, causing her to drop the cup, which immediately fell to the floor, breaking into pieces.

FIVE

"What are you doing?" Father Oliver asked as he moved into the room, closing the door behind him. "You shouldn't be here, Sister." He looked away from Eve and then down to the floor, discovering the dead woman near the bed. He immediately made the sign of the cross and dropped to his knees beside her. He felt her neck for a pulse and then bowed to pray.

Eve knelt down next to the desk to examine the mess she had made. "I ran into Anthony in the chapel. He told me that he had come by and found his" — she stopped, turning her gaze to the abbot beside the body, near where she was kneeling — "found her dead."

Father Oliver was still praying as Eve considered what she should do with the broken shards and the tea that had spilled on the desk chair and the floor around it. She saw all of the pieces scattered around her, knowing that she had broken what likely had been the cup the young woman had been drinking from. She realized that she had mishandled a very important piece of evidence in the investigation of Kelly's death, and now that the accident had happened, Eve wasn't sure whether to leave everything as it was or clean it up.

Maybe I should call the Captain, she thought, knowing that he would surely be able to tell her what action she should take. But just as that thought registered, she knew he would not be pleased that she had walked into a crime scene and compromised the investigation, and before he offered advice, she'd have to hear all about the bad decisions she had made.

She shook away the idea, deciding not to make that call.

"How long have you been here?" Father Oliver asked, startling Eve, who was still beside him, kneeling on the floor, trying to figure out what to do.

She stood up, making sure not to touch anything else. "I just got here," she answered. She looked at the clock on the small table next to the bed. "About fifteen minutes ago," she added.

He nodded but didn't move from his position beside the victim.

"What did Anthony tell you?" the vice superior of the abbey asked.

"Just that he had come to her room and found her this way." Eve turned once again to the body. "She's not been dead long," she said, still finding it difficult to believe that Anthony's little sister was dead.

Father Oliver didn't respond, but it was easy to see the question he had on his mind. *How long has she been dead?* That's what Eve knew he wanted to ask.

"She's still warm," Eve explained. "Like the tea, actually." And she turned her attention once again to the spill around her, knowing she was going to be lectured by the police for what she had done. She thought again about the strange smell she had sensed before the monk entered the room but decided not to share her findings.

"Do you have any idea what might have happened?" he asked. "Did she choke on something perhaps? Was it a heart attack?" He was staring at the body.

"I don't know," she responded, recalling Anthony's rambling about it being a murder, about having given her something that would have led to a homicide.

"What else did Anthony tell you?" he wanted to know.

And Eve suddenly remembered the monk

42

had said that Father Oliver knew what he had found and given to Kelly, pages of some kind, he had said, and that his superior knew about what had transpired between the two siblings.

"He told me why they argued at dinner," she replied, hoping Father Oliver would share what he knew.

Father Oliver only nodded and turned away, the distress written on his face.

She continued, hoping to hear something from him that might lend an explanation to what had happened. "He said he told you what he had found and that he planned to tell his sister what you had instructed them to do. He believes someone murdered her before he could get to her and take back whatever it was he had given her."

"He told you that he thought she was murdered?" Father Oliver asked, without offering up any information about what he knew. He stood and faced Eve.

She nodded. "He thinks someone she told about this discovery came to her room tonight and killed her."

Father Oliver glanced over Eve's shoulder to the desk. She watched as his eyes searched across Kelly's possessions.

"Did you find anything here?" he asked, turning his attention back to the nun.

She shrugged. "Nothing out of the ordinary," she answered. "But then I'm not sure I know what it is that I should be looking for."

There was a pause.

"Anthony told you what he found, what Kelly had," Eve remarked, watching him closely, hoping for a revelation.

"I have not seen these pages that he said he discovered. I only learned about them tonight after dinner. I've been to the services and then to my room. I don't know where they were kept. So I wouldn't know what to look for either, what she kept them in or where."

Eve glanced over at the desk, feeling the urge to dig through the pile of books, open drawers, and look under the mattress. She considered asking the abbot to assist her, but she knew she would compromise the scene even more if she started moving things around. And she still didn't know what she would be searching for.

"Is this discovery important enough to cause someone to commit murder?"

Father Oliver didn't answer at first. He dropped his shoulders and lowered his gaze. "Like I said, I never saw what he claimed to have found."

"Yes, but you have an opinion. You know

what this discovery was. Is it really that significant?"

He hesitated and then looked back at Eve. "I can't say for sure, but yes, if Anthony is right, if what he says is true and what he unearthed is really what he and Kelly thought it was, and I suppose if the wrong people were to find out about it . . ." He paused again, appeared to consider the question once more, and then rubbed his forehead.

He shook his head. "I don't really know," he confessed. "But it might not be murder, though, right?" he asked. "Surely something else could have happened."

Eve didn't respond.

He continued, "We don't really know anything that occurred in this room." It was clear he was trying to convince himself of something.

Eve shrugged. "Kelly was in excellent physical shape as far as I could tell. She was young, a marathon runner from what Anthony told me, gave up meat when she turned twenty. She hadn't mentioned any symptoms of a heart problem or displayed any behaviors that could be linked to a disease or a sudden death."

"But her death, it could be of natural causes?" he asked, sounding almost desperate, Eve thought.

"I guess so," she replied. "The cause of death will be determined in an autopsy, which will have to be conducted because this is such an unlikely death."

"Maybe she had a drug overdose or an allergic reaction to something."

Eve studied the man. Something was bugging her about his questions, about how he'd been acting since arriving at the guest room.

"There's no blood, so she wasn't shot or stabbed, right?" He was sliding his hands through his thin white hair.

Eve shook her head. "No blood."

"So maybe it's not murder, maybe it's something natural that happened. Maybe it was her time and God's angels came to bring her to her eternal rest."

Eve didn't respond but only watched the abbot as he searched for some action other than homicide that had caused the young professor's death.

"What is it?" he asked, feeling the nun's stare.

"You didn't knock," she said.

He stood watching as Eve tried putting things together.

"When you arrived here, you opened the door without knocking, and you didn't seem at all surprised that Kelly is dead."

"If it was murder," he said softly, not responding to the statements Eve had made, "then how do you think she was killed?"

Eve watched him as he waited for her reply. She looked again at the victim and then at the pot of tea that was still situated on the tray on the dead woman's desk, then back to the abbot, standing by the door.

"Poison," she finally replied, hoping to get answers of her own. "I think Kelly was poisoned."

Father Oliver closed his eyes once more and bowed again to pray.

Six

"Wait," Eve said, interrupting the abbot's prayer. "Tell me, why are you here?" she asked. "It's Grand Silence. It's after midnight and you're visiting a guest, a female guest at that. You walked in without knocking. I don't understand, Father; what made you come to this room?"

Father Oliver walked over and sat on the bed, dropping his head into his hands. He looked tired, weary, and Eve assumed that the new orders handed down and the consequential fallout covered by the local media, the departure of the nuns from the abbey, all friends of his, had all finally taken a toll on the vice superior. Now he would have to deal with this suspicious murder happening on the premises.

"Anthony came to my room to tell me," he reported. "Just now, I assume just after speaking to you in the chapel, he came to my room, woke me, and told me what had

48

happened."

"Just now?" she asked, realizing that Anthony had left the chapel where she had instructed him to stay, and hoping he hadn't disappeared again. "Where is he?"

"He's still there," Father Oliver responded. "He promised he would stay in my room until I got back, and we would return together when the police arrived."

"But you haven't called them yet?" she asked.

He shook his head. "I just wanted to see for myself, see that she was really dead." He paused. "Like you, I guess."

She looked away, understanding the vice superior's meaning. She realized that she should have contacted him first before coming to the guest room.

"Did you call the police?" he asked, pointing out the fact that she had also acted hastily and perhaps inappropriately.

"No, not yet. I wanted to make sure there wasn't something I could do. I wanted to see if what he was saying was true before I called it in."

They watched each other.

"And we came because we both know that once the police show up, we will not be allowed in this room and be able to say proper prayers for the young woman's soul." It sounded like the abbot was seeking justification for their actions.

"And maybe, since we're here, we could search for those pages?" Eve spoke sooner than she wished she had; she wanted to take back the words, but it was too late.

The vice superior shook his head but made no verbal response. He grasped the cross hanging around his neck and asked another question: "How do you know there was poison?"

"What?" Eve responded, surprised by the change of direction in their conversation.

He waited for her answer.

Eve looked at the spilled contents from the cup that had broken. "The tea," she answered. "It smells like cyanide."

The abbot appeared confused.

"I read about it in a case my father was working on. Cyanide often has a certain smell; it's a little like almonds."

"And that's what you smelled in the tea?"

She nodded. "I think it's the only thing that makes sense."

"And they will find this out during an autopsy?" he asked without looking at the nun.

"Yes," she replied.

There was a pause in the conversation, and Eve didn't know what the monk was thinking. She didn't know if he had come to the room for the same reason she had, to check out Anthony's story, to see if there was anything that could be done for the young woman, or if he had believed the story and was here for the reason he said, to pray for Kelly's soul before the police were called and removed the body. Eve wanted to believe the vice superior's explanation but just couldn't shake the feeling that there was something else going on, some reason he was asking questions about poisoning and why he seemed almost reluctant to contact the authorities. Then the obvious crossed her mind.

"She was the opening speaker for the conference," he spoke calmly.

Eve stayed where she was, still standing at the desk, shards of the teacup scattered around her feet, unsure of his direction. "Yes, and she apparently had some interesting news about Sister Maria she planned to share," Eve responded, recalling how the professor had acted when Eve had run into her earlier in the day.

"It was more than interesting," Father Oliver replied. "It was groundbreaking."

Eve waited for more.

Father Oliver dropped his elbows onto his knees and his chin into his hand. "The writings . . ." He paused.

"Yes, what kind of writings?" Eve asked. She leaned closer to him.

"They were writings that were believed to be something from Sister Maria."

"Something found here?" she asked.

"Something transcribed by the people here in New Mexico," he added. "Something she wrote to them."

"The Jumano people?" she asked.

He nodded and then looked over at the nun.

"During one of the periods of her bilocation?" She couldn't believe her ears. A new piece of evidence that the Blue Nun had really been in New Mexico.

"Anthony found them at the pueblo church in Isleta. He was helping with their renovations and he found them." Father Oliver looked away. "I don't know any more about them than that."

Eve turned to the items on the desk, wondering if the pages were anywhere in the stack of books or in the thin white binder, wondering if Brother Anthony had come to Kelly's room to retrieve the pages.

"He found them and hid them." The vice superior shook his head. "It was wrong of him and he knows it. When he confessed the discovery . . ." He stopped. "When he confessed the theft had occurred," he continued, emphasizing the word *theft,* "he said that he had only stolen them to show to Kelly, that he knew what they would mean to his sister, and he was going to let her take a look at them and then report the finding, first to me, and do whatever I instructed him to do with the papers."

It was finally all making sense to Eve, the argument in the dining room, Anthony's rambling confession in the chapel. Anthony knew the trouble he was in even though his intentions had been pure, a brother simply wanting to give his sister a great thrill. *I would likely have done the same thing,* Eve realized as she thought about her sister, Dorisanne, how loyal the two were to each other, even if they were so different, how Eve had raced to Las Vegas to find her, how she'd do just about anything for her sister, how she, too, would love to find something to bring her happiness.

"And if he had come to me first, I would have given the same instruction I gave to him tonight, to take them back to the pueblo church where he stole them."

"Not to the archbishop?" she asked, surprised by the abbot's remark.

"No, these papers belong to the people of the Isleta Pueblo. The Jumano tribe is gone, but the Isleta people are still here, and they are the closest kin to the Indians who were visited by Sister Maria. It was to their priest, their mission church where the Jumanos traveled to ask to be baptized, asked for a Catholic priest to visit them where they lived. The papers belong to them."

Eve knew the story. Most of the nuns and monks in Pecos knew the story. Sister Maria told the Jumano Indians where to go, and before they showed up at the church, the priest had been told about their coming. Later, when Spanish priests arrived at the pueblo, the Isleta priest sent them to the Jumano people. Once they found the tribe, over two thousand Indians were baptized and joined the faith. It was a great miracle and was the last time the revered nun was reported to have spoken to members of the tribe.

"Why did you ask about the poison?" There was still something odd about the questions he had asked earlier.

Father Oliver lowered his face once again. "Anthony was making tea," he answered quietly. "I saw him in the kitchen earlier. He was making a pot of tea, and he placed it on a tray and left the dining area. I think he brought it here."

Seven

Eve felt her legs weaken and she moved to the chair and sat down. "He didn't kill his sister. He wouldn't do this," she said. "I know Anthony. He's not capable of murder."

She glanced up to see Father Oliver's response, but there was none. "He loved Kelly," she added and then turned her attention once again to the dead woman at her feet. "And Anthony would never hurt her."

"Yes, yes, of course," the vice superior responded. "It's just the way he came to me tonight, the things he said."

Eve recalled how Anthony had confessed that he had killed Kelly when they were together earlier in the chapel. She shook her head. "But he didn't do this," she said. "He just thinks he was the reason this happened, that he brought this evil to her." She paused. "He would not murder her."

"Right. I know this, of course. There has to be some other explanation. He was preparing tea for himself, taking it to his room."

Eve tried to slow her breathing. She held her hand to her chest. "Somebody else brought her this tea."

He took another look at the victim. "Or maybe she took her own life," he suggested. "Could she have done this to herself?"

"Suicide?" Eve responded. "No, it doesn't make any sense. She was excited when I talked to her today. She was looking forward to breaking the news about this discovery." Eve remembered the last time she had talked to Kelly. "I think she believed this could push the beatification process forward for Sister Maria, and she wanted that as much as anyone."

She shook her head. "And her clothes . . ." She nodded in the direction of the suit hanging on the closet door. "Having the clothes you are planning to wear the next day hanging on the closet door as if you are making preparations for the event . . ." She shook her head again. "No, she didn't take her own life."

She glanced down at the items on the desk. "And we would know that for sure if we knew whether or not the pages from

Sister Maria were still here." She turned her gaze back to the vice superior, wondering if he would be willing to make a search.

"We will need to call the police," the abbot said, not taking Eve's hint but rather stating what she knew to be the obvious. "We need to call them right away."

"The police." Eve nodded, glanced at her watch, and then noticed once again the broken cup at her feet. "They're going to want to know everything." She was saying this as much to herself as to the abbot.

Father Oliver nodded. "Yes, and we will tell them what we know." He sounded sure of himself, confident of his decision. "We will tell them every detail of this night," he continued.

Eve didn't look at the vice superior. She was trying to make sense of all that they knew, everything that had happened, the details.

"We will tell them why we came to the room in the first place, how Anthony told us what he had found, what we saw when we arrived, and" — he paused — "what we know about the siblings, what we saw that transpired between them." He seemed to be rehearsing what he intended to say to the police. "We will tell them everything we know. It's the only way."

She didn't respond. Eve knew that if they told everything they had experienced that night, if they both reported everything that Anthony told them before they came to the room, including a confession of murder, and if they reported having witnessed the argument that the siblings had in the dining room, and if the vice superior then also told the officers that later in the evening he saw Anthony fixing a tray with tea, then an arrest would likely be made, an arrest that no one at the monastery would believe, an arrest that she didn't think should happen.

"We don't have to tell them everything," she responded softly, clear on how things would appear to investigating officers.

The two locked eyes.

"We can tell them if they ask," she said. "But we don't need to tell them until they do." She waited. "Not until we have a chance to figure things out, not until we know who could have stolen the writings, who else knew about them, who she might have told."

A thick silence fell between them.

The vice superior shook his head. It was clear he understood what Eve was suggesting. "I made a vow to be truthful in all things."

"Yes, as have I," Eve replied. "And I will be."

"But only if the right question is put forward to you?" He studied her. "Only if they ask a question that they will not even think to ask without hearing all of the information we have?" He closed his eyes. "Is that not still deceit? Is that not also being untruthful?"

Suddenly Eve thought about the recent history of their community. She thought about the interviews held, how he had claimed support for the change even though he had told her he was not in favor of what was happening. She remembered the vice superior's position, what he said in private to the residents of the monastery and what he stated on public record.

"Do you believe what you told the reporters about the archbishop's decision? Do you really believe it was right to make the sisters leave?" She spurted out the questions and then cleared her throat and watched him, waiting for his response.

He made no reply, but it was clear he understood what she was doing, how she was bringing to light his own indiscretions.

She studied the pieces of the broken cup scattered around her and shook her head. "I'm sorry," she said, making an apology.

"It's just that I know Anthony would not murder his sister."

"Then the police will discover that truth as well."

Eve didn't respond right away; instead, she recalled a conversation she'd had with the Captain and how her father had discussed how quickly and sometimes carelessly a police officer would manage an investigation. Yes, he was proud of the work he did as a detective for the Santa Fe Police Department, he had explained, and he admired his colleagues still in the same line of duty, but he confessed that they, too, often chose the easiest path in making an arrest. This was one of the reasons he had retired from the force, one of the reasons he had chosen to be a private detective. In private work he felt he was better able to sift through all the details without feeling pressured to make a hasty judgement.

"What about your friend?" the abbot asked, pulling Eve away from her thoughts.

"What friend?"

"The one on the police force. The one who always came to the monastery to see you, your father's former partner."

"Daniel," she replied.

"Yes, what if you contact him first? What if you call him, tell him what we know, tell him that we are certain of Brother Anthony's goodwill, his innocence, and let him manage the details?"

It was a good idea, Eve thought. He was the right one to call. She wasn't sure if he would actually be given the position of lead investigator, but the monastery was in his jurisdiction, and contacting him first would at least make things easier for everyone involved.

She would do as he suggested. She would contact Daniel. And she was just about to say all of these things to the abbot, agree to his idea, when they both heard the sirens moving in their direction.

· Eight

"Who would have called them?" Eve hurried over to the window and pulled open the curtains. There was no car approaching the monastery grounds, but she could make out the red lights coming in their direction.

Father Oliver stood up from the bed. "Could someone else have come to the room? Do you think another guest may have seen her and then called for help?"

Eve shook her head. "I think they would have come to find you first, don't you?"

"I don't know," he answered.

"If someone else had found her, they would have stayed. They would have made the call and stayed."

"Not if their phone was somewhere else. Maybe they ran back to their room or to their car and they called and just haven't come back to the room yet." He was searching for an explanation.

"Do you think Anthony might have told

someone else?" she asked.

"No, I specifically instructed him to stay put. There is no one else who knows about this," he noted. "Unless another guest came by or saw something or heard something and made the call."

Eve let the curtains fall back together and turned to the abbot. "Maybe it was the killer," she suggested. "Maybe the killer has been watching us all along and made the call as part of a strategy because they know how things look for Anthony, maybe even set the clues in motion to cast the blame or suspicion in his direction. Maybe they saw him making the tea, knew his plans, and wanted to stage it like he did this, and maybe once they saw us here in the room, maybe they became afraid we would tell a different story, ruin their plans to pin this on Anthony."

Father Oliver didn't respond. He bowed once again, closed his eyes. A few seconds passed.

Eve ran her hand through her short hair, bit her bottom lip, and watched. She knew they didn't have much time, that the police would be arriving at the main entrance very soon; or if they had been given directions to the guest room, they would be arriving there in a matter of minutes. She shifted her weight from side to side, blew out a breath, watching the man as he prayed.

She hated to interrupt her superior's private intercessory prayer, but she also needed him to help her figure out what to do about everything, about how to explain what she was doing there, about what she had touched, about the broken teacup. She wanted to know what he planned to tell the police once they got to the room. She turned away from Father Oliver and peered out the window once more, searching for the patrol car she could hear, knowing that it was getting closer. *This is one of those times we don't need to be praying,* she said to herself, shaking her head, feeling her patience grow thinner and thinner.

"I will go and meet them," the abbot said, breaking his silence and grabbing Eve's attention. "They will likely stop at the main entrance, go to the main door. I will meet them there, tell them what I know, and bring them here," he added.

Eve studied him. She thought he might be trying to tell her more than just what he planned to do, but she wasn't sure.

Should she pick up the pieces of the broken cup while he was meeting them? Should she leave things as they were? Could she take a peek through Kelly's things to see if the Maria de Jesus de Agreda pages were there somewhere on the desk? She wasn't sure what to ask.

"Should I stay here?" was finally the question she posed. "Do you want me to stay here with the body and wait until you return?" She watched him very closely, searching for the instruction she thought might be hidden behind the words he spoke.

He shook his head. "No," he answered clearly. "I think it would be best if you go find Brother Anthony. I think you should find him and be with him. This is going to be a very difficult time, and I'm sure the police will want to talk to him at some point once they see what has happened." He hesitated. "I will go and meet them at the front steps. I will introduce myself, give a brief explanation about what has happened, what I saw in this room, and then bring the officers here for the rest of their investigation."

"You're going to tell them that you came in here?" Eve asked.

"I will tell them Brother Anthony told me what he found in his sister's room, and yes, I will explain that I had come to the room to see if I could help her, to see if she was really dead."

"Who do you think called?"

He stood and turned to Eve. "It doesn't matter who made the call. They're here, and I was going to call anyway after I took a look around." He seemed to be preparing himself. He took in a deep breath, closed his eyes. When he opened them, he appeared calmer, more decisive.

"I will tell them that I came to the room, that I touched a few things in and around the victim's body, that I may have compromised the scene, but that I was just trying to check on Miss Middlesworth to see if there was anything I could do." He locked eyes with Eve, staring at her as if he were giving her more instructions.

Eve, however, wasn't sure what else he was asking her to do, what action he thought she should take in that moment. Then it clicked. "You want me to leave?"

"I think it's best," he replied, appearing relieved since she had gotten his unspoken message. He walked past her and placed his hand on the doorknob to open it. "I will tell them I have been here, that I was in the room, that I touched her and prayed for her. I will tell them that I came after hearing from Brother Anthony."

The sirens were growing louder.

He opened the door. "When I'm gone, you should probably go around the back of the guest quarters and by the offices and then go to my room from that side. Anthony will still be there."

Eve watched as the abbot made his departure. She didn't quite understand everything Father Oliver seemed to be saying to her, but she knew that she had only a few seconds if she intended to search for the pages or for any other clues that might be in the room. The time was very limited before she would need to make an exit without being seen by the approaching officers.

The door closed behind him, and Eve hurried over to the desk and began rifling through everything that was there. She flipped through the books, opened the binder, and picked up every page and notebook still on the desk, understanding that she was leaving prints on everything but deciding that she would have to worry about that later.

She pored over the entire desk. There seemed to be nothing that resembled what must have been the pages written by Sister Maria, nothing that appeared old or brittle, no pages tucked inside a folder pocket or envelope, just the books and the professor's papers. "Who did this to you? Who took the writings?" she asked, still searching.

She was just about to leave when she glanced down once again at the dead body and suddenly noticed the victim's hand, the one held to her heart. Eve walked closer and bent down.

Kelly's hand was slightly clenched, and Eve could see that something was being held in it. She leaned in closer, and when she studied the curled fingers, she could see that the victim had grasped at something, torn something that had been close to her, something belonging to the killer, perhaps.

Eve turned Kelly's hand over, and when she did a small fragment of blue fabric fell out, its edges frayed and clearly ripped from a larger piece of cloth.

Without time to consider the consequences, Eve grabbed the scrap of material, made the sign of the cross over the victim once more, stood up, and moved toward the door. She opened it carefully, stuck out her head, and looked to the left, in the direction of the front entrance of the monastery.

There were two black-and-whites already there, and she could hear more sirens coming. She watched as a couple of officers got out, and she could see Father Oliver standing at the top of the steps. She headed out of the room, turned, and quietly closed the door. She stuffed the stolen piece of blue material in her pocket and dashed in the opposite direction without ever noticing the curtain as it fell back into place in the room next door.

NINE

Eve ran behind the long building only recently dedicated to guesthousing, past the small parking lot at the end, which was filled with cars, and down behind the administrative offices, the wing of rooms that used to house her and the other sisters, to the back door of the main facility near the chapel. She pulled on the handle, opening it, and slipped inside. The hallway was dark and quiet, lit only by the Exit signs near the doors at both ends. She knew that to get to Father Oliver's room on the south wing she needed to walk through the main entrance, where the main door and large windows opened onto the parking area out front.

There was a clicking sound, the hot water heater still working after late-night showers, she presumed, something she became used to when she lived at the monastery, often walking the halls late at night. She heard the scratching sounds of pigeons nesting in

70

the eaves of the old building and the ticking of the grandfather clock, a gift from a benefactor that had been placed across the hall from where she stood. These were all the sounds she recognized and remembered from the long nights when she couldn't sleep, leaving her room at the north end of the monastery where the nuns had lived for years, sitting in the chapel for hours or working in the kitchen, preparing for the morning meal.

She closed her eyes, steeling herself to walk toward the front entrance, hoping Father Oliver and the officers had already gone from where the abbot had met them upon their arrival.

She moved past the chapel doors, stopping only a minute to peek through the narrow windows, making sure Anthony hadn't returned there after speaking to the vice superior. The only light was the large candle still burning inside the red cylinder next to the altar, but it was enough for her to see that the pews were empty and that no one was inside. She thought of the young monk, how distressed he was when she first saw him in there no more than an hour before. She hoped Father Oliver had calmed him, something she had been unable to do, and that he was at peace in the abbot's room, waiting for guidance and instruction. She could only hope that he hadn't heard the sirens and made some unwise decision to meet the officials outside and make the same confession he had made to her.

Eve headed in the direction of the main entrance, observing no overheard lights turned on and hearing no conversation between the abbot and the police or between Brother Anthony and the officers. Thinking that the coast was clear, she peeked around the corner, saw three police cars parked in front and an ambulance, its red lights still glowing, backing away. From where she stood she could make out several voices, but it appeared as if no one had come inside; rather, the conversation, the voices, seemed to be moving farther away.

She breathed a sigh of relief, thinking that Father Oliver was doing exactly what he said he would do, meeting them at the front and then leading them in the direction of the guest quarters and to the room of Kelly Middlesworth. Following his direction, Eve headed to the other side of the monastery.

She had gotten past the entryway and made the turn to the south end, the long hall of rooms where the monks resided, when she heard footsteps and the swishing sound of a long robe, a noise she probably knew better than any. One of the monks must be up, she thought, understanding that the sirens and the lights most certainly had awakened everyone sleeping in the monastery proper as well as in the guest quarters. She glanced down the darkened hallway but didn't see anyone. She paused, expecting a monk to be following her, heading in her direction, but when she turned back around, the footsteps had stopped and there appeared to be no one else there.

She hurried in the direction of Father Oliver's room at the end of the wing and was standing right in front of the vice superior's room, her hand on the knob, when the door next to his suddenly opened.

"Sister Evangeline?" It was the sleepy voice of Brother Matthew, one of the older monks, one of the men who had lived in the monastery for more than four decades. "Sister Evangeline, is that you?"

She drew in a breath, pulling her hand away from the abbot's door, and turned in his direction. "Brother Matthew," she answered him, smoothing out her voice. "I am sorry if I woke you."

He stepped out into the darkened hall, glancing in both directions. He was wearing a heavy brown bathrobe held together by both hands. His hair, hanging in long white locks, was messy and uncombed. "I thought I heard sirens. Are there police officers on our grounds?" he asked.

Eve smiled. "They are certainly loud, aren't they? It's being handled, Brother Matthew. I hope you'll be able to go back to sleep."

"Has something happened? Have you come to wake Father Oliver?"

Eve hesitated. "Father Oliver has gone to greet the officers; I have come to get something for him."

The old monk narrowed his eyes at Eve, the fake smile still plastered on her face. She stuck her hands in her pockets.

"There was someone in his room," he said. "I heard weeping. I was awakened by the sounds of a man crying, not by the arrival of first responders."

She didn't reply, waiting for more.

"I have been praying since I first heard him."

More sirens were heard in the distance.

"But I didn't come out. I didn't come next door because I am sure Father Oliver gave prudent counsel. The young man came to the right place if he seeks guidance."

Eve lowered her eyes.

"Brother Anthony," he said, suddenly getting the attention of Sister Evangeline. "It's

74

our young brother Anthony. I heard him weep, and I recognized his voice when he made a grave confession. And I heard Father Oliver offer him absolution for his sins."

Eve didn't know what to say. *Does Brother Matthew also know of the murder of the young professor? Is there now someone else involved? How many of the others living on this wing heard the same thing?* She glanced down the hall, waiting for other doors to open, other men to join the conversation. But there was nothing.

"He left just before the police arrived," Brother Matthew explained. "Only a few minutes ago."

And without a reply, Eve quickly turned and opened the door to Father Oliver's room. The older monk was right. There was no one inside. She stepped in. The bed was unmade and the closet door stood open. The bathroom light was on, and Eve could see that the small room adjoining the one in which she stood was also empty. A lamp revealed a piece of paper positioned on top of the small wooden desk. She walked over to see what it was and immediately discovered that it was something signed by Anthony, a letter, perhaps, but she wasn't sure and didn't take the time to read it right then. Instead, she kept the piece of paper in her hand and headed out of the room to ask the older monk what else he knew about the night visitor to Father Oliver.

Out in the hallway she saw Brother Matthew's door was closed, and beneath the door she could see that the light in his room had suddenly been extinguished. Surprised that he hadn't waited for her, surprised that he had apparently gone back to bed, she walked over, planning to knock, wanting to talk more and needing to ask the old monk questions about Anthony. Just as she leaned in and started to knock, however, she heard the voices moving in her direction.

TEN

Quickly, Eve stepped back and glanced around. She thought if she hurried, she could make it to the exit only a few feet away from Father Oliver's door, but just as she started to head in that direction, she realized that she was too late. From behind her a light came on.

"Excuse me, are you looking for someone?" the voice called out.

Eve froze for a second, and then, realizing there was no way out of this, she turned around as two men came toward her, a light in the next hall creating shadows as they moved. She tried to sound cheerful. "I heard all the racket, the sirens and everything. I wanted to see if Father Oliver knew what was going on." She dropped her hand behind her back, trying to fold up the letter and stick it in her pocket. "But he's not answering. I guess that means he's somewhere else on the grounds."

There was a pause as the two men before her seemed to be studying her. "Don't I know you?" one of them asked, the older of the two.

Eve didn't reply. She squinted, trying to see who was talking to her.

"I've seen you before," he added, switching on his flashlight and shining the light in Eve's face.

Eve covered her eyes and figured she'd been recognized from one of the many activities she attended with her father, but she waited for him to figure it out for himself.

"You're Jackson's girl, the oldest, the nun." He waited. "You live up here?"

Eve gave her best smile. The bright light had been lowered, turned off, but the bursts of color were still blurring her vision, and it was still hard to make out the identities of the men in front of her. She wasn't sure that she knew either of them, but she thought it was good that one of them knew the Captain. With the letter folded and shoved into her back pocket, she walked closer and stuck out her hand.

"Evangeline," she responded. "Evangeline Divine. And yes, I still belong to the Benedictine Order here," she added, deciding not to reveal everything about her situation.

The older officer took her hand. "You came home to take care of Jackson last year," he commented. He was about sixty, with graying hair and a bulging midsection, and he was chewing on a toothpick.

She nodded, squinting up at the nameplate pinned to his shirt underneath his jacket. "Jared Bootskievely," it read. She smiled, feeling somewhat at ease.

"Detective Boots," she said, recalling her father's colleague and friend. It had been awhile since she had seen him, but she certainly remembered the nickname.

He grinned and leaned back on his heels. "Evangeline, the nun," he said. "And your sister . . ." He pushed the toothpick from side to side and seemed to be thinking.

"Dorisanne," she replied, filling in the blank.

"Dorisanne, right," he said, clapping his hands together. "The Vegas dancer."

Eve nodded.

"You two were quite a pair." He thrust the flashlight back into its holder on his belt and rested his hands on his hips, nodding.

Eve shrugged, unsure of what to say. She cleared her throat nervously.

"Man, I was so sorry to hear about Jackson," he continued. "But I understand from

Hively he's doing okay now, one-legged and all."

He turned to the officer at his side. "Captain Jackson Divine, spelled like *divine,* served on the force for more than thirty years, runs a PD agency up in Madrid. Good guy," he explained. "Used to be paired up with Daniel Hively. You know him, right?"

The other man nodded.

"Yeah, good ol' Captain Jack. But whatever you do, if you meet him, don't get that last name wrong. Don't call him Captain Divine," he added, mispronouncing the last name. "He hates that."

The younger officer turned and looked again at Eve. "Detective Earl Lujan," he said, introducing himself.

"He's new," Officer Bootskievely noted, pointing his thumb at his partner. "Just transferred down from Taos."

Eve turned to the other man, suddenly feeling a strange flutter in her stomach. With only the distant light, she couldn't see much, but he appeared to be about her age, dark-skinned, probably from the pueblo, Eve assumed, recognizing the last name as a familiar one in Taos. She nodded and held out her hand to him, and he shook it. "Evangeline Divine," she said, unable to

80

pull her eyes away from the man standing before her.

There was an awkward pause.

The older officer cleared his throat. "So, anyway, one of the monks pointed us in this direction to find your guy. Oliver, same one I guess you were hoping to see." Officer Bootskievely stepped toward the vice superior's door. He leaned in. "He didn't answer?" He turned back to Eve, who immediately realized that she was still gazing at the other officer.

"Um, no." She quickly looked away, feeling slightly flushed but trying to shake it off. "He's not there," she added, not giving away any clue that she knew exactly where Father Oliver was.

"Yeah, we're the last ones up here. I guess some deputies got the call first, over at the county office. Sent an ambulance and another set of paramedics. Then somebody got smart and called us in Santa Fe." He winked at Eve and elbowed his partner.

Eve nodded again. She was starting to feel like one of those bobblehead dolls Doris-anne used to collect.

Detective Boots studied her. "You don't know anything about where the other officers and the man in charge might be, do you?"

Eve reached up and fingered the cross necklace she was wearing. "Um . . . I came from the chapel," she explained. "I went there earlier to pray, and as far as I know there was no one else in there, and I didn't see anyone else down the other hall." *At least,* she told herself, *it isn't really a lie.*

"What's down the other hall?" the seasoned detective wanted to know.

"Offices," she answered, deciding not to explain about the recent changes from residential quarters to administrative offices, with the nuns forced out. "And the dining hall is on the other side of the main entrance. I don't know if you saw anything down there when you came in."

He shook his head. "No, it was dark and quiet. Only saw the one monk, young guy, tall, blue eyes. He said he had been awake awhile and was watching everything out the window."

The description he gave sounded to Eve a lot like Brother Anthony, and she wondered what he was doing in the dining hall and where else he had gone. She thought about the time and guessed that it had been more than an hour since she had last seen the monk.

"He was the one who told us the head honcho lives down here."

Eve nodded again and then stopped herself from speaking for a moment. "Yes, that is true," she finally responded, trying to figure out a way to leave the conversation and find Anthony. "Father Oliver is the vice superior of the abbey, and this is indeed his room."

"Which he's not in?" Boots asked.

"Right, which he's not in," Eve replied.

"So, besides this main building, chapel, offices, dining hall, and residence wing, what other buildings are on the property?" Detective Bootskievely wanted to know.

And finally here was the out she was looking for. "The guest quarters," she answered. "If you just go out the main entrance like you came in and head left, you can't miss them. I'm sure everyone must be down there."

"Uh-huh. Guess you're right," the man responded. The toothpick moved to the other side of his mouth and he reached up and took it out. "You tell your daddy Boots said hey. Maybe I'll come over to Madrid sometime and take him out to lunch."

"I'm sure he would love that," Eve responded.

She felt the officer studying her.

"You don't want to go down there with us? You don't want to know what's going on?" Boots asked.

She turned away and shook her head. "I don't want to get in anybody's way," she said, trying to smile.

"Good nun response, I guess," he replied.

"I guess," she answered, nodding again.

"All right, good to see you, Sister." And the older officer turned to walk away.

Detective Lujan, still not having said anything but his name, peered at Eve and gave a slight smile. "It was nice to meet you, Evangeline." And then he paused. "I don't think he's still in the dining room. He seemed to be in a hurry, to pray, maybe."

Eve was stunned and was about to explain she didn't know who he was talking about, but before she could say as much, he turned and followed the other officer, leaving her alone with her thoughts.

ELEVEN

"Anthony," Eve whispered. After checking the young monk's room and finding it empty, she made her way to the dining room without running into any of the other monks or any other police officers. She chose not to switch on the lights, keeping herself and the room in the dark.

"Anthony," she whispered again as she headed from the dining area toward the kitchen. She quietly pushed open the swinging doors, calling out his name once more. There was no one around.

Eve stood in the familiar space where she had spent so many hours when she lived at the abbey. Of all the rooms at the monastery, the offices and the gathering spaces, the chapel and the gardens, the kitchen had always been a place where Eve felt completely at home. Even though there were far better cooks than she among the residents at the monastery, she had come to love the work that was done in this place. Baking bread, making soups and stews, roasting chiles, and even brewing beer — there was so much about cooking and preparing meals that Eve loved.

Here, even if silence was being observed, the men and the women, the nuns and the monks, worked together like musicians in an orchestra, stirring and measuring, peeling and tasting, and this gift of creating the community's shared meals was a very high honor for the nun. If she was able to contribute even a small thing to the bounty spread on the table for her brothers and sisters at breakfast, lunch, or dinner, she felt whole inside, complete. And as she stood just inside the doors of the kitchen, she felt a twinge of sadness that the nuns would no longer be there, the women who were suddenly banned from it all. A long breath poured from her, and she shook away her thoughts of the changes going on around her and returned to the matters at hand, trying to imagine where Brother Anthony had gone.

If he had been in the kitchen or the dining room as the officers said he was earlier, it was clear he had left. If he had been working on the morning meal or getting himself something to eat, he was nowhere to be found. Eve walked back to the pantry where they kept nonperishable supplies and peeked in. Not there. Then she headed down a short hall, over to the large walk-in freezers, and, knowing it couldn't be seen from anywhere else, turned on a light. She was alone. Realizing she was not going to find Anthony there, she walked back into the kitchen and then into the dining room, pulled open the blinds, and looked out a window in the direction of the guest quarters.

Several monks and guests had gathered around the main entrance, and she could still see the lights of the patrol cars and ambulance flashing in the distance. A news van from a local television station had also arrived and was heading past the window where she stood, over to where the action was taking place. As soon as it passed by, she turned and noticed a vehicle exiting the grounds.

It was a pickup truck, an old one, white, with a taillight out. She couldn't make out the numbers on the license plate and she couldn't see who was driving, but she did think it was odd that a vehicle was leaving the premises. She wondered why the police hadn't stopped it, but when she turned back to see what was going on at the guest quarters, there was so much commotion she was sure no one was paying close attention to who was coming and who was going.

Someone was putting up yellow tape around the front room of the guest quarters, marking the area as a crime scene and no longer just a guest room. The death of Dr. Kelly Middlesworth, Eve realized, was no longer a secret between her, Father Oliver, and Brother Anthony. The news was about to be known by everyone.

She shook her head and closed the blinds, making her way to one of the tables in the room. She dragged out a chair and sat down, pulling the letter out of her back pocket that she had taken from the vice superior's desk and unfolding it. She spread it out before her and, turning on the flashlight app on her cell phone, began to read:

Dear Father Oliver,

I realize now the horrible sin I have committed. I cannot take back the evil that has been done to my sister, and I am deeply sorry for all of these things that have happened and see now that I have to go. I meant no harm to the other monks at the abbey, to you, or to my dear Kelly. I know I can never be forgiven for my sins. I can only pray that

God will have mercy on me.

                    Your devoted son,
                        Anthony

Eve switched off the light, folded the letter back up, and placed it on the table. She
knew it should be turned over to the authorities; it would certainly be seen as relevant
to the crime. It didn't exactly bear a confession to murder, but Eve knew enough about
the law to realize that if the police added
this letter to the eyewitness report from
Father Oliver that he had seen the young
monk preparing the tray with tea near the
time the victim was killed, along with the
many reports from those who had seen the
siblings argue at dinner, and the fact that he
was now missing, things wouldn't look good
for Brother Anthony.

Eve rested her elbows on the table, clasped
her hands together, and tried to sort through
everything that had happened in the last
few hours.

Dr. Kelly Middlesworth had been given
writings, their existence apparently un-
known by anyone but the two siblings and
now the abbot and Eve and the murderer.
These pages, of words that were being
ascribed to Sister Maria de Jesus de Agreda,
had been written apparently for the Jumano

Indians, the tribe that the revered nun was said to have appeared to while she was in residence in Agreda, Spain. If Eve's math was right, these pages would have to be over four hundred years old and would surely elicit a tremendous response from theologians, archaeologists, historians, and religious scholars. These writings were so important, she had been told, they could possibly even push forward the beatification of the Spanish nun.

Brother Anthony had found the pages in Isleta while working at the pueblo parish, and he took them, without permission, with only the thought to delight and surprise his sister. Kelly, obviously clear about the value of such a treasure, had revealed to her brother earlier in the evening that she planned to tell everyone about the discovery at the conference scheduled for the following day. This revelation caused him to become angry and created a rift between the siblings. It also seemed to Eve that Kelly had not only changed her speech for the following day to include this new finding but also told someone else, someone who must have gotten to her room sometime after dinner, found and stolen the writings, and ultimately killed her.

Eve leaned back in her chair and closed

her eyes. Kelly was dead. And even though there was more than enough circumstantial evidence against Anthony to make him look like the murderer, she could not accept that he would have killed his sister, no matter how angry he was. It didn't really matter, however, what *she* thought because he was now gone, having disobeyed the abbot and fled the crime scene, adding even more evidence against him. She thought again about the letter and knew that if she'd read it correctly, Anthony had left the monastery. *But where did he go? Did he run away? Was this a suicide letter? Is he in peril just as Kelly was?*

Evangeline was clear that she was in over her head in this situation. She knew she had helped her father find the killer of the movie director in Madrid, and she knew she had been smart enough to help her friend and her father's former partner, Daniel, find her sister, who had gone missing in Las Vegas, but trying to find a murderer who appeared to have left no clues as to his or her identity, or even trying to find Brother Anthony and convince him to return to the monastery and tell the authorities what had happened or persuade him not to harm himself, all of this was more than she knew how to handle. She considered her options, understanding she would have to make the call. At a time like this, only one person could really help her figure out what she should do.

TWELVE

"What time is it?" The question was more of a growl than recognizable words.

Eve cringed. She hated waking the Captain. "It's after two," she answered, counting the hours she had been up and the minutes since the police had arrived at the abbey. She was still in the dining room and still alone, although the sounds of voices were building around her and she could see lights coming on in various parts of the building. With all this action she knew she wouldn't be by herself much longer.

"Then this better be good," came the reply. "You in jail for speeding? You turn your bike over in a ditch?"

"What? No," she responded, starting to think she shouldn't have called him after all.

"You break into the animal shelter, vandalize the premises, and set all them dogs and cats free again? Have you been arrested again?"

Eve sighed. "Why do you always bring that up — and I wasn't arrested, anyway. I just got put on probation. That place was horrible. Those animals were neglected. It needed public attention. And in fact, I never would have been caught in the first place if your partner, Daniel, hadn't ratted me out to you."

"You do the crime, you do the time."

"Yeah, whatever. That was a long time ago." She was now completely convinced that she was mistaken to have made the call.

He cleared his throat, making such a racket that Eve had to hold the phone away from her ear.

"If you aren't in trouble, then why did you call?" He yelled the question after all of the coughing and hacking.

"There's been a murder," she explained, imagining her father trying to sit up in bed, reaching for his glasses and a tissue, holding on to the phone while turning on the lamp that sat on the table beside him.

"Did you do it?" he asked. "Because if you did it, you should be calling a lawyer and not your father."

Eve didn't answer at first, the question surprising her.

"No." There was a pause.

"Why would you think I would commit a murder?" she asked.

"Because the last thing I remember you saying before you left this morning to go back to the convent was that these changes handed down from the diocese made you so mad you were thinking about protesting, making waves where you shouldn't be swimming. Besides, we all are capable of murder, Evangeline. Just put any one of us in the right place at the right time with the right circumstances . . ." He cleared his throat again noisily. "We could all do it. Even you."

Eve shook her head. Her father's take on human behavior never ceased to amaze her. She knew lots of people wondered about her decision to become a nun, but if they spent much time with the Captain, she was sure most folks would think she chose the vocation just to try to rid herself of all the garbage he had stuffed into her head while she was growing up.

"I did not commit a murder," she responded. "It happened at the abbey. One of the conference speakers, a sister to one of the monks, was killed in her room tonight. It was poison, found it in her tea, smelled like almonds —"

"Cyanide," he interrupted.

"I know," she replied. "She hadn't had a lot of it, but she's dead, regardless."

"Suicide?" he asked.

"No, not suicide. She was preparing to give the most important speech of her life this morning."

"At the monastery?"

"Yes."

There was a pause.

"Is this victim a nun?"

Eve thought it sounded like he was laughing. She felt her face flush. "I don't even know why I called you. What are you implying? That a nun can't make an important speech, that a Benedictine sister doesn't have something important to say to the world? You think that just because she's a woman, she can't speak to men?"

"Whoa there, Sister. Don't get all high and mighty with me. I'm not the one who pushed the girls out of the monastery and all the way to the back pew in church. I'm not saying anything like that. I'm just asking you questions about the victim." He blew out a heavy breath. "How many times have I told you that you will never solve a mystery if you let your emotions blind your clear thinking?"

She tried to settle herself. She knew he was right, and she also knew he loved to get

96

a rise out of her.

"Kelly Middlesworth was not a nun," she said, trying to sound as unemotional as she could. "She was a religion professor in Texas. She was speaking on the subject of Sister Maria de Jesus de Agreda."

"That one you're so keen about," he interjected. "The one you think has not been treated fairly by the church."

"The nun I think should be made into a full saint, yes," she answered a little too quickly, and she paused. "Dr. Middlesworth had been given something related to Sister Maria that I think was worth a lot of money, and I believe she told somebody who wanted this item bad enough to kill her for it."

"How did you find out about the murder?"

Eve hesitated. This was the part she was less enthusiastic to share. "Her brother found me in the chapel tonight. He told me about this item the victim had. He told me he had given it to her secretly and then had gotten very upset because she was planning to tell others."

There was no response, and she knew he was still waiting for her to answer his question.

"He found his sister dead in her room and

he showed up at the chapel and told me."

"And you called the police?"

"Not exactly."

"You went to see her for yourself."

"Yes."

"And you compromised the crime scene by entering it before the police."

"Yes, I did that too."

"Have you called the police?" he wanted to know.

"No, but someone did," she replied, thinking again that she had not yet discovered who had placed that call.

"Who's out there?" he asked, referring to the officers from the Santa Fe Police Department.

"Detective Boots and his new partner, some county deputies, I don't know who else," she answered.

"Bootsey?" He laughed. "Good heavens, he hasn't retired yet?"

"I guess not." And she suddenly recalled the other officer with him and the way she felt when they were introduced.

"What else?" he asked.

She wondered how it was he could tell there was always something else, how he seemed to know when she was holding back information. "While I was looking around the room I broke the cup she drank from, the one with the cyanide."

He sighed. "And . . ."

"And I found a letter her brother wrote, one he left for Father Oliver, one in which he explains that he's leaving the monastery, that he's sorry for what he's done and he's gone to make amends."

"And do you still have this letter?"

The question, coming not from the Captain in Madrid but from inside the door to the dining hall, startled Eve so much that her right hand flew open, dropping her cell phone to the floor.

THIRTEEN

"Evangeline!"

She heard her father calling for her as she knelt down to retrieve the phone. "I . . . I'll call you back," she replied, hitting the red button on the little screen, ending the conversation, and trying to make out who had just entered the dining room.

One of the light switches was turned on and she could finally see who was standing at the door. He walked toward her. Eve grabbed the letter on the table and shoved it into her back pocket. "How long were you standing there?" she asked, wondering how much of the conversation with the Captain he had heard.

"Long enough to know you've called for help." He hesitated. "And that you found a letter." He had gotten to the table where she sat and stood next to her.

Evangeline could see the man more clearly now, and he seemed taller than he had when they first met in the hallway by Father Oliver's room. He was about six feet, she thought, thick black hair that appeared to be pulled back and tied in a ponytail that she couldn't see but assumed must be hanging down his back. He was wearing what she knew to be the detective's uniform, a dress shirt and black trousers, a nondescript dark tie. In only one way did his dress deviate from that of all the other city detectives Eve had seen, and that was the black leather jacket instead of the standard all-weather sport coat. He had dark eyes and broad shoulders, and he wasn't standing so close that he was trying to use his position to intimidate her. Instead, he angled himself so there was room for her to get up from her chair and move away if she wanted. She wasn't, therefore, threatened by him, but she still felt nervous with him standing so close. Her pulse rate quickened and her hands started to sweat.

"Officer Lujan," she said, taking the space given and getting up from her seat. "I thought you were with your partner at the guest quarters." She stood near him, trying not to appear anxious or guilty.

"I was," he answered, glancing around the dining room and then turning his attention back to her. He stepped back a bit, giving

101

her a little more room, and he smiled. "There were more than enough personnel down there."

She nodded and smiled in return. "It does appear as if the word got out to everyone in the county and in Santa Fe." She looked toward the window. "I just saw a news crew drive past." She turned back, realizing the blinds were closed. "I was over there and watched," she tried to explain, realizing as the words left her lips how ridiculous she sounded. "Before I came here and sat down." She closed her eyes and shook her head. *Could you just shut up?* she asked herself.

There was a pause. She could feel him watching her. *Probably trying to see what other dumb or incriminating thing I can say on my own.*

"So, the victim has a brother who lives here," he noted, watching Eve carefully.

She nodded. "Yes, yes, she does . . . did," she added, correcting herself and, unfortunately, letting it be known that she was aware of the reference, that she had knowledge of what had happened on the monastery campus. "Wait. I'm sorry, who are you talking about?" She was hoping he hadn't caught the misstep.

"The woman in the guest quarters, the

sister of the monk you came to find. Anthony, I believe is his name."

Nope. He hadn't missed a thing.

"Yes, I thought Brother Anthony might still be here and I came to find him."

"To tell him what happened?"

She nodded her head, hoping that gestures didn't really qualify as lying.

He glanced around again. "He's not here?"

She shook her head and reached for the cross necklace around her neck.

He studied her. "Is that a special crucifix?"

She looked down at the pendant. "My mother gave it to me," she answered. "A gift when I joined the order . . . when I became a nun."

He nodded and smiled slightly. "I have one too," he said, and he pulled out the necklace he was wearing. It was on a silver chain and was not a crucifix but instead a cross that appeared to be made from stone, exactly what kind Eve didn't know. It was crude, and she had to look closely to make out that it was a cross and not just a round piece of white stone.

"It's sacred buffalo stone — from my grandfather on the Shoshone Indian Reservation in Nevada." He looked at the stone hanging from his neck and then placed it back beneath his shirt. "He gave it to me when I was a boy," he added. "Said he saw a white buffalo the day I was born."

"What does that mean?" she asked.

Detective Lujan shrugged. "Not sure," he answered. "He seemed to think it meant I would be protected."

She thought about the explanation. "I would imagine that's a good sign for a police officer."

He nodded. "That's why I wear it," he noted. He took in a breath, changing the direction of the conversation. "Do you know where Brother Anthony is?" he asked.

Eve relaxed because she was able to be completely honest with this answer. "I don't."

"But you were searching for him."

It wasn't a question so she didn't respond.

There was a lull in the conversation, and she was hopeful that he was finished with the interview. She waited.

"And the letter?"

This was a question, she knew.

She nodded without speaking.

"Can I see it?"

Eve reached behind her and pulled out the letter. She handed it to the officer and then leaned back, sticking her hands into her pants pockets, her fingers finding the piece of material she had taken from the victim's room. She clutched it, waiting for him to finish reading.

He refolded the piece of paper and handed it back to her. "So, he knew what happened before you got to him?"

She took the letter, holding it in her hand. "He told me earlier, then he told Father Oliver, who met me in Kelly's room. I was trying to find him when you and Detective Bootskievely arrived. This was on Father Oliver's desk. And when you told me he was here, I came to try and change his mind."

"Change his mind about leaving?"

She nodded. "He didn't kill his sister," she explained. "He's much too kind and he loved her very much. He didn't do this."

"But you were worried how it would look, what we might think."

She studied the officer. "I was," she replied. "There's some pretty strong circumstantial evidence you're going to hear. And I'm worried about him too. He doesn't sound too stable in that letter."

She felt the cell phone vibrating in the pocket of her jacket and knew it was the Captain.

He watched her a few seconds. "I'll need the letter eventually."

"But not now?" she asked, surprised he

wasn't taking it.

He shook his head. "I'm sure you'll keep it safe."

She nodded, the phone still vibrating.

"You should probably answer that," he said as he made his exit.

FOURTEEN

By the time Eve had gotten her father fully on board about what had happened, the detective had left the dining room. While she watched Detective Lujan exit, Captain Divine explained on the phone that he would come to the monastery first thing that morning and that he would call Daniel, his former partner and an acting detective, and fill him in on the murder and everything Eve had told him.

Eve planned to go to her room, the only sleeping quarter left in the sisters' old residential wing. She knew that Father Oliver had decided to leave one room unchanged in case a nun might wish to return to visit the old community. When he took her to the last room on the hall after she arrived, he explained that he thought it would be better for them, for her, to stay in familiar territory instead of having to bunk in the new guesthousing. And he was right.

As sad as she was to be back and for things to be so different from when she was a resident there, Eve was glad she was staying in the main building of the monastery. She had not wanted to stay in the row of rooms that had been recently built for the nuns but never used by them. She was relieved to feel less like a guest than she already did. The expulsion of the nuns bothered her greatly, but she still loved the monastery, and regardless of the recent history, it was still comforting to be in the place filled with so many memories.

Once she made it past the area around the main entrance, after greeting the five or six monks standing around talking about what had happened and feigning her ignorance about everything, she headed past the chapel and down the hall to the last room on the right. She opened the door and was surprised to find Father Oliver sitting at the desk, waiting for her.

"I'm sorry, Sister, to be in your private quarters. I didn't know where else I might find you." He stood up, bowing his head, and dropped his hands to clasp them in front of him, the rosary he had been praying with clearly visible.

She shut the door and walked over to him, taking him by the hand. "It's okay," she said, squeezing his hand before sitting down on the bed across from the desk.

As she studied him, seeing him in brighter and clearer light than when they had last been together in Kelly's room, Eve could see how much the vice superior had aged since she'd been away. Even though she had been in Madrid and away from the monastery only a few months, his hair had gone from salt and pepper to just salt, and it was curly and longer than he usually kept it.

There were new wrinkles around his eyes, two deep lines furrowed between his brows. He was slumped and his color was ashen. The thought that he was sick crossed her mind, but she knew his appearance had more to do with stress than it likely had to do with some disease or illness. It was easy to see that he was taking the transition at the monastery harder than anyone. And now he was dealing with this, a murder and one of the monks implicated and apparently missing.

"Anthony was gone," she said, unsure if he knew.

He nodded. "I saw Brother Matthew. He told me that he heard him leave and heard the conversation in the hallway between you and the police officers." He sat back down in the chair. "I hoped maybe you had found him. I hoped maybe he would come back here with you. Have you seen him at all?"

She shook her head and suddenly remembered the letter. She pulled it out of her pocket and handed it to him. She watched as he unfolded it and read.

He rested his elbows on the desk and ran his hands over his face. "What is he doing? Where has he gone?"

"I don't know," she replied. "But Daniel, my friend, the one I said I would call, he's going to come this morning. He'll understand when we tell him that Anthony didn't do this. He'll help us find him."

Father Oliver nodded.

"I met two detectives from the Santa Fe department. Bootskievely and Lujan," she said. "Did you see them?"

"They came down later," he explained. "But yes, I met them both. The deputies made the report to them, and I could see they would be handling everything from that point on." He added, "They seem like good men."

Eve shrugged. She waited for a few seconds before asking the question she had been dying to ask when she first saw the abbot.

"I told them what I know," he said, understanding the inquisitive look she was giving him. "I told them that Anthony had come to me earlier in the evening and shared with me what had happened. I explained that he was very upset and confessed that he had stolen something from the Isleta church and that he had planned to return it after he showed it to his sister. I went on to say that he had told me that when Dr. Middlesworth refused to hand the papers back over to him and explained that she planned to share them at her keynote address at the conference and that she had shared the news with other people, he was angry. I told them about the argument at dinner and how I had seen him afterward in the kitchen but had not spoken to him, and then a few hours later he came to my room to tell me that he had found her dead. And that he did not know where the papers were."

Eve did not respond, the one concern still bothering her.

He shook his head, understanding. "I did not tell them about the tea," he said softly. "But I'm sure they will ask me later, when they want to know what I saw him doing in the kitchen after dinner. They will surely ask who could have brought her the tea."

Eve glanced away, knowing how difficult these last few hours had been for the vice superior, realizing the difficult place he was

111

in of trying to protect Anthony but also trying to tell the truth as he knew it.

"It gives us a little more time," she said.

"Time for what?" he wanted to know.

"Time to find out who really did this, time to find Anthony and make sure he's okay, time to make sure we get to him before the real murderer does, time to find out who Kelly told about the pages."

Father Oliver's appearance changed. Eve noticed a kind of spark in his eye as he turned to her.

"What?" she asked, sensing that he was remembering something.

"A man arrived about a half hour after the two detectives showed up." He sat up a bit in his chair.

"What man?"

"He appeared very distraught, started weeping when he was told what had happened," Father Oliver continued. He shook his head. "But there was just something strange about his timing, about how he came into the room."

Eve didn't want to interrupt.

"Dr. Peter Pierce," he said, nodding. "Dr. Middlesworth's associate or maybe boss, I'm not sure."

"Was he staying in one of the guest rooms?" Eve asked, leaning forward.

Father Oliver shook his head. "He was wearing a suit, carrying a briefcase. I think he had just arrived, drove in with all the police cars and ambulances."

"That is odd," Eve commented. "Has Anthony ever mentioned his name?"

"No, not to me," he answered.

"And he started weeping?"

The abbot nodded. "He walked in before anyone could stop him, before they had covered the body, and he dropped to his knees and began to scream and cry. His behavior seemed sincere," he added. "One of the deputies took him to his car. I didn't see him after that." He looked over at Eve, watching her. "What are you thinking?"

She chewed on her bottom lip, a habit she had when she was deep in thought. "Just that his timing is pretty ironic and that we don't really know when he arrived on campus." She shook her head. "And we still don't know who called the police."

FIFTEEN

Sister Eve got about three hours of sleep, and she hadn't intended on having those. She had borrowed one of the monastery's laptop computers and was planning to spend whatever time she had left before morning came researching Dr. Peter Pierce and trying to find as much information about him as she could.

She stayed in her room, choosing not to risk showing up in the same place as the two investigating detectives, waiting to be out and about until after Daniel arrived, trusting that he would keep her out of any line of fire. At first, after the vice superior left, having brought her the computer from his office, she sat at the desk, but then she decided to move to the bed just to stretch out her legs. Before she knew it, the sun was high and bright and she was waking to the sounds of someone knocking on her door.

"Evangeline," the familiar voice was calling. "You in there?"

She jumped up, trying to shake off the sleep, throwing aside the bed linens in haste. "Just a minute," she exclaimed, running her fingers through her hair. After straightening her shirt, tucking it into her pants, and then smoothing them both down, she opened the door.

"Late night?" the Captain asked as he barreled in carrying something under his arm.

Eve glanced down the hall to see if anyone else was with him, but it appeared that he had arrived alone.

He took a seat at the desk, dropped what he was holding on the floor, and started rubbing his thigh as she shut the door. "I don't think I got Peggy on right," he commented as he pushed and pulled at his prosthetic leg.

Eve glanced down beside him. "Daisy!" She walked over, bent down, and scooped the little cat into her arms. "What are you doing here?" she asked, giving the animal a good scratch, and turned to her father.

He shrugged. "Your cat is driving me batty," he replied.

"Not sweet Daisy!" Eve sat on the bed and the cat settled in her lap.

"There," he said, bending his prosthesis

back and placing his foot on the floor. He looked over at the bed and then back at her. "You get some sleep?"

She nodded. "I guess I did." She continued rubbing the cat and then slid her fingers through her hair again, trying to get rid of the bed head she knew she must have. "What time is it?"

"Later than you think," he replied. "And yes, I've already had breakfast and my shot," he explained before he was asked.

"Did you get in touch with Daniel?" she asked.

"Not before Boots did," he answered.

She stopped petting Daisy and glanced up at him. "What are they saying?"

"It's officially labeled as a homicide," he responded. "They smelled the cyanide right off. They did tell Daniel that the cup was on the floor, broken, and weren't sure whether she had it in her hand when she fell to the floor and dropped it or if someone else had tampered with the evidence." He raised his eyebrow at Eve.

She turned back to the cat and then placed her on the floor. She watched as Daisy sniffed around the room, and then she began to straighten the linens on the bed.

"They're running it for fingerprints." He waited.

She shrugged. "That should help," she responded.

"Not if there're several prints found," he said.

She sat down near him at the foot of the bed, watching as Daisy headed over to the window. "I was careful," she finally said.

He nodded his approval. "And you're right about the brother, about her brother, the monk."

Eve inhaled sharply.

"They got eyewitnesses that saw the dinner fight, a guest who saw him around her room before the coroner's estimated time of death. He was seen in the kitchen after whatever late-night prayers you people pray."

He waited as if he expected her to interrupt him by giving him the proper name of the service, but when she didn't, he went on. "And there's also apparently a letter that's quite incriminating, seen by one of the investigating officers, which is in the possession of a certain nun." He cleared his throat.

She rolled her eyes, pulled out the letter that she had kept in her back pocket, and threw it on the desk in front of him. He glanced over it and turned his attention back to his daughter. "And there's the annoying fact that he's missing."

She fell back on the bed, her head on the pillow. She was tired, and even though she had just woken up from at least a few hours of sleep, it was clear to her that it was not enough.

"Daniel's holding off on a search," he added. "He said he wants to talk to you as soon as you're up for it."

She nodded. "They got anything else?" she wanted to know.

He shook his head as he unfolded the letter and began to read it. "I told Daniel about these missing writings," he said. "He's going to talk to your boss about that."

"Is he here?"

"Who, your boss?" Captain Divine asked, looking up from the letter. "I wouldn't know that."

"No, Daniel," she replied.

"Oh, I doubt it." He folded the letter back up, having read it. "He was going to check on the autopsy, make sure the fingerprints were at the lab, read the reports, get the tox screen results. He should be here anytime."

Eve nodded, realizing it was going to be a very long day.

"There's somebody else here who knows

the victim pretty well . . ." He hesitated. "My guess is that it's better than pretty well. Looks a lot like a grieving lover."

"Peter Pierce," Eve said, recalling the news from Father Oliver about the man who showed up after the police.

The Captain nodded. "*Dr.* Peter Pierce, some religion professor from UT. He taught with the dead girl."

"I've heard about the guy; I was trying to google him when I fell asleep."

"Google him? Is that something a nun is supposed to be doing to a stranger?" He grinned.

She ignored the joke. "What else did they find in the room? Was there a cell phone? A computer, date book, anything?" She knew that she had not seen a phone anywhere on top of the desk and recalled that she had not seen Kelly's computer, only the bag that she carried it in. She assumed if those things were missing that whoever had stolen the pages had also stolen anything that might link the murderer to the victim.

The Captain shook his head. "Not privy to the details," he answered. "At least not until Daniel takes over. Then I figure we can know anything they do."

"That'll be nice," Eve responded.

"Tell me about this blue lady everybody

keeps talking about, this conference you planned to attend."

Eve sat up. "I tried to tell you before I left. You weren't so interested then."

"Well, let's just say a murder changes the things that interest me."

She smiled, happy to share her knowledge. "Sister Maria de Jesus de Agreda," she answered. "She was said to have bilocated to several Indian tribes in New Mexico and Texas at the same time that she was in residence at her convent in Spain."

"Bilocated?"

"Two places at once," she answered, guessing that he had never heard of this spiritual gift. "She was in Agreda, Spain, but the Indians here said she was with them too."

"Two places at once," he repeated. "That sounds like something you've been trying to do, be here as a nun and be at home as my partner."

She dropped back down on the pillow. *Here we go again,* she thought, throwing her arm across her face. "No, I do not have the gift of bilocation," she answered him. "But I do think Sister Maria should be beatified and made into a full saint," she added. "They said her writings were not in full compliance or were not considered pro-

120

foundly biblical, so they stopped the process of making her a saint until they could find better evidence to argue against this decision."

"You think these writings the victim had would support the process or halt it altogether?"

Eve didn't answer right away. It was, after all, a very good question. Before she could give a reply, however, there was another knock at her door. She sat up suddenly, wishing that she had taken a shower and changed clothes because this day was certainly getting started.

Sixteen

Eve watched as Daisy darted under the bed, and then she got up from her place to answer the knock. Assuming it would be Daniel, her father's former partner, she was talking as she pulled the door open. "I hope you brought breakfast." She finished the sentence right as she stood face-to-face with the person on the other side.

There was a slight hesitation before he replied, "No, I apologize for that. No breakfast."

It was not Daniel.

"Oh, I . . . I was expecting . . . I thought you were somebody else," she said, managing finally to get the words out, her face flushing.

"Somebody with your morning meal, perhaps? Apparently a nun's life isn't as ascetic as I had heard."

Eve stood at the door for a few moments without a response until her father broke the awkward silence by clearing his throat.

"Oh, I'm sorry, please come in." And she stood away from the door, giving her visitor room to walk in.

He remained where he was but turned from Eve and glanced over at the Captain, who was still sitting at the desk. "I'm Detective Earl Lujan," he said with a smile. Unlike Eve, he had apparently changed clothes from the night before. He was freshly shaven, wearing a clean and pressed shirt, a different tie, and a sport coat, clearly ready for a new day.

Eve glanced down at her clothes, wishing she had at least changed her shirt or even brushed her teeth. She tried not to get too close.

Her father nodded. "Jackson Divine," he responded. "You're Bootsey's partner," he added, recognizing the visitor's name.

"Yes, I have been recently assigned with Detective Bootskievely. He's spoken of you, Captain."

"He's a good man," Jackson noted. "Easygoing, smart, doesn't have a lot of hangups; but whatever you do, don't let him pick the restaurant when you're out. He can find places with the hottest chile I've ever eaten."

The man at the door laughed. "Wish I had gotten that advice sooner. I've already had my tongue and tonsils on fire twice, and we haven't been partnered a month. And what's worse is that before I came to work at the Santa Fe department, I thought I could eat anything. I love spicy food, and I've always had an iron gut when it comes to chile."

Jackson shook his head. "He take you to that Vietnamese place next to the engine emissions garage? Tell you they had the best noodle soup in New Mexico?"

"Pho sate," he replied. "And yes, that would be incident number one," he added, shaking his head.

"The second happen at a Mexican food truck at the rodeo grounds?"

"You know him well," Lujan responded. "He recommended the red sauce on my breakfast burrito."

Jackson threw back his head and laughed. "He pulls that crap on every rookie on the force. I can't believe he's still doing that."

Eve was still at the door, holding the handle and extending her arm, inviting him in.

There was another awkward pause in the room.

"I don't think he's coming in," Jackson said to his daughter.

She didn't respond.

"What I'm saying is that you can put your

arm down unless that's some kind of special religious greeting you don't give to family members."

Eve's face darkened another shade of crimson and she dropped her arm. Daisy stuck her head out from under the bed, taking a peek around.

"Sister, I am truly sorry to stop by so early," the detective said softly, turning his attention back to Eve. "But it turns out that I'm going to need the letter." He waited a beat before continuing. "As I suspected, I'm afraid it's become important to the case."

Eve nodded and walked over to the desk. Her father handed her the letter.

"The victim's brother a suspect?" Captain Jackson asked.

Eve watched the visitor at the door as she handed him Anthony's letter written to Father Oliver.

"We haven't gotten that far," Detective Lujan replied. "But this could be related to the death, and we just aren't at a place where we can rule anything out." He took the letter, still folded, and placed it in the inside pocket of his jacket. "You haven't seen the victim's brother this morning, have you?"

Eve shook her head. "No," she answered.

"Because of course it would be really helpful to us if we could ask him a few questions. Maybe he has an idea of his sister's mindset during the last couple of days, or maybe he knows if she had any enemies. He might even know of some of her connections in Austin or around here that we could also talk to."

Eve shook her head again. "I don't know where he's gone."

The detective nodded as if he believed her.

"What about the other professor?" Eve asked. "The one who showed up in Kelly's room after you and your partner arrived."

A slight smile emerged on the police officer's face. "Detective Hively mentioned earlier today that you were pretty good at picking up on clues and details. In fact, he told me that you did some significant detective work with your dad last year." He glanced back in Jackson's direction and then again at Eve.

She shrugged. "I just heard that a man came into the victim's room and seemed to be very emotional, apparently having just driven up to the monastery."

Detective Lujan nodded, not giving anything away. He reached for his wallet and took out a business card. "I should have given you one of these last night," he said, handing the card to Eve and not taking her bait. "If you hear from Anthony, maybe you can give me a call just to let me know he's okay."

Eve held the card in her hands, reading his contact information.

"Well, aren't you the cutest thing?"

"I'm sorry, what?" she asked, the surprise evident in the tone of her voice. She glanced up.

"It's the cat," Captain Divine said, eyeing his daughter closely.

Eve looked at Detective Lujan, who had squatted down and was calling Daisy out from under the bed. She watched as her pet slowly moved past her and over to the outstretched arms of the man at the door. He picked her up and held her in his arms, looking very much at home with Daisy in his embrace.

Eve couldn't believe her mistake. She closed her eyes and shook her head.

"I'm a cat person too," he announced, apparently not recognizing her blunder. "Well, really, I'm a sucker for any animal."

"Sounds as if you two have a lot in common," Jackson noted, still watching his daughter.

Eve shot her father a look. He held up both hands in protest.

"You like animals?" Detective Lujan asked.

She nodded.

"She tried to make the Catholics build a shelter out here for all of the strays she brought in." The Captain leaned back against his chair. "That's just one of the reasons she got in trouble."

Eve suddenly wanted the conversation to be over. "Thank you for stopping by, Detective Lujan," she said, reaching out to take Daisy from his arms. "I will definitely let you know if I hear from Brother Anthony. And now, I really have to go because I'm late for chapel."

The police officer handed her the cat. "Lauds," he noted. "And I'm afraid you missed that," he added, brushing the hair from his coat.

Eve turned so that she could see the clock on the desk. *What time is it?* she wondered. *And how much of this day have I slept through?*

"They're serving breakfast now," Detective Lujan responded. "It's after eight. Oh, and I heard a little about the other nuns being sent away. I'm sorry about that."

Eve dropped her eyes.

"I guess you're the last to leave."

She didn't respond.

128

"Well, anyway, I'm sure we'll see each other again, Sister, if you stay, that is."

There was a pause and Eve still made no reply.

"I'll be around," he said, backing away from the door. "So nice to meet you, Captain Divine."

And she was just about to correct what she thought would be the common mispronunciation of her family's last name when she suddenly realized he had said it perfectly. She stood at the door, watching as he turned and headed down the hall.

"You already in trouble?" came the question from behind her.

Seventeen

"What is it with all of you?" Eve spun around and asked Daniel. He had apparently entered the building from the other end of the hallway. "Can't a person have time to get ready before folks just start showing up at her door in the morning?"

He stopped before getting all the way to where she stood. "Hey, is that what you call the ministry of hospitality around here?" He grinned. "Because if it is, Father Benedict may be rolling over in his grave."

She put Daisy down and held out her arms. Detective Hively came over and gave her a big hug. "Now that's what I'm talking about," he said. "Hello, Little Sister."

Eve released her father's former partner. "Where have you been?" she asked, still somewhat shaken from her last visitor. She dropped her arms and turned back to the door to her room, managing to get a good look down the hall where Detective Lujan had just headed. She walked in when she could see that he was already gone. Daisy was sitting on the bed.

"It's only eight o'clock," Daniel answered, following her into the room. He saw Jackson and gave a quick salute. "Partner," he said, greeting him.

"What have you found out?" Eve's father wanted to know.

Daniel gave a disapproving look first at the Captain and then back at Eve. "Is this the way you greet people here? No 'How you doing, friend?' Or 'Come in and have a seat, Daniel'?"

"Come in and have a seat, Daniel," Eve and Jackson said at the same time, and then they couldn't help themselves and both let out a laugh.

"That's more like it." Daniel sat on the edge of the desk, angling himself so that he could face father and daughter.

"What time did you get here and what did Lujan want?" he asked.

"I think the sister here might just have a crush on the new policeman," Jackson said.

"What?" She shook her head. "I do not." She rolled her eyes and gave her attention to the detective sitting by her. "Did you drive the Beemer?" She had been with him when he picked out his new car, and she was curious to see if he was driving it today.

"Don't change the subject. And no, I am not driving the Beemer. It's not shipped yet. And I don't plan to drive it when I'm working. It's for the weekends." He winked. "What did the detective want?" he asked again.

"I had a letter from Brother Anthony," she answered.

"The victim's brother who's also a brother," Daniel retorted.

Eve nodded and sat back down on the bed next to her cat.

"What did it say?" he asked.

"That he was sorry for the evil he had done and that he had to leave to make things right," Jackson replied.

"I'm not a lawyer, but that doesn't sound very good" came the response.

"He's upset," Eve explained, wanting to set him straight. "He's upset because his sister is dead and he thinks that because he gave her some writings he brought this danger to her."

"Well, it appears as if he's right about that," Daniel noted. "Do I want to know how it happened that you got the letter?"

"He left it in Father Oliver's room. I went to find him and found the letter instead," she replied.

"And this was after you were at the crime scene, dropping teacups and damaging the evidence?" the detective asked.

Eve looked over at her father. "Did you tell him everything?"

He shrugged. "It's my experience that the whole truth is best."

She fell back against the pillow and crossed her arms over her chest. Daisy hopped down, getting out of the way.

"Anthony came to the chapel, told me how he had found Kelly dead and about these writings he had discovered. I told him to wait there, but he went to Father Oliver's room to make a confession after I left. Later I ran into the vice superior in the guest room."

"Where the dead woman was," Daniel added.

"Where Kelly was, yes," she replied.

He appeared to be waiting for the rest of the story.

"Father Oliver sent me to find Anthony when we heard the police arrive." She sat up. "Which reminds me, who called the police in the first place?" This had bothered her before, and she had not yet received an answer.

Daniel shrugged. "Dispatch notes say it was an unidentified caller, male; that's all

133

we know."

Eve shook her head slowly. "See, that's so fishy to me," she noted. "Who else knew about Kelly other than Father Oliver and Anthony and myself? It had to be the killer. He had to have been watching and known we might mess up the way he left things."

"And how had he left things?" Daniel wanted to know.

"In a way that made Anthony appear like the guilty party."

"And just how was that?"

Eve did not want to elaborate, afraid she would make mention of Anthony taking his sister tea, and she wasn't sure she wanted to tell even her friend that slight bit of incriminating evidence.

"The caller could have been the brother." Daniel didn't push her. "You said that only you and the abbot were in the room. Anthony could have called and then got nervous and ran before our guys arrived."

"No," Eve answered. "That doesn't make sense."

"Well, Sister, it doesn't have to make sense. You said he was distraught, that he blamed himself. Maybe he thought turning things over to the authorities was the right thing to do." He leaned in her direction. "Which it is, and you know that, right? Call-

134

ing the police is the right thing to do when you have a dead person on the floor." He sat back up.

"Yes, I realize that," she answered him, sitting up as well and stuffing the pillow behind her back. "What else do you know?"

"The fingerprints haven't been processed yet, but they found a few sets of prints on the teapot and the desk." He waited to see if Eve would respond.

She did not.

"We're still waiting for the tox screen, but it does appear she died from cyanide poisoning. And no evidence supports that this was suicide."

Eve was hoping there was more, since this was information she already had.

"The professor who showed up later?" she asked.

"Dr. Peter Pierce, associate, perhaps friend, of the victim. He claims he flew in late last night to hear the speech scheduled for today by Dr. Middlesworth. He reported that she had called him at the last minute to come because she said that she had new material about her topic. He did not say that he knew what the material was, just that she had asked him to come."

"And you believe him?" Eve watched her friend closely.

"I didn't hear him," Daniel answered. "This is just secondhand."

She nodded. "Well, he would be my first suspect," she said.

Daniel shrugged. "Boots said he was pretty upset when he came in the room."

"That can be a show, Dan," Jackson offered, joining the conversation.

"Yes, it could be," he replied. "But at this point, we have no motive for him."

"Well, I hope you're going to dig a little deeper," Eve noted.

"No stone unturned," Daniel said, glancing over at his former partner with a wink.

"That's the way we always did it," Jackson agreed.

"So, what can I do?" Eve asked, rubbing her hands together.

"You can't do anything," Daniel answered. "The fact that you were present at the murder scene and then left it before the police arrived, probably dropping your prints everywhere, and because of your known relationship with the victim's brother *and* as one of the last people to see him before he ran off, well, you're what we'd call a person with vital information, Little Sister. You're a witness. All you can do is stay put and out of the way."

Eve started to laugh, but the look on Dan-

iel's face was serious enough that she suddenly understood that this was not teasing
from her old friend.

EIGHTEEN

Daniel and Captain Divine left only when Eve promised that she wouldn't go anywhere. She finally agreed to stay where she was because she decided that it wouldn't actually be such a bad thing to remain at the monastery and find out more about the writings Anthony had taken from Isleta and what they might mean. She might also get lucky and discover the answer to the all-important question: Who else might know about them? The campus library was full of books and articles about Sister Maria, and Eve thought that examining those resources might lead her to figure out what Anthony had found and what the writings might mean.

She wasn't sure what Father Oliver had decided to do about the conference scheduled to begin that day, the one she had been so excited to attend, but she guessed with the murder of the keynote speaker, it would be called off. No one would be up for speeches and panel discussions, knowing about the homicide. Daniel had even told her that many of the guests had departed once they were interviewed by the police and had given contact information. It seemed the murder had closed down the monastery for a while.

Before the Captain left, Eve went out to the truck with him to retrieve Daisy's sandbox and water bowl and other items essential to the cat's comfort and well-being. When she asked him why exactly he had brought the pet to her, he claimed at first that the cat was driving him crazy without Eve there to care for her, but then later he said he thought she could use a little company, implying that he knew ahead of time that Daniel intended for Eve to stay at the monastery and not return to Madrid.

When she got back to the room, Eve made a small space for the food and water bowls near the desk by the window, filling them both and positioning them on a small towel. She put the litter box underneath the sink in the bathroom, placing a piece of news-paper she had brought with her beneath it before emptying the sand into it. When she finished setting up her cat's housekeeping, she jumped onto the bed with Daisy, scratching her long, soft ears and rubbing underneath her chin. She was very glad to have the cat with her, and while she petted the little stray, she recalled some of the animals she had snuck into her room over the twenty years she had been in residence at the monastery. She soon lost count, as there had been so many neglected and abandoned cats and dogs.

"You know you're trespassing," she said to Daisy as she stretched out beside Eve on the bed. The purring soon started.

"Yep, it's true, you are not allowed to be in the living quarters," she added, recalling the many times she'd heard that very sentence from Father Oliver as well as from some of the older nuns who didn't want cats and dogs in the residences.

"You can stay outside but not near the front entrance, somewhere out back, and you cannot come in the rooms," she said, trying to sound strict.

Eve leaned back and threw her arm above her head. "Of course, I guess we're in the same boat now," she said. "I guess we're both actually trespassing these days. Neither of us is welcomed in this community."

Daisy snuggled inside Eve's arm, intending to take a nap. Eve moved aside and sat up. She knew there was too much to do to allow herself to fall back to sleep. Besides, she knew she needed to change clothes before somebody else appeared at her door. She thought a shower sounded like a good idea and headed into the bathroom.

She turned on the water, hoping to get it warm before stepping in, and it wasn't until she was starting to undress that she felt in her pants pocket and found the small torn piece of material that she had taken the night before from the victim's hand. She turned off the water, went back into the other room, and sat down at the desk, feeling a little guilty for what she had done. She placed the tiny square of blue cloth in front of her.

It was darker than the blue of her New Mexican skies but not as dark as navy. It was closer to the color of turquoise, the stone so popular in the jewelry native to the Southwest. The cloth felt like cotton, nothing synthetic, and the edges were frayed as if the piece had been torn from a larger piece of fabric. It was clearly something Kelly had taken from the last person who had seen her alive. It had to be from her killer, and as Eve smoothed out the small blue piece, she knew she shouldn't have taken it from the victim's hand or, at the very least, should have given it to Daniel,

141

who had only just left the room.

I just forgot I had it, she thought, knowing how lame her excuse would sound to the police. She picked up the piece of fabric again and placed it under her nose, checking to see if there was a particular odor to it. There was not. She slid it between her fingers, trying to imagine what the killer was wearing to have left such a small piece.

A robe? she wondered, recalling that the monks never wore that color and suddenly becoming hopeful that this could be evidence that the killer was not Anthony, because surely it could be agreed by everyone who knew him that he was never seen wearing anything this color. Of course, she knew it would be difficult to make the police believe that she had found it in the victim's hand. *"Oh, that's convenient!"* she imagined the officers saying when she handed it over.

She studied the scrap of material more closely and noted that it did appear to be from a more feminine article of clothing, perhaps because of the lightness of the fabric, the bright blue shade. She didn't know any man who would wear a coat or cloak that color. She touched her face with it, sliding it lightly across her cheek. She closed her eyes and then quickly snapped them back open.

The Indians from the area who had reported the visits from Sister Maria claimed she wore a blue cape; that's how she got the nickname, after all. Somebody, the murderer, Eve thought, was leaving a clue, letting it be known that he understood the significance of these undisclosed writings. He either wanted the authorities to think the Blue Nun had actually appeared to the victim or that the murder was in some way for her or by her. Eve shook her head.

If the piece of fabric was a clue, it didn't really make sense as to what meaning the clue held. She knew she should just turn it over to Daniel, and she told herself that was exactly what she would do. Only later, perhaps when they had gotten matches to the fingerprints in the room or when they had other evidence that didn't incriminate Brother Anthony.

Eve reopened the laptop computer and typed "the Blue Nun" into the small box for the search engine. She scrolled through all of the articles and videos about Sister Maria, most of which she had already read or seen. She went to the second page, clicked on an article from a religious journal, and began to read.

It reported what she had already read —

that the nun from Agreda was said to wear a blue cape when she appeared to the Jumano Indians. She made more than five hundred appearances, it noted, all of them while wearing this outer garment. The article also explained that this cape was said to have magical or miraculous powers. It reported that everywhere Sister Maria's blue cape was said to land, the flowers seen so widely in Texas, bluebonnets, were said to spring up. This state flower was named because the small blossoms looked like the bonnets worn by the pioneer women who traveled to the West. *Lupinus texensis* could be seen along highways and meadows all across the state, blooming from March to May.

The article noted that the legend of the flower in Texas had been told for generations and that no one could trace the origins of this story. Eve picked up the fabric once again and studied it. She turned back to her computer, planning to turn it off and go back into the bathroom to take her shower, when she glanced once again at the screen, the article still there. It was the names of the authors of the piece that captured Eve's attention.

Dr. Peter Pierce and Dr. Lauren Taylor-Pierce, University of Texas, from 2014.

NINETEEN

Peter Pierce is married? Eve wondered, suddenly very interested in this associate of Kelly Middlesworth. *Perhaps this murder didn't have anything to do with the writings of Sister Maria but rather something as pedestrian as a jealous wife,* she thought. She typed the name Lauren Taylor-Pierce into her search engine and found a bio that noted that Lauren Taylor-Pierce, like Peter Pierce and Kelly Middlesworth, was also a professor in Austin, in the Department of Anthropology.

It also appeared to Eve as if the married scholars had written several articles together about indigenous North American cultures and their religious traditions. There were some journal citations about Indian tribes in Mexico, the Aztecs and Toltecs, and the role of the Catholic missionaries who came with the Spanish conquistadores into that country, and a few articles about the New

Mexico Pueblo Revolt in 1680 and the consequences for the Catholic missionaries during that event.

Dr. Lauren Taylor-Pierce had written several articles about the Jumano Indians, finding a connection between them and the other Pueblo Indians in central New Mexico and western Texas. She had, in fact, written her thesis about this tribe and the theories concerning what had happened to them, searching out reasons as to why they were no longer in existence. She was cited as an expert in the Jumano culture, while her husband was noted as a religion scholar in the field of Catholicism and the Pueblo Indians.

Eve scrolled through the articles and books attributed to them both, even finding one that included the name of Kelly Middlesworth as one of the contributors, providing a clear connection between the murder victim and these two professional associates. Eve read through a couple of the articles, finding most of them too academic for her, before finally ending her research. She closed the laptop, and as she was taking in all the information she had just uncovered, she suddenly thought about the first case she'd worked on with her father. It had to do with the murder of a Hollywood director, and Eve remembered how quickly everyone had jumped to the conclusion that his mistress, Megan Flint, had been the one who killed him. It was assumed that she had been angry with her lover because he had not been honest with her about his plans to divorce his wife, causing her to snap and consequently kill him in some kind of jealous rage.

"Love can make a person do all kinds of crazy things," she remembered one of the police officers saying after Megan's arrest. *"Especially when there's another woman still posing in the family picture."*

She had never really thought that Megan would have murdered Charles Cheston, but she did eventually consider the possibility after Megan confessed to bouts of rage over the fact that her lover had not filed for divorce as he had promised. Even though Eve had never experienced that kind of jealousy or passion in a relationship, she had learned that angry lovers often made serious suspects in murder cases.

Eve picked up the fragment of blue material once again and wondered if the writings of the Blue Nun were used as a cover-up for the real motive for murder. Perhaps Dr. Pierce, *Dr. Lauren Taylor-Pierce,* had also heard about the grand discovery and decided this was the perfect opportunity to get rid of her husband's beautiful young associate. She could make sure that the spotlight was shining on the theft as the motive and perhaps even her husband as a suspect, moving the investigation away from her and her jealousy.

"So, what do you think? Was it the jealous wife who killed her?" Eve asked her cat, still lounging on the bed.

Daisy raised her head and then quickly stretched and returned to sleep.

Look at me! I never used to give a thought to the depravity of humans, Eve mused, realizing that as a nun she kept her focus on the goodness of humanity, the divine spark in each soul. However, as a partner to her father, a private detective, she was starting to notice and even expect to see a different side of people, and it was not the most favorable side, she thought.

"Maybe I'm wrong," she announced and picked up her cell phone. She searched the Internet and found the phone numbers for the University of Texas, including the contact information for the anthropology department. She punched in the number, waited a few seconds, trying to decide exactly what she would say if she did get through to the professor, and then hit the call button.

A recorded greeting came through on the second ring, explaining how to reach various people who worked in the department, listing their names and extensions. When she heard the number for Dr. Lauren Taylor, she punched it in and waited, glancing over at the clock and wondering what an anthropology professor might be doing on a Thursday morning.

As the phone rang, Eve considered what kind of message she might leave, deciding not to give away any information about what had happened at the monastery.

"Dr. Taylor's office." It was a real person answering. A woman was on the other end of the line.

Eve swallowed hard. She wasn't expecting to speak to anyone and suddenly began to regret the decision to make the call.

"Dr. Pierce?" she said after an awkward pause. "Dr. Lauren Taylor-Pierce?" she added, making sure she had dialed the right number.

"Dr. Taylor isn't in," came the reply.

Eve sighed, relieved not to be talking to the professor. She paused.

"Hello," the voice said. "Is there something I can help you with?"

"Oh, I'm sorry." Eve realized she had

149

hesitated a bit too long. "Is she teaching this morning?"

"No, Dr. Taylor doesn't have a class on Thursdays," came the reply.

Eve waited, trying to decide what to say or what question to ask.

"Are you a student of hers? You have questions about the midterm?"

"No," Eve answered. "No, I'm not a student. I'm a colleague; well, more of an old friend, actually, an acquaintance really." Eve was stumbling.

"Oh, okay."

Eve cleared her throat.

"Are you a reporter?"

"Um, I do some of that," Eve replied, shaking her head and rolling her eyes, hating to hear herself tell such a complete lie.

"Are you calling about the recent findings?"

"The recent findings?" Eve repeated.

"Yeah, the writings from the nun in Spain."

"Sister Maria de Jesus de Agreda?"

"Yeah, that's the one," the young woman responded.

"Has there been something new discovered?" Eve asked, wondering how many people actually knew about these supposedly secret pages.

"Oh, yeah," came the reply. "Dr. Taylor went to New Mexico to find out about it, some convent near Santa Fe. You from the *Journal*?"

"The *Journal*?"

"Yeah, she said someone from the *Journal for the Scientific Study of Religions* might be calling. That's why I'm in her office, taking her calls. She didn't want to miss any."

"Oh, okay," Eve replied. "Um, no, I'm not from the *Journal for the Scientific Study of Religions*. I'm from the *Journal of Native American Anthropology,*" she added, making up the name of a magazine. "We've spoken before."

There was a pause.

"I hadn't heard of that one," came the response.

"Right, well . . ." Eve was backpedaling. "We're a small journal focusing on . . ." She stopped.

"Native American anthropology."

"Yes, exactly."

"Uh-huh."

"When did Dr. Pierce leave for New Mexico?" Eve asked, changing the subject.

"*Dr. Taylor* left this morning," the young assistant answered, emphasizing the professor's maiden name. "And I wouldn't call her that if you want an interview," she added.

"Pierce?" Eve asked.

"Yep. If you knew her, you'd know she doesn't want his name connected to hers. It's been awhile since she did that."

"Oh?"

"You know, I'm at the computer and I'm searching for the *Journal of Native American Anthropology,* and there's not one coming up." The tone of her voice hinted at suspicion.

"Yes, well, that's because we're very new, haven't even put up the website yet. But we're working on that, and we'll show up on Google's list very soon. Just tell Dr. Pierce, I mean Dr. Taylor, that I'll be calling again to set up an appointment for an interview when she gets back."

"You want me to tell her your name?"

Eve thought for a second. "Daisy," she answered, looking over at her pet. "Daisy Cat." And she hung up, glad to be done with that call.

TWENTY

Eve decided that after her shower she should extend that special brand of Benedictine hospitality by finding the two college professors and introducing herself, thereby getting a better read on them. She hurried through the shower, dressed, and towel-dried her hair. After placing the towel back on the rack, Eve took a long look at herself in the mirror. She suddenly noticed the wrinkles around her eyes and the gray strands in her hair. She leaned in, getting a closer look, and shook her head. Studying herself this way seemed like a new experience, and she wondered why she was even doing it. She certainly didn't plan to change anything regarding her appearance. She wasn't about to start wearing lipstick or eyeliner like Dorisanne. She wasn't planning to get a color and cut for her mousy brown hair.

"I am what I am," she said out loud to

herself and then grabbed a comb off the small shelf and ran it through her hair once, put it back on the shelf, and looked again.

As she examined herself, she realized that one of the things she had always loved about being a nun was the lack of emphasis on appearance. It was such a different way to be a woman, she thought, remembering the way she strived for inner beauty, the ways she saw it in the other nuns. None of them ever struggled with whether they looked pale or were in need of shades of pink on their lips or cheeks. They didn't just take up new values of living lives of faith and seeking to be of service; they also gave up values of Western society that demanded makeup and fashion from women. And even though Eve could never remember having been as concerned about those things as her sister, there was a time when she paid attention to how she looked, worried that she didn't quite fit in. But once she took her vows, she'd never struggled with those issues again. In fact, there was a time she took down the mirrors in her room because she wanted to completely rid herself of the temptation of vanity. She wanted to spend her time and energy focusing on the contents of her heart and not on what was lacking in her physical appearance. She stared at herself in the mirror a few moments more and then shook her head. Eve turned away, leaving the bathroom and the mirror, and walked into the other room and searched for her rosary and phone that she remembered had been on the desk. As she grabbed those two things she noticed once again the small piece of blue cloth she had taken from the crime scene. She placed it in the narrow desk drawer and stuck the other two items in her pocket. She gave Daisy a quick scratch under the chin, promising to return soon, and she left the room, heading down the hallway to the front offices.

She rounded the corner and suddenly found herself squarely in the middle of what appeared to be a press conference. Father Oliver's back was to her, and standing next to him were the two investigating officers, Detective Bootskievely and Detective Lujan. All eyes that had been on the three of them immediately turned to her. Eve stopped and then started to back up. Daniel was standing behind the small but lively group of reporters and camera operators and he smiled when he saw Eve, waving her over. She changed direction once more and quickly moved behind the three men being questioned and headed toward her friend.

"You sure know how to make an entrance," he said in a whisper, elbowing her as she made her way to stand beside him.

"Why didn't you tell me there was a media event scheduled for this morning?" she asked, glancing around at the group of people standing in the entranceway.

"Didn't know about it," he replied. "It was sort of an impromptu thing," he added. "The reporter from Channel 7 found out the reporter from Channel 13 was here and she called the gal at Channel 4. I think they're all on each other's speed dials."

Eve watched as the cameras rolled and the young reporters took notes. She noticed a number of folks standing behind the media representatives and tried to see if Dr. Pierce and Dr. Taylor were in the crowd. She thought she would be able to recognize them from the photos she had seen when she researched them on the computer earlier. She searched the group, going from face to face, but didn't see anyone resembling either of them. She did recognize many of the visitors from the meals they'd shared earlier in the week. It seemed like some of the guests who had planned to attend the conference had stayed after all. Some of them met her eyes and nodded or shook their heads as they were hearing what had happened the night before.

156

"The Captain leave?" he asked.

She nodded. "He said he was going back to Madrid; he's got some other case he's working on," she responded, recalling a few details her father had mentioned. "Somebody thinks there's a ghost at the fire station," she added. "They're paying him to find out for sure."

Daniel nodded.

She turned back to the abbot as he was finishing up his statement. "What's he been saying?" she asked.

"Oh, just that there has been a tragedy at the monastery and that they're asking for prayers during this difficult time, and to give the brothers some privacy." He looked at Eve. "And that people need to let the police officers do their jobs and not get in the way."

She rolled her eyes at him and watched as Father Oliver appeared to turn things over to the two investigating officers. Detective Boots stepped up as Father Oliver moved away from the small podium filled with microphones.

"We don't have any further statements to make at this time," he announced, holding up both hands. "This is an ongoing investigation, and we will let you know when we have anything to reveal to the community. We need to contact family members of the deceased before announcing anyone's name. I hope you will honor that request, as I'm sure you all understand what a tragic event this is."

One of the reporters raised her hand and stepped forward. "Caren Cox, Action 7 News," she said as way of introduction. "I heard the victim was going to deliver a speech at the conference scheduled at the monastery for today through this weekend."

The detective shook his head. "We cannot verify any such statement."

Another reporter, obviously seeing what was happening and wanting to get in on the questions, moved to stand beside her colleague. "Cathy Niroo, Channel 4, Award-Winning News. Is it true this is being investigated as a homicide?"

The detective shook his head and held up his hands again as if to say he would not comment.

"Officer, at least give us that much. Is it a homicide?" Another reporter had pushed her way from the middle of the group to the front. "Barbara Trembley from the *Journal.*"

"We are calling this a suspicious death at this time. We have not ruled out any possibilities."

"I heard she was poisoned," came a voice

from the crowd. "And that her brother, a monk here, is missing."

Eve turned to the area where the voice had come from and noticed a man she hadn't seen before. He was of medium height and wearing a black leather vest, jeans, and a long-sleeved striped shirt. He had his arms crossed over his chest, wore black plastic glasses, and had long red hair pulled back into a ponytail, a full red beard covering his face. At first Eve thought she recognized him, but as she tried to focus on him more clearly, people kept moving into her line of vision.

She realized he hadn't made the comment, however; that had come from a young man standing beside him. But at first glance, the red-haired man appeared to be very interested in the remarks and in the response. He was watching the detective closely. She was staring, still trying to place him, when he suddenly turned and looked in her direction. She immediately glanced away.

"We do not have any information about other family members present at the monastery," Detective Jared Bootskievely replied. "And there has been no cause of death given at this time," he added. "We thank you for coming out here, and when we know something more, we will have a statement to deliver. If you'll excuse us, we have a lot of work to do." He backed away from the podium, and Detective Lujan and Father Oliver joined him as he headed in the direction of the abbot's office down the hallway behind them.

"Well, that will not give them the headlines they were hoping for," Daniel stated. "Who are you looking at?" he asked, following Eve's eyes as she scanned the crowd.

"A blast from the past," she answered, unable to spot the man again. "And not the good kind."

TWENTY-ONE

"I'm just going to walk over there and say my prayers," Eve said when Daniel questioned her about heading down to the guest quarters. Not coming up with a connection between the man with the red hair and the murder, she still hoped to find the professors.

"That's all you're doing?" he wanted to know.

"Well, if I happen to run into somebody who was close to Kelly, a colleague, let's say from Texas, I might want to welcome them here and ask if I can assist them in any way."

"If my facts are straight, you don't live or work here anymore," Daniel noted.

Eve smiled. "A sister in Christ is willing to help wherever she happens to be."

"A sister in Christ needs to stay out of trouble," he replied.

"Which is why I must go and say my prayers," she explained, turning to walk out the main entrance.

"If I recall correctly, there is no outdoor chapel in the vicinity of the guest quarters," Daniel responded.

"The last I heard, a person doesn't have to be in a church to pray," she replied, standing at the door.

"That's true," he said. "But if a person says they're going somewhere to pray and suddenly finds themselves someplace they shouldn't be — *like a crime scene . . . ,*" he emphasized, those four words spoken a bit louder, causing a few people around him to turn in his direction. He smiled at them and then turned back to Eve, his tone a bit softer. "Then that person might later wish that they had gone to church."

Eve waved to her friend without turning around to acknowledge his warning, expecting him to be at her heels.

"Stay out of the way, Sister," he called out.

She dropped her hand, and when she didn't hear him following, she hurried beyond the front door and down the path to the row of guest rooms.

The yellow tape was still wrapped around the first room, one end tied around the doorknob and then wrapped about two poles outside the room, with the other end tied onto one of the chairs that was sitting outside the door next to the small table. Eve could hear voices from inside the room but didn't recognize any, so she didn't stop.

As she passed the second room, she noticed that the door was partly open and she decided to peek in to see who had been staying next door to the victim. She quietly knocked on the door, opening it wider as she did so, allowing her to get a better look inside.

It seemed uninhabited. The bed was made; there was nothing on the desk. The curtains on the window were closed. No clothes, bags, or shoes anywhere. She wondered if the monk in charge of cleaning had already done his work that morning or if no one had been registered in the room next to Kelly's.

She snuck in and sat on the bed. She wondered if the guest in that room had heard anything and assumed that an interview with the person next door to the victim would have been one of the first interviews the police conducted. It was clear that someone in this room had the best vantage point for hearing or seeing anything suspicious. A thought came to her: *Kelly had to have known the killer. Otherwise, somebody would have heard a scuffle, a scream, something. Kelly let her killer in either because she knew that person or because the person gained her trust and she invited them in. Or with the unlocked door, the murderer just came in after Kelly had taken the poison.*

She stood up, even more resolved to talk to the professors who knew as much about the Blue Nun as the victim did. She walked out and moved past the other rooms, wishing she had gotten the list of assignments from the office at the main building so she could see which guest was in which room, and find out if the two colleagues had made a last-minute room reservation when it was decided they would attend the conference. She knew having that list would have made it a lot easier to find them and subsequently introduce herself to them, allowing her the opportunity to see what they knew about the murder and the discovery of Sister Maria's writings.

Eve knew she had not heard Kelly mention any colleagues from Texas that she expected to come to the event. And Eve recalled that the detectives in charge of the investigation had mentioned that Dr. Pierce had arrived at Kelly's room the night of the murder saying that he had only just gotten to the monastery.

Eve walked around the corner of the guest quarters and began looking over the cars

164

parked in front of the rooms and in the spaces in the small lot nearby. Most of them appeared to be from New Mexico, with the bright yellow license plates bearing the red Zia sun emblem that was also on the state flag, the state capitol, and highway markers. There were these as well as a few of the new turquoise plates, with the state name and USA clearly displayed.

Eve knew that this information had been added to both styles of license plates in the last fifteen years or so, since more than a few New Mexicans had been stopped while driving in other states and hassled to show an international driver's license because it was thought that they were visiting from another country, Mexico. Eve recalled her recent trip to Vegas with Daniel and explaining to a store clerk that she was from New Mexico after being asked if people spoke English there.

"No tanto," she had finally answered, "not so much." And the clerk asking simply nodded and smiled, making the final comment that Eve should be careful if she was living out of the States, that it was not always safe to be in those "foreign places." She and Daniel had a good laugh about that.

In the lot there was a van from California belonging to a group of students and professors she knew who had come from the Jesuit college in Santa Clara, and one from a seminary in Denver. She'd met people from both institutions, and they had enjoyed several meals together. There was also an old white truck just like the one she had seen the night before leaving the grounds. She wondered if the person had left after the commotion and then returned the next morning, and she made a mental note to try to find out who the truck belonged to. She continued searching and finally noticed, between the monastery station wagon and an SUV with Arizona tags, an old green Subaru with Texas plates. It was the only one she saw from the Longhorn State.

Eve walked over to the car, quickly finding on the back window a University of Texas sticker that marked the vehicle as one driven by faculty. The car was dusty, not uncommon for the vehicles in New Mexico, and there was orange mud on all four tires. She moved a little closer, glanced around, and seeing no one, cupped her hand on the driver's-side window and peeked inside. There was a stack of papers on the passenger's seat. She couldn't exactly see what they were, but they appeared to be something from students. She could make out red marks and a number in the right-hand corner of one. Paper cups and empty bags from fast-food places lay on the floorboard, and a gym bag and a pair of sneakers were on the backseat. She could see a few tennis balls on the floor and a couple of other stacks of papers under the canvas bag.

"Is there something I can help you with?" the voice from behind her asked.

Eve, startled by the question, whipped around and stood face-to-face with a tall woman, her long dark hair smoothed back into a ponytail, her hands held at her sides, and a piercing stare clearly focused on the woman peering into the windows of a car that didn't belong to her.

TWENTY-TWO

"You must be Dr. Taylor," Eve said, trying to sound as normal as she could and recognizing the professor from the pictures she had seen in her Internet search.

"I must be," came the chilly response.

Eve held out her hand. "I'm Sister Evangeline," she noted with her best smile. "I used to be in the community here," she added.

"Used to be?" the other woman replied, not taking the extended hand. She waited, giving the impression that she wanted to hear more.

"It's now a monastery for the Benedictine monks," Eve answered, dropping her hand. "The nuns . . . we have all found new places to live and serve."

"Was there some scandal?" Dr. Taylor grinned, raising her eyebrows, appearing to enjoy the idea.

"Only in the fact that we never had a say

in the matter."

"Well, you are a nun, right?" the professor asked, shrugging.

"That's true," Eve answered. "And we do take our promise to submit ourselves to the authority of the church quite seriously."

"Even when they kick you out of your home?" She watched Eve closely.

"Even when they ask us to move," Eve answered carefully. "Yes."

The professor didn't respond. Finally, she shook her head. "Well, that's the life you chose," she said.

Eve nodded, deciding not to explain where she was in her discernment process or to discuss her disappointment and anger about the situation at the abbey.

"So, in spite of your vowed submission, what are you doing here? Looking to steal a car and make your getaway?"

Eve felt her face flush, knowing her hand was clearly in the cookie jar. "I was just admiring the Subaru," she said cheerfully. "My father needs a new car, and I was thinking this might be a good choice. Is this the '05 model?" She faced the car, sliding her hand across the front, feigning interest in the small wagon. "Four cylinders?"

"I'm afraid I don't know anything about cylinders," the woman answered. "They teach you that in nun school?"

"No, not in *nun school,*" she said. "As a girl I spent a lot of time with my dad hanging out in the garage," Eve added. She glanced away from the car and back to the guest from Texas. "Are you here for the conference? Friends with the keynote speaker?" she asked.

The professor studied the woman standing before her. "I got here yesterday," she answered. "Yes, I know Dr. Middlesworth; we work together at the university."

Eve nodded.

"How did you know who I was?"

Eve recalled that she had acknowledged the Texan by name when she was startled by her earlier. More backpedaling, she knew. "Kelly showed me a picture."

Dr. Taylor seemed disbelieving. "Kelly Middlesworth had a photograph of me?"

Eve shook her head. "No, not a photograph, just online, some research she showed me, recent articles about the Lady in Blue. I read some of your work, and I recalled something you had written with Dr. Pierce, I believe, another colleague."

"Not just another colleague," came the response.

Eve waited. "Pardon?" she asked.

"Not just another colleague," the profes-

170

sor repeated. "He's my husband."

"Oh, I see," she said. "I didn't realize that," she quickly added.

"That's because it's not true," came a reply from behind Eve.

She turned around to see a man walking up to them. He was of a medium build and height, wore his brown hair long, and had piercing blue eyes. She instantly recognized this professor as well. Here was the man she had been searching for.

"Good morning, Lauren," he said, staring across the car at the other professor.

She did not respond.

"I hadn't heard that you were here," he noted.

Eve watched the two of them. The tension between them was palpable.

"I was here last night." She paused. "And you?"

Eve saw a smile form on his lips. "I arrived last night as well."

There was an awkward pause.

Eve cleared her throat. "I'm Sister Evangeline Divine," she said, making her introduction. "I used to be in community here at Pecos," she added, extending her hand again and then dropping it when she realized he was not watching her and was instead staring at the other woman.

The man looked away and extended his hand to Eve. "I'm Peter Pierce," he said, returning the greeting. "Dr. Middlesworth called me yesterday and asked me to join her here for her speech." Tears filled his eyes. "I got here too late." He took out a handkerchief and wiped his eyes. "She was gone before I arrived."

"Murdered, you mean," Dr. Taylor noted.

Dr. Pierce and Eve turned to her.

"She wasn't gone; she was murdered," Dr. Taylor clarified. She crossed her arms across her chest and narrowed her eyes in his direction. "I hate it when you don't state the truth, when you try to make something sound like it's not as dirty as it really is."

She paused and then faced Dr. Pierce.

"She was murdered. Your girlfriend was murdered. And you don't need to put on a show for the two of us. We're not investigators."

"This is not a . . ." He stopped.

"What are you doing here, anyway?" he asked, leaving the last response unfinished.

Eve waited for the answer. This was a question she had wanted to ask as well.

"I know about the writings," Lauren Taylor said, watching the man closely. "I know about Sister Maria's secret writings," she repeated.

He snapped around to face her.

"Yes, that's right. I know all about them," she noted. "You should be more careful in picking your assistants."

Dr. Pierce shook his head. His face had reddened.

The woman smiled.

"Did you think she was going to give them to you?" he asked.

"No, I didn't think that," she replied. "But I did think that after I told her a few things about you and your promises to her, she certainly wouldn't give them to you either." Dr. Taylor raised her eyebrows and shrugged. "Never underestimate the power of a scorned woman," she said smugly. "And never listen to the promises of a desperate man."

Eve watched the two, her gaze moving back and forth between them as if she were watching a tennis match. The dialogue went from one to the other, insult to accusation back to more insults. She was learning a whole lot about their relationship and a whole lot more about motives for murder.

"You were not scorned or victimized by my relationship," the man responded. "We both knew this marriage was doomed years ago, long before I started seeing Kelly, so don't start playing the role of the betrayed wife now. It's way too late for that."

The woman blew out a breath and shook her head. "You're right about that. I was betrayed long before Kelly came on campus." She sneered. "Did Dr. Middlesworth know that you seem to enjoy the Intro to Religion course the most? The freshmen, I mean? The girls?"

He started to move toward the woman, his hands clenched into fists and his face tight with anger. Eve quickly stepped between them as Dr. Taylor turned to walk away.

"Face it, Peter, your girlfriend is dead and those precious pages are not coming to you." Lauren paused and then moved back to where he stood. "Tell me, did she agree to marry you even with all those gambling debts? Or did you fail to mention that to her too?"

He started in her direction, but Eve held him by the arm.

"It's always good to see you, Peter dear," was the last thing they heard as she made her exit.

TWENTY-THREE

"How I ever fell in love with that . . ." He stopped and glanced over at Eve. "I'm sorry," he said, appearing to be trying to regain his composure. He waved away the thought and shook his head. "I don't know why she came," he added.

"Well, it sounds like it might have been the same reason as you," Eve replied, watching for his response.

"Kelly called and asked me to come; I seriously doubt Lauren received the same call." He leaned against the front of the car and slid his fingers through his wavy brown hair.

"When did she call?" Eve asked.

The professor seemed confused. "What?"

"Kelly. When did she call?"

"I'm not exactly sure," he said without giving a direct answer.

"You said yesterday, is that right? Is that when she called and told you about the writings her brother had found?"

He shook his head. "I don't recall; we might have spoken before yesterday."

"Did she make you aware that she told her brother about you?" Eve wondered how much the professor actually knew about what had been happening at the monastery between the two siblings. "Did she tell you that he was really angry at her for telling you about the writings?"

Peter peered closely at Eve. "What is your role here?" he asked, skirting the question again.

Eve didn't want to change the subject, but it was a viable question. She knew she was starting to sound like a police officer.

"I used to live here, be a part of the community," she answered. "Since the sisters had to leave, I'm deciding where to go. But I'm here this weekend because of the conference. I value the work of Sister Maria; I'd like to see the beatification process completed. I'd like to see her become a saint. She deserves it."

"You sound like Kelly."

"Yeah?"

He nodded. "Yeah. She wasn't a faithful Catholic, not like her brother and her parents, but she'd felt connected to this nun ever since she first studied her, was devoted to seeing her reach sainthood. It was almost like a personal challenge for her."

Eve thought about Kelly, how excited she was when she talked about the Spanish nun. The research, the facts, the story — she did seem to make this her life's passion; she did want to see Sister Maria make it to full sainthood. Eve glanced over at Dr. Pierce and saw that he was tearing up again. He cleared his throat and took a moment to pull himself together.

"But now she'll never get to see if that happens." He shook his head.

"What was she going to do with the papers?"

"What?" He didn't seem to follow the line of conversation.

"The papers that Anthony had given Kelly — what was she going to do with them?"

He shrugged. "She was going to report them today at the keynote, and then I'm not sure after that."

"Did you have any ideas for her?" Eve leaned in.

He turned to her and gave her a slight smile. "You're not very good at this, Sister," he said.

She was confused. "Not very good at what?"

"You want to know if I'm the killer, don't

you? You think I showed up last night and stole the papers and murdered Kelly."

Eve didn't respond.

"Well, I didn't, okay?"

Eve could hear voices coming near them. She glanced around and saw the group from Santa Clara heading to their van. It looked as if they were leaving.

"She was dead when I got here," he added.

Eve nodded.

Their conversation stopped while they watched the students and professors load their stuff in the back and get in their vehicle. She waved at them as they left the parking area.

"But if she hadn't been dead," Eve said, returning to the conversation, "what did you think she should do with the papers that were found? What advice had you given her?"

"If she had what she said she had, they were worth a lot of money." He gave Eve a measured nod. "Is that what you want to know? Had I researched how much money we could make on the discovery?"

"We?" Eve had heard the slip.

"I was going to ask Kelly to marry me. I bought a ring before she left, and I was going to give it to her when she got back. When she called me with this news, I thought it would be perfect to give it to her while we were here."

"And I suppose that if someone wanted to verify your claim that the ring was bought before you got here last night, you could produce that dated receipt."

The professor smiled again. "I sort of get the feeling that I need to have a lawyer present when I'm talking to you."

Eve returned the smile. "Do you need a lawyer, Dr. Pierce?"

He reached into his pocket and pulled out a receipt. "Not that this is any of your business, but I wasn't here at the time of the murder."

She took the receipt from him. It was from an airline company, a claim that he had bought a ticket for a flight that was in the air at the time of Kelly's death estimated by the coroner. She handed it back to him. "You could have bought two tickets, arrived earlier. That's not hard to check."

"How well did you know her brother?" he asked, surprising Eve. "Anthony? Hasn't he suddenly disappeared? Doesn't everyone think he did this? Wasn't there a big fight of some kind?"

Eve didn't answer him, but his question did confirm that he knew about the conflict at dinner; Kelly had spoken to him earlier the night she was killed.

They both noticed the detectives when the two men rounded the corner of the row of guest rooms. And then she got an idea.

"I'm not sure you know this, Professor, but in my role here at the monastery, I am often privy to stories of a sort of . . ." She paused before continuing. "How should I say it? Intimate nature."

The professor cocked his head. She had his attention even though she wasn't completely sure of what she was doing.

"Kelly and I talked, Dr. Pierce, yesterday. And she told me some things about her research, her concerns. She gave me something to hold for her, a page." Eve stopped, turned, and watched the detectives. She hoped she sounded convincing.

"A page from what?" The eagerness was easily detected.

Eve didn't answer. She paused, deciding less was more. "It was nice to meet you, Dr. Pierce. I'm sure we'll see each other again." And she started to make her exit.

"That's it?" he called to her.

She turned back.

"No condolences, no 'I'm sorry for your loss,' nothing?" He paused. "I thought you religious people were more empathetic than the rest of us. I thought you'd have more to say to me than that."

"I'm sorry for your loss, Dr. Pierce," she said with a slight smile.

He seemed to be studying her. "Go say your prayers, Sister," he responded as he made his way to a vehicle parked next to the Subaru.

TWENTY-FOUR

Eve was hopeful that the detectives would not notice her as she tried to exit the parking lot and head up to the main building, but she was too late. As Dr. Peter Pierce drove past her, Detective Bootskievely motioned her to join them. She took in a breath and headed toward them.

"You did a nice job with the press," she said to Detective Bootskievely as she made it to where they were standing. "I guess Our Lady of Guadalupe Abbey is now the headline story for New Mexico."

The older officer scratched his chin. "Somebody apparently tweeted from here."

"I'm sorry," Eve responded, not understanding the reference.

"Tweet," he repeated and then held out his thumbs like he was texting on a smart phone. "It's the latest way to get your news," he added.

Eve shrugged. "Sorry, I don't know about that."

Detective Lujan smiled, and Eve felt that funny tumbling feeling again. She tried to shake it off. "So, I heard the line you gave the reporters, but do you have anything new?"

Bootskievely shook his head. "It's still early, so at this point, everything's new."

Eve nodded, counting down the hours since the murder. It had not yet been twenty-four.

"You know Dr. Pierce?" Boots wanted to know, the apparent real reason he had called her over.

"No," she answered, guessing they were curious about her conversation. "I had heard that he was upset, and I just wanted to make sure he knew there were resources for him if he needed any support while he stayed here." She touched her chest first and then dropped her head, a kind of bow.

"Yes, yes," the older detective said. "Of course, you would be doing your ministry here," he added, nodding.

She felt Detective Lujan's eyes on her.

"We've asked him to stay awhile," Boots added, watching the car as it moved out of the gate and onto the main road. "He and the victim were apparently close."

Eve glanced back up at Boots. "Sounds like it, yes," she responded. "Colleagues at the University of Texas."

"Now, Sister, you might not know about tweeting, but I'm somehow guessing you know they were more than colleagues." Boots leaned back with his hands on his hips, exposing his badge and gun. He winked.

"I could certainly see that he was taking the news of her death pretty hard, yes," she answered, not taking the bait. "If you asked him to stay, why is he leaving the grounds?" She knew they had watched him exit.

"He's not under house arrest." Boots paused for a minute. "Going to buy deodorant. I don't know. He's free to come and go, just not go and stay away."

Eve nodded. It made sense even if she did worry he would disappear.

"How did he seem to you?" Boots asked.

Eve glanced to where she had been talking to the professor. "Sad, sure; upset." She turned back to the detectives. "Is he a suspect?"

Boots smiled, winked at his partner, and nodded at Evangeline. "Daughter of Captain Jackson Di-*vine*," he said, holding out the last syllable, making sure to pronounce it correctly. "Darling, at this stage, every-

184

body's a suspect."

She nodded.

"Even you," he said and then started to laugh.

The tease startled Eve, and she didn't quite know how to respond.

"All right, Earl, you get on the phone and call up forensics, see what news they got for us from the tox screen about the brand of poison our killer likes to use." He glanced back at Eve. "You ever hear from the monk?"

"I'm sorry." Eve was confused again.

He pulled a pad out of his front pocket and opened it, glanced down, and then closed it before putting it back. "Anthony," he replied. "The victim's brother, the one who's missing, the one who had a fight with her, stole something from Isleta. Brother Anthony, you heard from him this morning?"

"I have not heard from Brother Anthony," she answered sincerely.

"Well, if he calls you, you'll let us know, right?" Boots reached up and pulled at the collar of his shirt.

"I doubt he will call me," she replied.

"Yes, but?" Boots wanted a promise.

"Yes, if he calls me, I will definitely let you know."

185

"Good, that's good." He stretched and then patted his stomach. "I'm going to go back to the scene, take another look at things, try to figure out why the cup the victim was holding fell and broke like it did. So far, that doesn't quite make any sense to me with where she landed."

Eve felt her face redden and she quickly glanced down. When she looked back up, Boots was gone and Detective Lujan was watching her. "Well, it sounds like you've got some phone work to do this morning," she said, hoping to make an exit without any more questions.

"Why do I get the feeling that you know more than you're letting on?" he asked. "The letter from the brother . . . being in the abbot's room after we were called . . . now out here with the victim's . . ." He paused. "Colleague."

She immediately started shaking her head. "I wouldn't know why you have that feeling, Detective," she said, trying to give a smile for reassurance.

Before Officer Lujan could ask something else, another guest came out of his room, pulling a suitcase. As he got closer to them, he stopped and turned to look behind him in the direction of the crime scene. He let go of his bag.

186

"It's a real shame this happened," he said. "I was just talking to Dr. Middlesworth last evening, and now . . ." He shook his head, ran a hand through his hair, clearly distressed. "You just never know, do you?"

Eve reached out and touched the man on his arm. "This is a terrible day," she said.

He glanced down, nodding. "Yes, yes," he replied.

"Drive safely to your home," Eve said with a tenderness in her voice. "And may God bless you."

He reached out and took her hand. "Thank you, Sister," he said and then continued walking toward the parking lot.

Eve and Detective Lujan watched as he opened the trunk of his car, threw his suitcase in, closed it, and headed to the driver's side.

"Frequent guest here at the monastery?" the officer asked.

She shook her head as if to say she didn't understand the question.

"He called you Sister and yet you're not wearing your habit." He paused and still she said nothing. "No robe, no veil. I didn't know you're a nun when I met you, so he must know you live here, right? And you do live here? Right? For now, I mean?"

Eve glanced over as the man drove past

187

them out of the parking lot and toward the monastery's main gate. "We met earlier in the week." She hesitated. "And I have lived here for twenty years," she answered, not giving anything away.

Twenty-Five

Eve headed to the main office, wondering if she should have set the detective straight and explained that she was in the discernment process about being a nun. In fact, she was a little surprised that she hadn't told him, hadn't just made the announcement to him that she wasn't sure she wanted to be in a religious community any longer. But she was still confused and she didn't want to say that out loud, and she certainly didn't want to say it to a stranger.

She gave the matter no more thought, knowing she had other things more pressing to handle. She wanted to check the room assignments to see who had reserved the room next to the victim, and she also hoped to find Daniel to let him know about her encounter with the two married professors from Texas. If there were ever two likely suspects, she thought, those two fit the mold for sure. She was sure that he would be interested in the conversations, and she also wanted to make sure that she asked him about the tox screen results. Perhaps, if she knew the exact nature of the poison used to kill Dr. Middlesworth, she would be able to find out if any such ingredients could be found elsewhere on the monastery property.

When she arrived through the front door, there didn't appear to be anyone around, and she wondered if Brother Xavier, the monk assigned to greet visitors and help with accommodations for guests, had gone to the chapel to make preparations for midday prayer. As she glanced around to see if anyone else was nearby, the main phone began ringing. With no one else there, Eve did what she had done for years when she lived at the monastery: she walked around the desk to answer it.

"Our Lady of Guadalupe," she said into the receiver.

"I'd like to speak to Father Oliver," a faint voice from the other end responded.

Eve glanced down at the phone but immediately noticed that it was a different system from the one she was accustomed to using. Without knowing how to put the caller on hold, she responded, "I will try and find him for you." She searched the desk for a pen and paper.

190

"May I tell him who is calling?" She started to write, but there was a click and the line was dead.

"Well, I guess I won't," she replied to no one.

The phone started to ring again, and Eve suddenly understood why the monk responsible for the front desk had left. She let the call roll over to voice mail and looked down both halls, wondering then where everyone had gone. In addition to the phone ringing off the hook, she also realized that once the conference had been canceled, there would be a lot of work that had to be done. With so many registered guests leaving, all of the rooms would have to be cleaned and financial adjustments would need to be made for those requesting reimbursements.

New arrangements would likely need to be made for media and law enforcement officers if they intended to stay on campus. With so many things up in the air, she assumed that somewhere on the premises the monks had likely gathered in a private meeting to go over tasks that would need to be delegated and concerns that would need to be addressed. She could only imagine what a nightmare this was going to be for the entire staff, and she was glad that she was here and in a position to help.

With no one around to stop her, Eve simply made herself at home, taking the chair behind the front desk and booting up the computer. She hoped the monks hadn't made a change and that she still knew the correct password to unlock the screen and how to open the reservation program they used to assign guest rooms. She was reaching for the keyboard to start her search when she heard raised voices coming from down the hall. She tried to focus but eventually became too curious to stay where she was and got up from her seat, heading in the direction of where she had heard the noise.

Down the hall, she could see that there appeared to be five or six men gathered near the door of Father Oliver's office. Their voices were loud enough so that even standing where she was, she could hear some of the conversation.

"We have the right to speak to him," one of the men was saying.

Eve thought she heard Father Oliver make a response, but he was not talking as loudly as the visitors. Unable to hear him, she moved closer.

"He has something that does not belong to him," another of the men remarked.

As Eve got a better view, none of those

192

standing in the door appeared familiar to her. They varied in age and size, but she could see those with gray hair were standing near the abbot's desk, and those with darker hair, the younger men it appeared, were gathered behind them. They were all dressed in jeans, long-sleeved shirts, and cowboy boots. She could see them only from behind, but it was clear that they were quite concerned about something.

"He stole from us. He came under the auspices of helping us restore the church and instead he took what wasn't his."

Eve could see around the men and noticed Father Oliver sitting behind his desk. His hands were clasped before him and he continued to speak, but she still couldn't hear the reply.

There were more comments from the elder visitors, and as Eve tried to get a better look, she could see that a priest was in the center of the gathering, standing directly in front of Father Oliver, not a monk from the monastery, but a parish priest, a short man dressed in black, his hair pulled back into a tight braid. When she heard his voice, she recognized him as Father Jonas, the priest to some of the Pueblos in the area. She remembered having met him on several occasions when he came to Pecos on retreat.

He was cheerful and personable, and she had always enjoyed his visits.

Father Jonas was born and raised in Mexico, attended seminary there, and had told her once that he had always intended to serve in his home country. Once he had been assigned to the Pueblos, however, he never wanted to leave New Mexico, never wanted to leave this ministry. She remembered how passionate he was about the Native American Catholics, how deeply he felt for the parishioners living on the reservations. He had served the people of the Sandia and the Isleta Pueblos for years, choosing to make his home with them instead of in Albuquerque with the other priests. He and Eve had spoken numerous times about his deep respect and love for the people in his care.

Eve tried to make out what he was saying, but he was speaking more softly than the others, so she crept even closer to hear.

"I did not know of it until this morning," the priest said, the gentle accent still evident in his English. "We found the letter in the church. One of the deacons was changing the altar cloths and found it under the antependium."

Eve knew he was speaking of the cloths on the altar, one of which was known as the frontal cloth. She guessed that someone was making changes for the upcoming season of Lent, changing the colors from the white of Epiphany to the purple intended to be used for the forty days prior to Easter. She strained to hear more.

The priest was apparently reading the letter and she couldn't make out everything he was saying, but from what she could hear, it seemed pretty clear that the letter was written by Anthony, another letter of confession, another missal meant to explain his actions and his resolve to find and return the writings he had stolen.

"I have participated in a grave and sinful act, and I am prepared to suffer the consequences for this commission. I bear the guilt alone and recognize that I have brought great shame down upon my brothers and my father at Our Lady of Guadalupe. I will seek the guidance of Sister Maria. I will make things right."

She couldn't make out the closing remarks, but she could see and hear Father Jonas as he folded up the letter. "Where is the young man?" he asked.

Eve understood from the conversation she was overhearing that Anthony had left the monastery sometime after his sister's murder and made his way to Isleta to leave this letter for the priest to find. She leaned in, waiting to hear the abbot's reply.

"What are you doing?"

The question whispered into her ear startled her so much that when Eve swung around, she landed a punch right in the man's belly.

TWENTY-SIX

"Holy . . ." Daniel doubled over. "Why would you hit me so hard?"

"Why would you sneak up on me like that?"

She glanced behind her and saw that several of the men at Father Oliver's door had turned and were staring in their direction. She started walking toward the front desk, pulling Daniel along by the front of his shirt. "Oh, for heaven's sake . . . Man up! It didn't hurt you that much."

They rounded the corner.

He stood up with his hands on his hips. "You're right. You punch like a girl."

She flinched like she might hit him again, and he quickly reacted with the defensive move of crossing his arms in front of him.

She immediately laughed. "Some cop you are," she said.

"And some nun you are," he replied. "Okay, what's going on back there?" He motioned to the area down the hall.

She took the seat behind the desk. "What makes you think I know what's going on back there?"

Daniel gave her a look of disbelief. "Evangeline Divine," was all he said, clearly not falling for her innocent act.

"Fine," she replied. "Apparently it's the elders from Isleta," she said. "They're not very happy with us here at the monastery."

He waited.

"It appears as if Brother Anthony left them a letter too," she explained. "The writings that Kelly Middlesworth had, they came from Isleta; that's where Anthony found them, in the pueblo church. I guess they know they're missing, which means they knew what they had, which means Anthony didn't really discover them. They had already been discovered and were kept hidden." She was starting to sort through this bit of new information herself.

Daniel stepped away to get a better look down the hall and then moved back. He nodded as if he understood. "Is he still at the pueblo?" he wanted to know. "He must have dropped off a letter there sometime after leaving last night."

Eve shrugged as she tried turning on the main desk computer once again. "Or maybe before last night, who knows?" She hesitated. "It's strange, don't you think, that they wouldn't have ever told anyone about the writings? Why would they keep Sister Maria's writings secret and never even tell the church authorities?" She tried the old password as she continued talking to herself. "Of course, knowing what we do about the history with the Catholic Church and the Native Americans, I can't say that I blame them." She glanced up and Daniel was only watching.

"What?"

Daniel shook his head, apparently confused by Eve's questions.

"I'm only asking, how long do you think the Isleta elders have known about these writings and never told anyone?" she asked. Suddenly the computer came to life. She clapped her hands together, happy to know the password hadn't changed.

"I don't know the answer to that. Is he at Isleta?" He was asking the question again.

"Who?"

"Anthony."

"Oh no, I don't think so, especially since they're here searching for him. Somebody found the letter this morning and apparently got the elders together for this little Pecos meeting."

Daniel eyed her closely. "So we still don't know where Brother Anthony is," he noted.

Eve shot him a look. "He's not the suspect," she said.

"He's not the suspect," Daniel repeated. "Yet," he added.

"What does that mean?" Eve asked.

Daniel shook his head and leaned an elbow on the long narrow desk that separated them. "You know what that means," he answered.

She waited.

"It means he needs to show back up here as soon as possible, or he's going to be a suspect."

Eve rolled her eyes. "He's a monk," she said to her friend. "He's the victim's brother. He loved her. He wouldn't kill her."

"We have a letter of confession," Daniel replied. "We have lots of folks who saw them fighting at dinner."

Eve didn't respond.

"Some witnesses came forward," he said, the announcement quickly gaining Eve's attention.

He reached into the pocket of his jacket and pulled out a small notebook. He flipped it open to a page and started reading: "A witness reports she was sitting on the front porch of the main entrance about eight o'clock last evening when she saw a man dressed in a brown robe like the monks at the monastery wear. He walked out of the side entrance near the dining room and was carrying a tray and walking away from her. She watched as he headed down to the guest rooms. She's pretty certain it was Brother Anthony."

"That doesn't mean anything. Maybe it was tea or maybe it was scraps for the squirrels."

"She later saw the tray on the table at the victim's door. There was a pot and a cup and saucer, a small pitcher."

"That's completely circumstantial. She's only *pretty* certain," Eve responded, using the same words as the witness. "That doesn't mean it was Anthony. It could have been any of the monks. It could have been someone impersonating a monk."

He continued reading his notes. "Another witness saw Anthony preparing tea and placing the pot on a tray while he was in the dining hall, the same kind of pot, the same kind of tray."

"That still doesn't prove anything," Eve replied. "All of our pots are the same, as are all of our trays. Maybe he was fixing tea for himself."

"Another witness saw a monk who looked

a lot like Brother Anthony place a tray outside his sister's door after the service of compline. This witness was going to his room at the other end, after having been to the parking lot, when he saw a monk walk around the corner and leave the tray."

She held up her hands in protest. "Again, a monk who *looked like* Anthony? That's no proof of guilt. And it is still circumstantial. Somebody else could have walked past the pot of tea later and put poison in it." Eve was shaking her head. "It doesn't prove he's the murderer."

Daniel closed the small pad of paper and stuck it back in his pocket. "I would very much like to believe you, but that seems way too convenient."

"Not if the killer was watching. Not if he knew where Anthony was going."

"We have a confession, a handwritten confession from the guy, and apparently he wrote another!" He motioned toward the group down the hall.

"He thinks he caused his sister's murder. He thinks that because he gave her these stolen writings, he brought evil to her. That's all he's confessing to." Eve leaned back in her chair, dropping her arms to her sides.

"And I believe you," Daniel responded.

"But it would help his case out a whole lot if he'd just show up and talk to us."

Eve closed her eyes and blew out a breath. When she opened them, there was something on the screen in front of her, a name on the list of those attending the conference and staying in the guest rooms, that caught her eye.

TWENTY-SEVEN

There was the sound of a loud sneeze coming from around the corner, followed by a deep, booming voice calling out, "Is there a cat in this building? I thought I made it clear that there are to be no cats in our buildings."

Instantly, Eve jumped up from her seat, catching Daniel by complete surprise, while snagging the electric cord with her foot and yanking it from the socket. In a matter of seconds, the computer whirred, as did the printer, a small fan, and the lights on the front desk. Everything around her powered off. Eve's face was bright red, and while Daniel watched in seemingly utter amazement, she straightened to a soldier's pose.

"I don't know anything about a cat," she protested, a bit too loud and a bit too quickly, she soon realized. She closed her eyes and shook her head as Daniel maintained the surprised look on his face, waiting for an explanation.

There was another loud sneeze, closer this time, and then came the greeting, "Well, this is a surprise," and a stocky, barrel-chested man dressed in a black suit with a clerical collar made his way around Daniel all the way to where she stood. He held a handkerchief to his nose and blew loudly. "Sister Evangeline Divine."

The visitor was older than the others standing near him but not as tall. He was balding on the top of his head with thin strands of red and white hair curling in the front and the back. His hands were small but beefy, and he wore a gold watch on his left wrist and a large gold band on his wedding finger. A jeweled pectoral cross fell out of his front jacket pocket as he sneezed yet again. His blue eyes were turning red and watery, and his pale skin was beginning to splotch.

"Divine," she corrected him without looking him in the eye. "Divine," she said again, softer this time. She felt herself standing at attention. She couldn't help it; she always acted this way around the archbishop.

A young man in a long black cassock quickly came running up behind him. "I am so sorry, sir," he said, shaking his head. "I did not know they allowed animals in the monastery." He glanced around as if he might see the culprit. "I don't see a cat." He searched from one end of the room to the other. "Is there an animal in this building?" he asked Eve, who did not answer about the cat again.

"Never mind," groused his supervisor.

"Do you want a Zyrtec?" the assistant asked the older man and started patting his pockets, apparently trying to find an allergy pill.

"Well, of course I want a Zyrtec if there's a cat on the premises." The man blew his nose again noisily. He turned to Eve.

"Yes, yes, how could I forget? Evangeline Divine," he said again, correctly this time. "Sister." He bowed his head slightly.

She bowed in response.

"I'll get you a glass of water," the young seminarian declared, suddenly exiting the group. "The dining room is this way, right?" And he hurried down the hall as Daniel pointed in the right direction.

"Poor boy, he does try." The archbishop rolled his eyes when he noticed the pitcher of water sitting on a table beside the desk. He turned back to Eve and there was a pause. "Are you working here?" he asked, glancing around and not hiding the surprise in his voice.

She shook her head. "No, sir, I was just —"

"Hello," he said, cutting her off and turning his attention to the man he had only just noticed standing beside him. He held out his hand to Daniel, and the detective took it, giving a firm grasp and then releasing it.

"I'm Archbishop Donnelly," he added as an introduction, his Irish accent on show. He smiled. "Are you one of the professors here for the conference?" he asked and then continued without waiting for an answer. "I had hoped to be able to attend one of the lectures this weekend. I, too, am a fan of Sister Maria de Jesus de Agreda. I consider *Mystical City of God* a fine literary and theological document." He leaned in a bit. "However, I must admit that I agree with those who say her Mariology is incompatible with Vatican II."

Daniel didn't reply.

The archbishop turned over his handkerchief and wiped his brow. "Yet I still value lectures and conferences that allow theologians and religion scholars to bend the minds of priests and monks, keeping us up to date with the latest in our fields. Where do you teach, and do you read the sacred texts in Hebrew and Greek?"

Daniel looked first at Eve and then back to the archbishop. "I'm not a professor," he said.

"Oh, a participant then? Here as a devotee of Sister Maria just to aid in your private prayers and devotions?"

Daniel shook his head.

"On private retreat with the monks here at the abbey?"

"I'm Detective Daniel Hively," he responded.

The archbishop pulled back and waited for more.

"Here on police business," Daniel obliged.

"Oh yes." The archbishop drew out the words and placed his arms on top of each other in front of his chest. "The police business," he repeated and then crossed himself and bowed. He shook his head. "It is too dreadful even to say." He turned back to Eve. "I'm here to talk to Oliver about this." He blew his nose again. "However, it appears that someone else has his attention at present."

Eve nodded.

The archbishop seemed to be waiting for a response other than a nod.

Eve was confused.

"Who is that in his office?"

Eve thought. "Oh, it's Father Jonas and

some of the men from Isleta, I believe," she answered.

The man shook his head at the mention of the priest. "It's likely to be a long meeting, then, if Father Jonas has shown up. What is he doing here?"

Eve didn't answer. She was not about to tell the archbishop of the discovery at the pueblo church.

He waved off the question. "Never mind. Just go and tell Oliver I have arrived."

"Yes, sir." She started around the desk.

"Are the other nuns still in residence here?" He peeked behind the desk as if he thought a woman might be hiding.

Eve stopped and shook her head.

He glanced around once more and then sneezed again.

"Bless you," Daniel said and then smiled.

"Thank you," the archbishop responded.

Eve had started in the direction of Father Oliver's office when she suddenly stopped and turned back. "No, the others are all gone. They left after you . . ."

The archbishop quickly glanced in her direction.

Suddenly the young assistant hurried back into the room, interrupting. "Here's the water," he announced, sounding out of breath. "And a Zyrtec." He handed them both to his supervisor, who smiled and watched as Eve turned and headed down the hall.

TWENTY-EIGHT

Eve crept down the hall past Father Oliver's office, heading in the direction of the dining room. The abbot's door was closed and she could hear the two men talking, but even by leaning in as she slowly made her way past the office, she couldn't make out any of what was being said. All she could hear with any real clarity was the archbishop's sneezes. Apparently, even after a couple of hours, the Zyrtec hadn't done the job.

Daniel had left soon after the men from Isleta exited and the diocesan visitor made his way to Father Oliver's office. He claimed that he was going back to Santa Fe to get the results from the autopsy and tox screen. However, even with Daniel's promise that he wouldn't label the monk a suspect, Eve surmised that her friend was also going back to the police station to start a search for Anthony.

She knew that she needed to figure out

some things quickly if she was going to take the heat off of the victim's brother. She needed something substantial to place suspicion on the professors from Texas, but she was having difficulty finding any clear evidence that they were behind the murder. When she mentioned her idea to Daniel, his rebuttal had been a good one: *"If one or both of them were behind the murder, why did they stay and make themselves known? Why didn't they leave right after they did the deed?"* It was a very good question, and one for which she didn't have an answer.

She wanted to talk to Dr. Pierce and Dr. Taylor again, but at the moment she was hungry and decided to fix herself a sandwich before going back down to the guest rooms to try to snoop a bit more. She looked at her watch. The archbishop had been with the abbot a long time.

No doubt he's trying to find a way to get the writings for the diocese or for himself, throwing the Isleta church and Brother Anthony under the bus, she thought to herself and then immediately blew out a breath, crossed herself, and asked for forgiveness. *Why do I let him get to me like this?*

Knowing it was no good to keep her thoughts on the archbishop, she decided to change her line of thinking and focus on some other things that needed her attention. She wanted to ask Brother Xavier about the name she had seen on the guest room list, the one assigned to the room next to the victim, the name that was familiar, John Barr, the man she had seen at the press conference. She also wanted to find out from Father Oliver what the priest and the men from Isleta wanted. However, she couldn't seem to locate Brother Xavier, and she would have to wait for the archbishop to leave before she could speak to the abbot.

She found bread and peanut butter in the kitchen, some crackers, and a couple of small cartons of milk in the refrigerator. In spite of the archbishop's rant and his assistant's detective work of trying to locate the cat, she was not kicking Daisy out. She just needed to make sure no one else knew the pet was in her room. A little milk, she thought, would keep the cat happy and settled, not making noise and not outing her accomplice. Eve gathered the food items and started to head back to her room. The kitchen was empty, and when she noticed the time on the large clock over the door, she realized that the monks had likely finished midday prayers and lunch and were probably doing afternoon chores. The morning had already come and gone.

With both hands full, she walked back to the pantry and was searching for a plastic bag, something to hold her supplies, when she heard someone talking. It appeared to be a conversation that was going on in a small alcove just outside the rear door to the dining area. The door stood partly open, and she could see the shadow of someone standing on the other side. The person was apparently on the phone. She put her things down on a counter and walked closer so that she could hear the conversation.

"At this point, everybody's searching for him." The caller was male, and she instantly recognized the voice.

"If the police get to him first, you know what kind of light he'll throw on all of us. He's a thief and a liar, not to mention a suspect in the murder case." It was the young assistant, the seminarian, the man traveling with the archbishop.

"We know he's not at Isleta. They were already here, and it appears they're sending a search party as well. I talked to the priest, and he's convinced that they can find him before the detectives do."

Eve knew he was talking about Anthony, and from what she'd just heard, it was clear that Father Jonas and the men from the pueblo had created their own search party.

"If they find him, they'll make it bad for us too. They'll let everybody know that a Catholic monk stole the writings. It will be the missionaries versus the Pueblo Indians all over again. It could cause another revolt."

Eve noticed a car pulling out of the monastery, heading down the driveway that went past the partially opened door. It was Detective Bootskievely leaving, but he was alone, apparently without his partner. Detective Lujan must still be on the premises. The caller hesitated as if he was watching the vehicle as well.

"No, don't use his name anywhere. We have to keep him as far away from this as we can. No scandal," he emphasized.

There was a pause.

"Well, of course he knows; he's not an idiot. He didn't get the title of archbishop because of his great service to the poor. He understands what's at stake if the word gets out that a monk stole from the pueblo, but he also understands what it could mean for him if he gets to the papers first. You know he's wanted out of the Southwest since he first got here. He thinks this could be his ticket to Rome."

There was another pause while the assistant apparently listened to the caller on the other end.

"Look, the guy is more than likely still dressed like a monk. He can't be too hard to find. Ask around. See if anybody gave him a ride out of here. If he's been at Isleta, he's probably somewhere south of Albuquerque, maybe heading to Mexico. If what that dealer said is true, the papers are worth a lot of dough. He's likely trying to get out of the country and make the sale. Start by looking up the records to see if he has one of the property's cell phones, and try to see if he's used a credit card. Help me out here. You're the professional. He's a monk, not a hardened criminal, for heaven's sake."

Eve was trying to piece it all together. The archbishop had obviously told his assistant to find Anthony, but who was the guy talking to?

"We'll worry about that when we find him."

A detective? The idea seemed ludicrous to Eve, but that was certainly how the conversation sounded.

"My guess is that he'll be sent somewhere very far away from here. We don't really want another priest in jail! We've had enough of that publicity to last us a lifetime. No, I figure they'll stick him away in some remote monastery, never to be heard from again."

Eve drew in a breath. The office of the archbishop was now also searching for Anthony, and it seemed he would not fare any better if they found him first. She backed away from the door as the assistant finished his call. She watched as he walked around to the front entrance, and then she looked over at the meager lunch she was planning for herself.

I'm going to need more than just a peanut butter sandwich to fortify me on this journey, she thought. And she headed back to the kitchen to gather more food.

TWENTY-NINE

"Tell me that you aren't going to try and find him." The Captain guessed his daughter's plan without her giving a clue.

She didn't respond. She had made the call only so that her father wouldn't worry about her when he heard from Daniel or one of the other detectives that she had left the monastery.

"Evangeline, you don't know what or who you'll find out there. Let me go with you."

"No, I need to do this by myself," she answered. "If he thinks someone else is with me, he won't talk to me."

"I don't like this," her father replied. "Your monk friend Anthony may not be the killer, but with all I've heard of how he behaved after he found out about his sister, he doesn't appear to be mentally stable. I don't like the thought of you out there by yourself with him."

"I'll be fine."

She heard a long breath pour across the phone line.

"How do you even know where he is? The Santa Fe police have been searching all day. The Isleta police have even been helping. What makes you think you can find him?"

"I found something."

"Okay. I'm listening."

"I wanted to get a list of all the guests for the conference, go through them, see if anybody had a connection to Dr. Middlesworth."

"Makes sense." There was a pause. "And?"

"And I got it, the list of the guests," she replied.

"Anybody of interest?"

"Maybe a person of interest."

Another pause.

"Who is it and what makes them of interest?"

She held her breath.

"Evangeline."

She exhaled and gave in with a response. "There was a stack of letters in a folder."

"What kind of letters?"

"They're from a guy who used to come here. Well, I mean, I guess he still does come here." She didn't mention the name John Barr, and she didn't mention to the Captain that she had, in fact, seen him earlier that day. She also wasn't going to reveal the nature of this man's letters.

There were maybe six or ten of them, all mailed to Father Oliver at the monastery within the last year. As soon as she pulled out the first one, she knew the sender and remembered having seen him at the press conference. After checking, she saw that he was also on the list of those attending the conference. The old white pickup she had seen in the parking lot earlier was also likely his, and he easily could have been the one to have given Anthony a ride out on the night of the murder.

"What about this guy? What makes you think he's involved?"

Eve didn't want to say because she knew that once the Captain heard about John Barr, heard how she knew him, the kind of man he was, his unpredictable behavior, he would never let her go near him alone.

"I just think he might know something." She chose her words carefully. "He and Brother Anthony had a relationship; they were friends."

Eve recalled that Barr lived not far from the monastery, in a cabin somewhere north of Pecos near the little town of Tererro. He came down to the abbey just a few times every year, usually near Christmas and

Easter, even making a kind of pilgrimage, walking several hours to the chapel during Holy Week. When he visited he would never speak to the nuns, only to the monks, and then only to a few of them, Father Oliver, and for some reason that the others didn't understand, Brother Anthony.

While Eve lived in community at Pecos, John Barr's visits and his letters to Father Oliver were legendary. He wrote long missives in which he ranted and raved about the decline of the Catholic Church, about its fall from grace after Vatican II, establishing himself as a sedevacantist, one who holds that the post–Vatican II popes have forfeited their position through acceptance of heretical teachings connected with the Second Vatican Council.

Like the others with these opinions, John Barr always let it be known that for him, a man old enough to remember church history before that council, since the 1960s there had been no true pope in the church. He often wrote that the sedevacantists rejected the revised Mass rite and strongly believed certain aspects of the postconciliar church teachings to be false and that all the popes involved were false also.

He came to chapel for one of the services of the day and stayed, arguing for hours with Father Oliver about everything he saw as heretical going on at the abbey. He argued at him for speaking English during Mass and not the traditional Latin, for not facing east "toward the Lord" while presiding over Eucharist, and he argued most vehemently about the inclusion of women in roles that he believed were established only for the priests, the men, in services of worship and in equal standing in the community. And for whatever reason, while the other monks and nuns simply put up with the strange man from Tererro, Brother Anthony seemed to have undue compassion for him, always packing him a bag of food before he left and always walking or riding in his truck with him to the gate as he left, reminding him that he was prayed and cared for by those who lived at the community. She and the other nuns often chastised the young monk for being so nice to the man, claiming that in his kindness he demonstrated an acceptance of the man's harsh views and in essence caused him to turn his back on his sisters at the abbey.

"Was he there yesterday? Do you think he's the one who did this?"

"I don't know if he was here *yesterday*," she replied truthfully. "And no, I don't think he's the one who killed Kelly." She didn't want him to worry. "I just think he might know where Anthony is. He's a good person to talk to."

"You want to tell me where this person lives?"

"I don't know for sure," she responded. And that answer was true. She really didn't know where he lived, only that he stayed in a cabin just north of the monastery. She knew he made a living hunting and selling animal skins, and she did have a post office box number for him. She hoped this would be enough information to find him.

"I don't suppose you'll give me that name, will you?"

Eve thought about it. "I can't. I don't want to put you in the middle of this. It's best if you don't know any details."

She heard a clicking sound and knew the Captain was tapping a pencil on a cup. He did that when he was thinking.

"Take your phone and call me every hour."

"Okay. I will call you and let you know that I'm all right."

"Are you driving the Harley?"

"Of course I'm driving the Harley."

"I don't like this."

"I'm fine, Captain. I'll be fine."

"What should I tell Daniel? Because you know he's going to want to know where you've gone."

She hadn't thought about that exactly. She knew he had asked her to hang around in case they had other questions, and she had promised the other detectives that she wouldn't leave.

"Just tell him I needed some time away to deal with things. I am sad, you know. Kelly was someone I admired. I liked her." She waited, concerned he wouldn't go along with any of this.

She heard the long breath.

"Right," her father replied. "You took a trip to the desert because of your grief; you're following Jesus in the wilderness, that sort of thing."

She smiled. The Captain wasn't going to let her down.

THIRTY

Her afternoon and evening had been spent researching the sedevacantists and reading more of the articles written by Pierce and Taylor, waiting to leave until she was sure everyone had gone to bed. She timed her departure to be long after Grand Silence had begun and long before anyone would be up preparing for the Office of the Vigils at six thirty in the morning. Even though she didn't really have very far to drive to find the hometown of John Barr, she wanted to time her departure so no one would see her leave.

Eve gave her cat a bowl of milk and a little extra food, unsure of when she might return. She knew the Captain would check on Daisy even if he pretended he didn't care about his daughter's pet. She tidied up her room, packed the food she had taken from the kitchen, and tucked the folder of letters she had taken from the front desk at the monastery under her arm. She stood at the door and looked around the room, making sure she wasn't leaving any clues about where she might be going, and then remembered the small patch of blue cloth she had stuck in the desk drawer. She walked back to the desk, retrieved the swatch of material, stuck it in her pocket, and headed out the door.

The backpack was heavy, and she wasn't sure there would be room for the folder in her saddlebags on the Harley. She wasn't even really sure of why she had taken the stack of letters; all she needed was one with the return address, but since she had removed them from the front desk and didn't want to put them back, she also didn't want to leave them in her room, giving a certain clue to Daniel or the other detectives of where she had gone. She didn't know for certain if one of the police officers would really try to find her. She hoped that she would be back before anyone actually realized she was gone, but she wasn't certain about that and she wanted to make sure she had time to find Anthony and talk to him before the police or the archbishop's people found him.

She quietly opened the back door to the monastery, walked out, and then closed it behind her and headed to the rear of the chapel where she had last parked her bike. When she got to the place where she had left her Harley, she knew immediately that the Captain had gotten there first. Her bike was gone, and there in its place was her father's truck. She couldn't believe what he had done. Sometime after their last conversation, he had driven from Madrid to Pecos, left his vehicle, and returned home on the motorcycle. She was making a mental list of all the things she would yell at him about.

You stole my bike! You drove a motorcycle in the dark with one leg! You didn't think I could take care of myself and had to intervene, leaving me your truck! And you did not give me a choice! When I see you, Captain Jackson Divine, we are going to have a serious talk about your meddling in my life!

Eve shook her head and felt like stomping her feet, but she knew it would do no good. He had taken the bike and left the truck. She would have to do exactly what he had planned for her to do. She walked over and peered in the driver's-side window, half expecting him to be in the passenger seat. He was not, and she could see the keys had been left in the ignition, the same way she had always left her keys in the ignition of

227

her bike. No one stole cars at a monastery.

"Of course, I thought no one murdered anyone at a monastery either; I guess I'll have to start being more careful," she said quietly to herself as she opened the door.

As she got in, she found that the Captain had done more than just left her his vehicle; he had also fully stocked the truck. There were several blankets, a pillow, and an icebox on the floor on the passenger's side that she didn't peek in but knew would be filled with food. There was even a thermos on the seat. She opened the lid and smelled its contents. The coffee was still hot and freshly brewed and Eve couldn't help herself, she smiled at her father's attempt to keep her comfortable.

"I wonder if he's hidden a GPS somewhere," she thought out loud, but she figured he wouldn't have had time to buy one and she was pretty sure he didn't own a tracking device. She had tried to talk him into buying a GPS when they started working together, but he said that there was nowhere in New Mexico he hadn't been before and he didn't need some woman spouting off directions to him while he drove. He also claimed that he had never needed technology to help him find missing persons when he was a police officer, so he didn't need any help as a private detective. Eve felt pretty confident that he would not be tracking her.

However, she did reach underneath the seat and felt something else she was sure he had left her. Her fingers immediately wrapped around a pistol, the semiautomatic Colt Defender, the 9-millimeter model that he had bought for her and taught her to use when she came back from her trip to Las Vegas searching for her sister.

"If you're going to keep putting yourself in dangerous situations," he had said to her when she opened the box he'd placed on her desk at the private detective office, "then you're going to learn how to handle your business."

Eve had complained that it was not ethical for a nun to go around "packing heat," the slang she had heard to mean carrying a concealed weapon, but he refused to take no for an answer. If she wanted to work with him, wanted to engage in the activities of a private detective, he argued, she was going to learn to shoot.

It turned out she was a natural, even becoming a better shot than he was, and it actually became a source of pride for her as she acquired her license to carry a gun, even though she claimed she would not keep the pistol on or with her when she went out on business. Clearly, he had not listened.

There was also a note next to the firearm, and she pulled out the loose piece of paper to read:

Eve,
    Just take the gun with you. Just because you have it doesn't mean you have to use it. But if you're foolheaded enough not to let anyone go with you, you're going to take the Colt.

And it was signed, "Your father."

Eve reread the note and especially the two words that ended it. She studied them. As far as she could remember, the Captain had never sent her a letter the entire time she lived away or traveled from home. He had never signed a card or note. All the birthday greetings and checks during college came from her mom. She signed the cards and letters for them both. And seeing this one, seeing his handwriting, his closing, that title written out like that, touched her.

She would not fuss with him about stealing her Harley and driving it in the dead of night with his one leg. She would not give him a hard time for fixing her food and packing her supplies. She would not argue with him about the truck or the concealed revolver. Captain Jackson Divine must be softening up in his old age. He had written her a note. He had called himself her father. Small things for many daughters, but to Eve, this wasn't something she had ever known from him. It changed everything about her response to what he had done.

She got all the way in, pulled the seat belt around her waist, started the engine, turned on the heat, and adjusted the mirrors. Even though he had seemed so displeased with her decision when they spoke on the phone earlier, when she had let it be known that she was going out on her own, he had given her his blessing. He had even filled the tank with gas. In all the ways he knew how, the Captain had shown his love.

She backed out of the parking spot without turning on her lights, drove as slowly and quietly as she could away from the main building of the monastery, out past the guest rooms, and down the driveway. She drove out the gates, the familiar sign catching her eye as she left: *Vaya con Dios,* translated as "Go with God." She smiled and nodded at the sentiment and was sure she had gotten away without being seen. She never noticed Detective Lujan as he stood near the chapel watching her as she

231

drove away.

"Let's find the path to Tererro," she said to no one in particular, hoping she could find her way.

THIRTY-ONE

Eve drove in the dark, north on New Mexico State Highway 63 past the town of Pecos. She passed the lake and the Lisboa Springs Fish Hatchery. She continued on the winding road, forging a path through the canyon, along the river, finding her way to Tererro and over to the Bert Clancy Wildlife Area, where she pulled in and waited for the sun to rise.

She knew the road ended just a few miles farther north, that beyond the town of Cowles there were national forest camping sites, hiking paths, and places to hunt and fish, but there were no more paved highways beyond the Hamilton Mesa. She had driven to the top of the southern finger of the Sangre de Cristo Mountains, the back side of Pecos Baldy and Round Mountain, and had landed in a spot not too far from the Holy Ghost Campground, one of the places she had discovered and loved to visit when she lived at the monastery.

Eve parked the truck and opened up the thermos the Captain had left for her and poured a cup of coffee. It was just before four o'clock in the morning and the roads were empty, the area around her still and quiet. She sat and drank coffee as she thought about where she had landed. She thought about the Holy Ghost Campground and Creek and all the stories she had heard through the years about the place surrounded by blue spruce and ponderosa pines. There had been one story in particular that she suddenly recalled about a group of church kids being massacred by some bikers.

As far as she knew, the story about the massacre had never been validated. There were never any police reports or newswritings, and it had grown into an urban myth and ghost story that was often told around campfires, leaving campers nervous and afraid. She didn't feel nervous about her parking place, but as she thought about the tale, she reached over and locked her doors.

Sitting there in the dark, she remembered another tale, an older one but just as gruesome as the story about the kids and the bikers, this one about a priest killed in the area near the contemporary campground in

1680 during the Pueblo Revolt. Some New Mexicans claimed that the name was attached to the area after it was believed that the murdered priest, beheaded and burned, still walked the trails around the creek, trying to find his way home. This was known as the one and only "holy ghost story" and always got a laugh when it was described that way.

She finished her drink, dismissing the memories, and tried to imagine where John Barr lived. She knew he had mentioned a cabin to some of the monks, but she wasn't sure if it was somewhere close to the highway or down one of the many forest roads, out somewhere that might be hard to find. She also wondered how she was going to find the exact location, who would give her such information, and what the man would say when she drove up to his house.

There was also the question of whether Mr. Barr had actually given Anthony a ride out of the monastery the night of the murder. Eve was pretty sure it was his truck she saw exit the grounds, but she never saw Anthony in it. It was of course logical, she thought, that catching a ride with the man he had befriended was a perfect departure for the monk, but she was unclear of how the two of them found each other in the melee that was going on after the police had been called.

Had John Barr seen Anthony in his sister's room? Had he searched for him later and found him in the dining room? Had he approached Anthony after witnessing an action that Eve didn't want to believe happened? Did he see Anthony take the tea to his sister, and was he now hiding Anthony? Was Anthony really the killer after all?

She had so many questions, and she wasn't even sure that she would find John Barr or that he would answer them if she was given the chance to ask. He never had been what she might call a guy "easy" with conversation. He rarely spoke to the women, going out of his way not to have to interact with any of the nuns. He seemed interested only in arguing with Father Oliver as long as the abbot would allow.

She did know that Anthony never seemed to have the same experience as the others with the man from Tererro, that he dismissed the accusations of the community members who called him delusional and mentally unstable. When questioned by the others, he always sided with the visitor, claiming that Mr. Barr simply disagreed with the changes in the church and desired to please God just like they all did.

"He's just a wounded soul," Anthony had said once when one of the other monks questioned his compassion for the angry guest. "He served in Vietnam; he struggles with what he had to do as a soldier and how he was received when he returned. He feels as if the church spent more time loosening restrictions and turning its back on the orders of God than it did in offering help and comfort to the veterans of the war. In his mind," the young monk continued, "everything fell apart in the 1960s — the country, the government, the youth, the church, especially his own life. He just has strong opinions, that's all."

Eve remembered how the other monks refused to believe their brother, saying instead that the man needed mental help and that he posed a danger to those in community at the monastery. One of the nuns, Sister Jeanne, started calling him John the Baptist because they shared the same initials, JB, and because Barr seemed just as odd as the man who was known to have "prepared the way" for Christ. John the Baptist, the cousin of Jesus, was a man who lived in desert caves, ate honey and locusts, wore animal skins, and preached repentance. The name actually caught on for a while until Brother Anthony reprimanded

237

them, asking them to stop.

However, even Father Oliver, who never denied John Barr's request for counsel, warned Anthony that the monastery visitor was not to be left alone or allowed entry to the rooms of the residents. Even though he never would give a concrete reason for his caution, Father Oliver seemed to be of the same mind as the others, and he was concerned for the safety and well-being of the community members. He seemed to have additional information about Mr. Barr that troubled him, even though he refused to tell anyone else or ban the visitor from the monastery. As long as Eve lived there, John Barr made a trip to visit at least once a year, usually twice, always creating a kind of nervous tension for everyone there. Everyone, she thought, except for Brother Anthony, who never ceased to welcome the man with a kind heart and a generous spirit.

Eve recalled that she and the other nuns simply chose to stay away from the man. They greeted him, offered him food, and served him, but they all remained on edge when he was there. His visits were not frequent enough or disruptive enough to warrant discussing a specific policy regarding their hospitality toward him, but it was partly because of John Barr that the community devised a plan in case there was a dangerous episode on the grounds. Emergency numbers were listed and code words formulated for various crisis situations.

At the time, it was actually a surprise to Eve that the nuns and monks had decided to have these conversations, but she understood that just because they were a religious community didn't mean they were able to ward off all evil and pretend they didn't need to know how to react in case of uninvited trouble. They agreed to leave the doors unlocked and continue to minister with the gift of hospitality, but they also decided that they would come up with a plan for what to do if violence entered their gates.

Eve checked the truck doors once again, making sure they were locked, and then leaned back against the seat and closed her eyes. She intended to rest for just a few minutes, to nap just for an hour or so, just take a break before the sun rose and she figured out a way to locate John Barr. She had noticed driving in that there was a café and a post office in Tererro. She hoped that someone in one of the two places might give her the information she needed to find the cabin of the man who might be able to tell her the whereabouts of Anthony.

THIRTY-TWO

It was the horn blowing that finally woke her up. The sun was high in the southwestern sky, and when she looked at her watch, Eve couldn't believe her eyes. She had slept for more than five hours. It was after nine in the morning, and the horn blowing behind her, the one that woke her up, came from a garbage truck there to empty the Dumpster right where she had parked. She hadn't even really noticed it when she pulled in earlier and stopped.

She waved at the driver, signaling her apologies, and started the engine of her truck. She backed out and then drove to the entrance to the wildlife area lot. She paused for a moment to check her bearings and try to figure out where she might go to find the street address of John Barr, who she might ask where the man lived. Eve had lived in New Mexico all of her life, and she knew that residents of the more rural areas of the state known as the Land of Enchantment were often suspicious of strangers and tended to be very tight-lipped about giving out information about neighbors and fellow citizens. She needed a strategy to ask the locals where to find Barr's cabin.

She noticed a full parking lot at the café and a few people coming and going from the post office. With a stack of Barr's letters showing a return address of a PO box, Eve decided that the mail station might be the best place to start. She pulled onto the main road, making a quick left into the parking lot shared by the Tererro Café and the United States Post Office. She parked the truck in a space, took in a deep breath, turned off the engine, and opened the door. She hoped she could charm the mailperson into giving her directions.

A man was coming out as Eve headed up to the door; he waited, holding it open, and greeted her with a "Good morning." She smiled, returned the greeting, and walked in.

The boxes, all with small keyholes, were to her right, and the front desk, the area with an employee standing behind the counter, was to her left. She could see the woman working there had watched her come in, so Eve decided to go immediately to her and just ask for the information.

"Good morning," she said as she made her way to the counter. She noticed the woman was wearing a name tag. She was Rosemary B. There was no last name, and Eve wondered if there was a maximum number of letters allowed for post office employees and Rosemary had used all of hers up with her first name.

"Hello," the clerk replied. "How can I help you?"

Eve cleared her throat. "I have a friend." She smiled.

Rosemary made no response.

Eve pulled out the folder with the stack of letters written by John Barr and addressed to Father Oliver at the monastery. "His name is John and he lives here." She opened the folder so that Rosemary could see the accumulated mail, hoping that granted her some element of trustworthiness.

The post office worker glanced first at the letters and then back to Eve. She gave away nothing with the look on her face.

Eve closed the folder. "Anyway, I was driving around here and I thought I might drop in on John, you know, surprise him."

Still nothing from Rosemary. Someone was entering from the rear of the building. Eve assumed it was one of the carriers coming in for the mail to deliver.

"I'm a nun," Eve said, not at all sure why she thought that might help.

Rosemary nodded. "You camping in your truck?" she asked, obviously having seen her in the parking lot near the office.

She shook her head, glancing behind her at the cars in the lot. "No, just driving through." She turned back to face her. "Anyway, I thought it would be nice to drop in on John."

"Right, you said that," Rosemary replied. She was suddenly sounding bored.

"Well, you see, all I have is his post office box number." And she opened the folder once again and pointed to the return address.

Rosemary didn't look away from her, didn't follow her pointing finger.

Eve smiled again. "So, I was thinking maybe you might tell me how to find John, give me directions to where he lives, a street name or something."

There was a pause.

"You try to call him?"

Eve hadn't anticipated the suggestion. She shook her head, the smile still plastered on her face. "I don't actually have a phone," she said, lying.

"There's one over at the café," Rosemary noted.

Eve turned around once more and looked toward the restaurant only a few feet away from where she stood. She turned back around. "Actually, I'd rather drop by his place," she said. "So I just thought if you could give me directions to where he lives . . ."

A man came around the corner. "Hey, Rosemary," he called out. He had a large canvas bag thrown over his shoulder. "Oh, sorry," he added when he noticed Eve was standing there. "Didn't know you had a customer."

Eve nodded in his direction and glanced back at Rosemary. She was still waiting for the woman's answer. She remained hopeful that the direct request might still work and that the post office worker would give over directions to Barr's residence.

"We're not really allowed to give out home addresses of our customers."

There was a pause.

"Oh, sure, I understand," Eve replied, trying to sound easygoing and not at all bothered by the post office rules. "It's just . . ." She suddenly noticed that the man behind Rosemary was now watching her. She stopped in midsentence and leaned in so that she was closer to the woman behind the counter. She lowered her voice. "It's just that I wanted to pop over and surprise him, and I don't know where he lives."

"I could call him and just verify that he knows you, that it's okay if I give you the information."

Rosemary had her there, she thought. And this was a terrible idea. He would know someone was looking for him, and if Anthony was with him, he'd tell the young man that they had found him. And then there was no telling where they might run. Eve tried to think.

"But that would ruin the surprise, wouldn't it?" She made a face, tried to appear disappointed.

Rosemary shrugged. "That's the best I can do."

"Who's she trying to find?" The man behind Rosemary asked the question, and Eve's hopes were raised. Maybe he'd tell her the address.

"John Barr," Rosemary replied. "She has a stack of letters he wrote, says she's his friend, wants to see him." She turned to face her colleague. "She's a nun."

The man laughed. "Then she ain't no friend of his." He put down the large canvas bag and opened it. He pulled out a stack of letters. It appeared as if his job was to sort them.

Rosemary turned back to Eve and shrugged again. "It's a policy. We can't give out personal information."

Eve brought up a hand and pinched the bridge of her nose. This was clearly not working. "Okay, I'll go over to the café, give John a call, and get the address from him."

Rosemary responded with a kind of humming noise, a sort of "uh-huh," as if she didn't believe Eve.

"You all have a good day," she said and turned to walk out of the office.

THIRTY-THREE

She peered ahead at the café and assumed breakfast was being served. A few trucks and cars were still in the lot. Since she'd told Rosemary that she was going over there and knew that she could see her from where she stood behind the counter at the post office, she might as well make good on her word. Besides, breakfast, she thought, wasn't a bad idea. She left the truck where it was and walked across the paved lot for both establishments and in through the café's front door.

As soon as she entered, it was clear that she was the stranger and everyone else belonged. She met the eyes of the diners, most of them men, before the waitress walked out from the kitchen carrying a tray of plates, the food hot and steaming, in one hand and a pot of coffee in the other. There was a pay phone in the corner just inside the building, the one Rosemary had mentioned. Behind the counter, a television was on that was muted with closed captions and seemed to be giving the local morning news from Albuquerque.

"Just take a seat wherever you like," the woman said as she made her way to the first booth, where two men were sitting. They made some comment about being glad that their meals had finally arrived and that if it had been much longer, they would be eating lunch.

Eve didn't stop at the phone or the counter; she walked past the waitress to the third booth by the window. She slid in on the side where she would face the TV and watched as the garbage truck across the street finished collecting the Dumpster trash and pulled out onto the highway. She hoped the driver wasn't planning to come over to the café, as she didn't really want to be eyeball-to-eyeball with the man who had caught her sleeping in her vehicle.

"You want coffee?" The server had delivered the plates and was now standing beside Eve with the pot still in her hand, the tray resting under her arm.

"Yes, please," Eve responded and watched as she filled up the cup in front of her.

"You camping in your truck?"

Eve began to wonder if everyone had seen

what had just happened in the lot across the street, if everyone had noticed she had been parked at the wildlife area. She could feel the folks around her listening. "No, not really," she answered. "I got here early, just before sunrise; thought I'd pull over and rest."

The waitress nodded with a smile, feigning only mild interest. She waited with no further question.

Eve didn't seem to understand why the server was still standing beside her. She inspected her uniform and noticed the name tag. Her name was Jennifer, and she looked to be about forty years old.

"You know what you want?" Jennifer asked. She was pretty, her dark hair pulled back in a ponytail, and she was dressed in a mustard-yellow uniform that was not very flattering.

"Oh, I'm sorry, no." Eve glanced around the table until she spotted the menu stuck behind the napkin holder and the salt and pepper shakers.

"Take your time," Jennifer said and walked away.

"Order up," came the announcement from the kitchen.

Eve turned and noticed the cook. He appeared to be older, sported a short white beard, and was wearing a chef's hat, a T-shirt, and a white apron. He placed a couple of plates on the shelf and then moved away, likely going back to the grill, she assumed.

Eve pulled out the menu. The dishes were the usual New Mexican fare. There was a breakfast burrito, ranch-style eggs with chorizo, sausage-and-egg tostados, and her favorite, huevos rancheros served with black beans and home fries. She closed the menu and placed it back behind the napkins.

She poured some cream into her coffee while she glanced around the place. It looked like it had been serving meals for years, and yet somehow Eve had never noticed the café when she took her camping trips to Holy Ghost. She was always so excited about her destination, she had never really driven past the campground turnoff to see what else might be down the highway. She realized as she took in the place that she had never eaten at a restaurant when she headed north to camp; in fact, that was part of the draw for her. No services, no luxuries, no people. She always came to the area for solitude. Going out to a restaurant was never anything she'd intended to do.

As she peered ahead, the man in the booth facing her direction seemed to be watching her. Eve smoothed back her hair and straightened her blouse, thinking she must look like she just woke up. She wondered if she appeared homeless or destitute, if that was part of the reason Rosemary wouldn't give her any information. She glanced down at what she was wearing — her crumpled shirt, old gray hoodie, wrinkled jeans — and realized she certainly didn't look like a nun and she certainly didn't look like somebody a person should trust with private information. She smiled at the man watching, who then looked away.

Eve turned her attention back to the highway and watched the few cars and trucks that passed by. It was not the busy season, she knew, because the campgrounds in the national forest in that area of the Santa Fe Mountains hadn't opened yet for the season. It was still a few months before the road would be busy with tourists and hikers.

"You decide?"

Jennifer had returned.

"Huevos rancheros," Eve answered.

Jennifer nodded. "Good choice," she noted and then asked the question Eve was accustomed to hearing in New Mexican restaurants, "Red or green?" referring to the kind of chile Eve preferred. She topped off

251

her coffee while she waited.

"Red," Eve replied.

A couple walked past, apparently having just finished their meal. The woman handed the waitress fifteen dollars.

"Keep the change," she said as she walked behind the man and headed out the door.

"Thanks, darlin'," Jennifer said and turned to walk away. "Huevos with red," she yelled to the cook.

Eve sat back in the booth. She liked the feel of the Tererro Café. It was comfortable and nothing fancy, and she thought that maybe when the campgrounds opened she'd come back, maybe even bring the Captain, take a drive around instead of just parking and staying at Holy Ghost. She knew her father would appreciate a place like this.

She glanced up at the television and was immediately captivated by the images on the screen. It was a report about the murder and showed a reporter standing near the front steps of the monastery giving a run-down of what had happened and who was involved. She noticed Detective Lujan standing near the young woman as the camera panned the area, and Eve felt her stomach do a flip. Since the sound was turned down, she was unable to hear the report, but captions told the story.

"The name of the victim is not being released to the public at this time," read the words scrolled across the screen. "But the Santa Fe police spokesperson will say it was a woman and that she is not from New Mexico. Monastery officials ask for privacy during this time and will be closing their guest quarters for an undisclosed period of time."

And then what Eve heard next was like an unexpected gift, coming from the booth in front of her.

"Hey, Jen, isn't that where your crazy boyfriend walks every year, carrying a cross on Good Friday?"

Eve turned as the waitress came back into the main dining room.

THIRTY-FOUR

"John Barr is not my boyfriend, and I don't know where he walks with that cross on his shoulder." She headed over to the men sitting in the first booth and began clearing their plates and refilling their cups with coffee.

"Pecos," the man with his back to Eve replied. "The monastery at Pecos," he repeated. "That's the only one around here."

"I thought he walked to Chimayo like all the other Catholics," the other man added. "He just walks to Pecos?"

"It's more than twenty miles from his cabin," the first man noted. "He's way out there past Panchuela. I mean, unless he stays with Jen at her place the night before he walks." He was clearly teasing the waitress. "That would save him a couple of miles, plus maybe he'd actually have a reason to carry the cross and repent of some sins."

Eve watched as Jennifer rolled her eyes. "You want another sopapilla or are you done?"

She picked up an empty plate.

"Nah, I've had plenty." He reached for his coffee cup. "Tell Ralph I'll have some trout to bring by later tomorrow if he wants to serve fish over the weekend."

Jennifer nodded.

"And tell your boyfriend to call before he starts walking. They may not have a room for him at Easter."

The other man facing Eve laughed.

Eve couldn't believe her good luck. She just needed to find out for sure exactly where John Barr's cabin was. She knew Panchuela; she had seen it on the map even though she had never camped that far north. Surely, she thought, there were only a few places where his house could be. There couldn't be that many roads up around Jack's Creek and the surrounding campgrounds.

Jennifer quickly appeared again at her side, this time placing a plate on the table in front of Eve. "Huevos with red," she announced and poured more coffee without asking.

Eve smiled. She wasn't going to ask anything right away. Besides, it appeared as if the other diners were leaving, and she'd rather ask Jennifer about directions without an audience. She took a bite of breakfast and looked back up at the television. The weather report was being given, and Eve watched as the meteorologist stood in front of a state map, giving his forecast while holding a small dog in his arms.

Eve thought about the news report and wondered if Father Oliver was not only closing the gates to new guests at the monastery but also asking the others already staying in the lodge to leave. She wondered about Dr. Pierce and his wife, Dr. Taylor, and if they would soon be making an exit. She wondered if the detectives had interviewed them and whether they had become as suspicious of the two professors as she was.

"Jen, we'll see you in the morning," one of the men at the front table said as they slid out of the booth.

"Make sure you ask Ralph about the trout," the other one added.

"Ask him yourself," Jennifer called back. "He's finished cooking."

The man sighed and turned to his friend. "I'll catch you later," he said. "I'm going to go to the kitchen for a sec."

The other man nodded as he threw some money on the table. He looked over at Eve before leaving, raising his chin in her direction.

Eve nodded in return.

She enjoyed her breakfast and finished a third cup of coffee before the waitress reappeared, this time carrying a basket with sopapillas.

"You want more coffee?" she asked.

Eve shook her head. "I think I've reached my limit," she replied with a smile. "I could take a glass of water, though," she added. She listened as the man going fishing started a conversation with the cook. He was explaining how long he planned to be out on the river and where he thought the trout were most plentiful. In a few minutes he was walking out the front door.

Eve looked around and realized she was the only diner left in the café. She must have been the last of the breakfast crowd as Jennifer went from table to table, taking up creamers and adding a sheet of paper to the menus, probably highlighting the day's lunch specials, Eve thought.

She took a bite of sopapilla, added a bit of honey, and quickly took another bite. The soft doughy pastry was good at any meal, but she particularly enjoyed having them at breakfast. It always reminded her of her mother, a woman who always made her own tortillas and fried her own sopapillas. Eve and Dorisanne always claimed their mother was the best cook in the state, and because of her kitchen skills and expertise at the stove and the oven, neither of the daughters had bothered to learn how to bake and cook. When Mary Divine got sick, she tried to teach her daughters the family's favorite recipes, but Dorisanne was clearly no longer interested in learning and Eve was so wrapped up in her life at Pecos in the religious community she didn't have time to pay attention.

Their mother had written down all of the recipes, saying that perhaps at some time her daughters might want to cook, but so far neither Divine girl could come anywhere close to their mom when it came to making a meal.

"You want a few for the road?" Jennifer had another basket in her hand. She was offering Eve some more sopapillas.

Eve smiled and patted her belly. "I think I should just stick to one," she answered.

"Sure?" Jennifer tempted her. "We can't save them for lunch. Ralph is going to make another stack."

"Well, in that case," Eve responded, "I'll

take them."

Jennifer grinned. "Let me get you a bag," she announced and headed toward the kitchen.

Eve drank some of her water and took a couple of small containers of honey. She reached in her back pocket to get some cash.

"Here you go," Jennifer said as she placed the bag in front of Eve. She also pulled out a small pad and tore off the top page. It was the check for breakfast.

"Can you tell me what the camping is like at Panchuela?" This was the direction she decided to take. She was worried that to ask about Mr. Barr specifically might sound a little too nosy for a stranger.

The waitress shrugged. "What exactly do you want to know?"

I want to know where your so-called boy-friend's cabin is, Eve thought but instead answered, "Are there a lot of trails?"

Jennifer shook her head. "I'm not much of a hiker," she replied.

"Is the road to the campground a good one or does it get pretty muddy up there?"

She thought for a second. "There's just the forest road into the campground and I think the rangers keep it pretty cleaned up. Not now, of course; they're all closed until Memorial Day."

"Right, I'm just scouting for some places for the summer." She waited a second. "So, it's not hard to find the camping sites?" Eve asked. "The road goes right up to them?"

"State Road 223 ends at Jack's Creek. Take that, and just past Windsor you'll go west. As far as I remember there are just turnoffs from the main road going to the listed campsites. Panchuela is the only thing off the road out there. There're a couple of cabins on the way, a few locals live out there, but there's not too much else north of here. If you stay on 223, you won't get lost." She seemed to be studying Eve. "You going out there by yourself?" she asked.

Eve nodded. "Yeah, I like camping alone. I go to Holy Ghost all the time and camp by myself."

Jennifer raised an eyebrow. "Well, be careful when you do that. There're some crazy people around." And she turned and walked back to the kitchen.

THIRTY-FIVE

Eve knew she needed to call the Captain. He had made it clear that he wanted hourly phone contact while she was gone and she hadn't talked to him since she left the monastery. She pulled out her cell, which she realized had been turned off, and started to punch in his number. Immediately she could see that he had already tried to reach her. Several times. She decided not to listen to the voice mails since she was pretty sure they would all say the same thing, simply growing in volume and intensity.

He picked up on the first ring.

"EVANGELINE DIVINE, YOU BETTER HAVE A GOOD EXCUSE FOR NOT CALLING ME!"

He was screaming so loud she had to pull the phone away from her ear.

"I'VE GOT DANIEL UPSET AND SUSPICIOUS AND NOW THAT TAOS

DETECTIVE KEEPS RINGING ME UP ASKING ME WHERE YOU ARE!"

He continued to shout, and Eve waited until she thought he was through. She did feel herself perk up a bit when he mentioned Detective Lujan.

"DANIEL DOESN'T BELIEVE YOUR *GRIEVING IN THE DESERT* STORY!"

There was a pause. Eve pulled the phone back to her ear to listen.

"ARE YOU STILL THERE?"

She jerked it away again and waited. "I'm sorry," she finally responded. "I fell asleep," she added.

"It's after ten o'clock," he said, his voice back to a normal volume.

"I know, I know," she replied. "I'm sorry. I guess I was more exhausted than I thought."

Eve had left the parking lot of the two Tererro establishments and driven back to the wildlife parking area where she had been earlier. There was another truck in the lot and a couple of men were getting out. They were carrying fishing poles and were dressed in waders. They glanced over in her direction.

"Where are you?"

She started to say her location and then stopped herself. "Why did you take the

262

bike?" she asked, using the diversion tactic.

"Because I didn't want you out somewhere in the middle of the night on that thing." He paused only briefly. "And don't change the subject."

"I'm okay," she noted, still not revealing her location. "I just need to check out a house. I'll be back at the monastery before vespers."

"What time is that?" The Captain could never remember the daily hours at the community.

"Five o'clock."

"It's going to take you six hours to check out a house?"

She realized that was not the answer he wanted to hear.

"I said I'd be back before five o'clock; that could be anytime this afternoon," she said, trying to sound comforting, trying to assure her father that she was not in any danger.

There was no reply, but she could hear him breathing. She waited.

"Look, something else has been discovered," he announced. "They've found something else."

She didn't say anything.

"You still there?"

"Yes," she answered. "What else has been discovered? Does it have anything to do with Anthony? Is it evidence that he isn't involved in the murder?"

"They found some money in his room."

Eve couldn't believe what he was saying. "How much money?" She knew the nuns and monks rarely had any personal cash. The vow of poverty was a real one for those choosing the religious life. Community members had cash only if they were making small purchases for themselves or were planning to go shopping for the entire monastery.

"About a thousand dollars," came the response.

This was indeed very unordinary, and she understood that it didn't look good for the young monk. It gave rise to the suspicion that he was not who he appeared to be. It created doubt about his vows, about his intentions, about everything.

"Well, it was put there by someone else." She couldn't believe Anthony would have access to that kind of money. "It has to be someone setting him up, the same one who called the police. It has to be the killer still trying to pin the murder on the victim's brother."

She heard the long breath of exasperation.

"Eve, I don't want you confronting this guy alone. Go back to the monastery and tell the detectives what you know. Let them search for Anthony; they won't hurt him."

"No, they'll just take him in and question him for hours, giving more time for the real killer to get away."

"It's Daniel we're talking about here. He's not going to arrest the boy unless there's proof, unless there's a confession."

"They say they have a confession," Eve argued. "They have the letter. They have eyewitnesses putting him at the scene. Besides, Anthony is likely to confess just because he's so messed up about this." She hesitated. "No, I will find him first and let him know everything. I want to be with him if he goes to the police. I have to make sure he's safe and that he doesn't say something stupid to them."

"And you won't even tell me where you are?"

"It doesn't really matter where I am. He's probably not even here," she said, trying to sound convincing. "This was just a long shot that I thought I should try."

There was no response.

"I'll be back this afternoon," she said, glancing at the clock on the dashboard.

Another car pulled into the parking lot. A young couple looked as if they were going hiking. Eve watched them as they got out of their car and loaded up with backpacks and hiking sticks. She envied their ease, their simple plans for a lovely mountain walk.

"Leave your phone on," he instructed her.

Eve pulled her attention back to the conversation she was having with her father. "What were you thinking leaving me the gun?"

"I told you that if you were going to engage in dangerous endeavors, you were going to be prepared."

"It isn't a dangerous endeavor," she pointed out. "Anthony is a friend and he is a monk. He is not a killer."

"You didn't think he was a thief either," the Captain replied. "But he is," he added.

"He borrowed some old papers, some very interesting old papers, to impress his sister. He was going to take them back."

"That's not what the tribal officials believe."

"How do you know what they believe?" She wondered how much her father had learned about the visitors who had come to the monastery. She wondered if he knew about the archbishop's stop as well.

"Daniel."

"What did he say?"

"He said that the governor from Isleta was gravely concerned about the monk who had been working on the church. He and the priest say that more than just these writings have been stolen. They claim other things are missing."

Eve shook her head. It just wasn't true and she knew it. Anthony was not that guy. He would not steal for personal gain. She had to find him to get him to go back and explain the truth. "I'll call you when I get back," she said.

"Eve."

"Yes?"

"Just take care of yourself, okay?"

"Okay," she answered softly, and then promptly ended the call.

Thirty-Six

The road from the little town of Tererro wound around the Pecos River, becoming more and more narrow before the pavement ended at the tiny village of Cowles. Eve kept heading north on the dirt road before she found the marked path to Panchuela, west of the recreational area known as Jack's Creek. She made the turn, slowing down as she headed toward the campground. Just as the waitress had reported, there were driveways off the road, a couple of them leading to cabins that she could see from the road. She slowed at each one, trying to see if there was something identifying the houses, something letting her know which one was Barrr's, but there was nothing. She couldn't even see the end of the second driveway to make sure it was, in fact, a house, but she assumed it must be since it was in between two other private residences. She drove down to the end of the road, stopped, and then turned around at the entrance to the campground. She faced the direction from which she had just come.

Assuming that no one was at home at any of the houses, Eve was at a loss to figure out which one was Barr's. *Should I just knock on each one, snoop around?* she wondered. *And what is it that I plan to say to the man, anyway?*

Eve thought once again about the new information her father had given her. Money found in Anthony's room, a lot of money. It was more circumstantial evidence against him. Whoever was pinning this murder on the monk was covering all the bases. Give him motive with a witnessed argument with the victim. Show him to be less than honest by making sure everyone knew the writings that had been in his possession were stolen from the Isleta Pueblo. Make him look guilty with a confession letter. Place him at the scene of the crime with what turned out to be the murder weapon. Have him disappear and then plant a large amount of cash in his room. Eve hated to admit it to herself, but even she was starting to wonder about the innocence of her friend.

She shook her head at everything pointing in the monk's direction. Motive, opportunity, confession, running away; the evidence, circumstantial or real, was certainly mounting against him. She turned off the engine and waited for something to happen, but what that something would be she didn't have a clue.

Her phone started to ring and she glanced down, noticing Daniel's name and number. She quickly powered it off. She knew having a conversation with him, even though he was a personal friend, would not be helpful at that particular moment. Plus, she didn't want to lie to him about her whereabouts and she knew he would ask. It was better, she thought, just not to have a conversation than to have one that would be mired in deceit.

A few minutes passed and she turned the phone back on, noticing the indicator that there was a new voice mail, which caused Eve to remember the other messages she had not heard. She had assumed that all of the ones noted were from the Captain, but she thought as she waited at the end of the road that perhaps there were others. She scrolled through the screens until she found the one listing the voice mails. She wasn't too far off. There were five from the Captain, all of which she deleted without hearing. And there was the new one she knew to be from Daniel. She decided not to listen to that one either. But there was also a seventh voice mail listed, one with a New Mexico area code but not a number she recognized. It had been recorded at six thirty that morning, a few hours before she had awakened. She touched the play icon and waited.

"Sister." It was a voice that was familiar but not one that she immediately recognized.

"I'm calling because you weren't in chapel again."

There was a hesitation and Eve felt her pulse quicken.

"You missed lauds and Mass yesterday, and today you're absent from the Office of Vigils. I'm just wondering where you are."

"Detective Earl Lujan." Eve whispered his name.

"So, anyway, if you'd like to talk about Sister Maria and what the victim had in her possession at the time of her death, what it all means, or if you just want to run past some of your ideas or theories about suspects, you can reach me at this number."

There was another pause.

He cleared his throat.

"I saw you leave," he added, surprising Eve with his announcement. "It doesn't really matter, of course; you're certainly free to come and go as you like. I just thought it was a strange time to drive away, that maybe you're upset or . . ." He paused again. "I don't know."

Eve closed her eyes. She had been seen making her exit, and she worried that maybe he had followed her or maybe he had told Bootskievely and Daniel.

"I haven't told my partner, if that's what you think," he said as if he had read her mind. "I just want to make sure you're okay."

She listened closely as he gave his phone number and then ended the call. And then, without fully understanding why, she played the message again. And oddly enough, one more time. Finally, she powered off her phone once again and placed it on the seat beside her.

"What is this?" she asked herself, refer-ring to the unusual emotions she felt, the flips her stomach was making, the strange way the detective kept showing up in her thoughts. *I do not need this,* she thought, without completely understanding what *this* actually was.

She yanked the rearview mirror so that she could look at herself. She smoothed down her hair, pulling loose strands behind her ears, and slid her fingers across her eyes. She rubbed her chin, sliding her hand down her throat until she felt the crucifix necklace she wore, the one Earl Lujan had noticed and consequently revealed his own sacred jewelry. She fingered the cross, watching herself in the mirror, and then placed the pendant under her shirt and flipped the mirror back.

He had watched her drive away from the monastery at three in the morning. He had not followed her, at least she didn't think he had, and he did not tell his partner or probably anyone else what he had seen. And yet he was concerned. Or so he said. Maybe he was just suspicious. Maybe he was watching her, actually had her under surveillance, because he found her with Anthony's letter and because he could tell she knew more than she was saying.

Detective Bootskievely didn't concern Eve; he seemed to discount her knowledge or interest in the murder and seemed to be paying attention to the concrete things of the case, the toxicology report, fingerprints, witnesses. The other detective, however, Earl Lujan, the rookie officer from Taos, seemed to have his attention pointed right at her. He showed up everywhere she was. He let her keep the letter and then he took it. He knew when she didn't go to chapel. It was weird, she thought, but she knew she needed to be careful and she needed to control these strange responses every time he showed up.

Eve gently slapped her face a few times, trying to be as alert as she was able, not just to try to find John Barr and then talk to him to see if he knew anything about Anthony, but also not to let a police detective use her to get to the monk. She didn't want to be some avenue to their suspect, some source of information of where they might find Anthony to interview or arrest him. She knew she had to be at her best, careful not to be followed or tripped up.

And yet, even as she imagined that Detective Lujan distrusted her and was keeping his eye on her because of suspicion, she couldn't help thinking there was something else between them, something she wasn't sure she knew how to name or understand.

Eve was about to start the engine and drive back to the monastery. She didn't know how to find out which cabin was John Barr's, and the thought of knocking on all three doors looking for the missing monk seemed more and more to be a wild-goose chase. She figured she should simply go back to Pecos. She decided that she could probably do more to help Anthony's case from there.

She was putting the car in gear to move forward when suddenly a white truck pulled out of the driveway of the second cabin, a white truck with a broken taillight. She kept her grasp on the gearshift and froze. She couldn't believe what, or rather whom, she was seeing.

It was John Barr, the red hair and beard obvious as he stopped and made the turn. Eve stared in shock as he drove away with no one else in sight.

THIRTY-SEVEN

Eve pulled out after the truck turned off the narrow forest road and onto the state highway, heading south, back to Tererro or perhaps to Pecos, she didn't know. Slowly and carefully she followed it to the end of the road and watched the truck just as it disappeared down State Road 223 about a half mile beyond her, the road curving beside the river.

She sat and waited, realizing she had two options. She could follow John Barr, hoping he would stop at the café or go back to the monastery, and she could talk to him there, ask him about Anthony, let him know that she was trying to help the monk, get to him before the police, hope he would let her come back with him to his house or take her to where Anthony was. The second option was slightly more dangerous but an option nonetheless: while he was gone she could go to his house and take a look around.

After all, she thought, maybe Anthony was inside. Maybe John had gone out for supplies or food for them both, and while he was out of the house she could take the chance to talk directly to Kelly's brother alone. Maybe the two of them could discuss his decision to leave the monastery so that she could find out what he was thinking. Maybe if she had a few minutes alone with him, he could explain what he knew about Kelly's present situation and even suggest who the killer might be. They could talk about what the police were doing, what action they were taking, and maybe she would even be able to convince Anthony to go back to Pecos with her. Maybe she could just go up to the house, knock on the door, and finally locate the missing monk.

She put the truck in reverse and backed down the dirt road until she got to the second driveway, where she made the turn and continued driving in reverse up the path. She figured heading straight out might come in handy if John Barr returned and she was caught on his property. She was pretty confident that even if he came back and parked in front of her, trying to block her, the driveway was wide enough in some places that she would be able to skirt past him. She knew, however, with her driving skills, she could do that only if she was heading forward.

She backed all the way up the long driveway, in between the ponderosa pines, the Douglas firs, and the Engelmann spruces, snaking beside a small creek, feeling a slight incline, gaining elevation, all the way to the front of the cabin. She stopped, put the gearshift in park, set the brake, and turned off the engine. She yanked out the keys and held them in her hand as she tried to decide whether to take her phone too. She quickly grabbed the cell phone and placed both items in her front shirt pocket.

She stepped out of the truck and softly closed the door, leaving it unlocked, making it easier to jump in if she needed to get away in a hurry. She stood in the driveway and looked around, listening for any sounds of people or animals. There was only silence. Like her favorite camping spot just a few miles up the road, it was very quiet where she stood.

All she could hear was the babbling noise of the running creek, the cawing of a small gathering of crows overhead, and the sound of leaves rustling around the forest floor in the late-morning breeze. There were thick rows of evergreen and pine trees on both sides of the house, and she couldn't see anything or anybody else around her. It was a very private location, and it was easy to see why a man troubled with demons and who seemed so socially awkward might feel comfortable there.

She turned her attention to the man's house. The cabin was rustic and small, not like many of the weekend retreats and vacation homes built along the Pecos River in that area of northern New Mexico. It did not have a large wraparound porch with wicker furniture or a tall stone chimney. There were no river rocks artistically placed for a front walkway or railings crafted from twisted blond aspen branches.

This was a workingman's house, Eve thought, nothing fancy, and nothing particularly beautiful. It was not built for show, not built to entertain city friends or give the appearance of wealth and ease that the second homes in the area often did. But to Eve, the cabin looked sturdy and dependable, a simple residence built with his own hands by a man who lived in the woods and wanted shelter and privacy, and nothing more.

She walked up three steps made with stones to the front door, glancing in the large window beside it as she knocked. A small homemade bench sat beneath the window. A snow shovel leaned against it. She waited and watched. There was no movement from inside. She knocked again, this time calling out Anthony's name, hoping that he would realize it was her and come out.

"Anthony," she said, a bit louder the second time. "It's me, Eve. I just want to make sure you're okay."

Nothing. She tried the doorknob to see if it was unlocked. It was not.

Eve knocked again, waited, and then moved on the top step to her left as far as she could. She leaned in and pressed her hands against the glass in the window, trying to get a good look. She blinked a few times to get her eyes accustomed to the darkness from inside, and in a few minutes was able to get a good view of everything in that part of John Barr's cabin.

The front room was large, with a woodstove on the southern end; a sofa was against the window, and there was a chair, a big recliner, a small table with a stack of magazines or books on top, on the north side, facing the window. There was a narrow kitchen straight ahead from where she stood, with a stove, a refrigerator against the back wall, and a small round table and one chair situated in the corner. There appeared to be no one inside.

She headed down the front steps, returned to the driveway, and moved around to the rear of the cabin. There was a back entrance that looked like it must open to the kitchen, an old door with two small windows just at eye level. She tried turning the knob, but that door was locked as well. She moved around past the kitchen and to the south side where another window was located; this one was about four feet above her head and, to Eve's delight, cracked open. A screen was in place but a little bent, so it didn't appear to be secure. Here, she decided, was her opportunity to take a quick look inside.

She walked around to the front of the house to make sure John Barr hadn't returned home. When it was clear that she was still alone, she pulled the bench from beside the front door all the way around to where she had seen the window and placed it underneath. She took in a deep breath, readying herself for what she was about to do.

First she positioned the bench, making sure it was sturdy and secure, and when she was confident it was so, she stepped up onto it. It was just the right height as she stood face-to-face with the window that was apparently located on the back wall of John Barr's bedroom. Without too much effort she reached into the slight opening, pressing against the screen, and with just a little shove, knocked it to the floor. She then placed both hands underneath the window and was able to push it open, allowing herself enough space to crawl through. Headfirst, she entered the bedroom, landing on the floor right beside a twin-sized bed, making a loud thump. She rose up and immediately gasped as she came nose-to-nose with a black dog, a big one, quietly watching everything from the bed next to where she lay.

THIRTY-EIGHT

"Holy cow!" Eve jumped to her knees, but much to her surprise, the dog only yawned, looking at her with slight interest. This was an old dog, she thought, clearly not kept by Barr to guard the premises. Eve waited a second, but as soon as she realized he was not going to attack, she got up on her knees beside the bed and petted the large animal. The dog was male, and she made a guess that he was over twelve years old. It was also soon evident that the big mutt was blind, his eyes glazed over with a thick film, unable to focus on the woman who had just entered his home.

"Well, look at you," she said, giving the dog a good scratch. The dog leaned forward, his nuzzle touching Eve's face, and she was instantly given a firm, wet lick that stretched across her mouth and nose.

"Okay, okay," she said, wiping her face but still petting the dog. "You don't have to be that generous with your welcome!"

Eve stood up and took her first glance around the room. There was a closet on the front wall near the door, a dresser and tall straight-backed chair next to it. There was just the one bed, topped with several old quilts and with a small table beside it, a lamp on top, a small alarm clock, and a book, the Bible, a very old edition, situated next to a rosary and a pair of reading glasses.

She moved toward the bedroom door, noticing the few knickknacks on the dresser, an ashtray that held coins, a small cigar box, a picture of a couple taken a long time ago, and a stack of handkerchiefs. She turned to notice that the old dog was not joining her. He was not getting up from his resting place.

"So, are you here alone?" she called out to the pet. She turned back to him, and it appeared as if he was deaf as well, having dropped his head back onto the pillow, clearly not paying the unexpected visitor any attention.

"I'll take that as a yes," she answered herself and moved into the hallway, hoping still to find some evidence that Anthony was close by. There was a small bathroom on the right, a toilet and sink, a narrow shower. Eve walked in and noticed a cup with a toothbrush on the back of the sink, a towel hanging on a rack, shampoo and soap in the corner of the shower. Everything appeared neat and clean, and she was a bit surprised that a man living out in the canyon alone like Barr would take such effort to keep his cabin clean.

It was clear that John Barr didn't have much, but it seemed to Eve that what he had was kept tidy and straightened, with everything in its place. She walked a few more feet and found herself in the living room, the room she could see from the front window, the same window that this time she was looking out as she entered the area. She could see her truck outside but nothing else along the driveway or coming in her direction, hoping that meant she had more time to snoop around.

There was no television or phone that she could see anywhere around. She did notice a small radio on a shelf near the kitchen, an old one, a transistor type that appeared to run on batteries, and an antique clock that was ticking away the seconds. There was a thick wool blanket on the back of the sofa, magazines and newspapers stacked in the corners, and the recliner facing the window was old, the fabric worn. Next to it was a tall lamp, its base made from an old butter churn, and a stack of books placed near.

She walked into the kitchen, peeked in the refrigerator, and discovered Barr didn't keep much food on hand. There were several bottles of water, a large helping of cheese, a bag of tortillas, salsa, a couple of jars of mustard and ketchup, and plastic bags of sandwich meat. She closed the door. A big bag of dog food sat next to the appliance. Food and water bowls were positioned next to the sink on the floor. Two cups, two saucers, and one spoon were drying on a rack, but that was not really proof there had been two people in the house.

"Mr. John Barr, have you entertained company?" Eve looked around at the meager belongings of the single man, realizing she was finding nothing of consequence.

She went back into the living room and walked over to the stack of books she had noticed by the recliner and picked up the one on top. As she did, she immediately noticed that all of the books in the stack were about Sister Maria de Jesus de Agreda.

In addition to the books, there was a folder of articles from magazines and journals about the Spanish nun. She put down the books and flipped through the contents of the folder, finding in addition to the articles a map with markings near one of the places she knew that scholars had declared as being the spot where the Lady in Blue appeared to the Jumano Indians, a map of the Manzano Mountains with a star near the village of Punta de Agua, a place near the national monument known as Quarai at Salinas Pueblo Missions. It was the site where a large tribe of Indians resided around the 1600s and one of the places where it was said that the Blue Nun appeared to them. She put the folder down, thumbed through the books, and thought about John Barr's apparent curiosity concerning the Blue Nun.

Nothing in the collection seemed strange to Eve; she'd probably had copies of the same books and articles at one time or another. And there was nothing that connected him to Kelly. This was no obsession with one particular scholar, just interest in Sister Maria, and this information that she had gathered about John Barr gave no clue to the whereabouts of Anthony. Surely Barr was interested in the Blue Nun or he wouldn't have been at the conference.

She finished snooping through the books and papers and reorganized the stack exactly as it had been before she rifled through it, and then glanced around a final time.

This was clearly a house of one man and

one man only, a man and his blind, deaf dog, Eve thought, and it did not appear that he was hiding a fugitive. It could be true, she thought, that he may have given Anthony a ride from the monastery to some other place, but it certainly didn't appear as if the monk had ever been in this cabin. She sighed and headed to the bedroom to make her exit, but something stopped her at the door.

It was just a flash of color that drew her eyes to it. In fact, she noticed it only after she had taken a few minutes to glance one last time around the bedroom. She turned to her left and saw it just behind the closet door, hanging on a nail or hook of some kind. She walked over to the closet, opening the door only slightly, and at first she thought it was just Barr's bathrobe or a towel from the shower. However, even though she couldn't put her finger on it, she was sure there was something familiar about what was hanging there, something she was certain she had seen before.

She opened the door wider, getting a better look, and immediately felt the air leave her body. She froze for a minute and then swallowed hard as she raised the bottom of the long cape that was hanging on the door, quickly discovering the seam that was ripped from the back of the cloak.

She reached into her pocket, her hands suddenly shaking uncontrollably, and pulled out the fragment of material she had taken from Kelly Middlesworth's fingers. She held it up to the blue cape.

It was a perfect match.

THIRTY-NINE

"Hail Mary, full of grace . . ." Eve said the words out loud, praying the prayer as she closed the closet door and made her way to the window as quickly as she could. The old dog raised his head, lifting his nose as if something had captured his attention, sniffing and sniffing until he slowly got up from the bed, moving toward the front of the house.

Eve didn't wait to see where he was going. She hurried to get out of the window, placing her hands on the floor, sliding out feet-first and dropping to the bench beneath it. She leaned in, feeling for the screen, and quickly snapped it in place and pulled the window down to where she remembered it had been. That was when she heard the old dog bark. Someone or something was heading in her direction.

She wasted no time jumping from the bench and then picking it up, carrying it as fast as she could, and placing it carefully once again by the front door. As she ran toward the truck, hoping to get in and down the driveway before whatever or whomever the dog smelled got any closer, she started feeling in her pockets for her keys.

She knew that she had been cautious enough to stick the piece of torn material back in her pocket and careful enough to keep her keys on her person. What she realized as she hurried to the driver's side of her father's truck was what she had not been cautious with and what had consequently fallen out of her pocket somewhere in her entry or escape out the window: her phone. She had lost it, dropped it somewhere in John Barr's house. She stopped for a second, thinking about going back to look around, when she saw the truck coming up the driveway. It was too late. John Barr had returned.

Eve tried to calm her breathing and to appear as comfortable and natural as she could. She reached up and rubbed her neck and tried not to think about what he would eventually find in his house. She had just made it to the door on the driver's side of the truck. She turned back to the house where she could hear the old dog barking, took in one deep breath, plastered a big smile on her face, and turned back around to greet the man in the oncoming truck. She watched as John Barr exited his vehicle and walked toward her. It was clear that he was not pleased to have company.

"Hello," she said with as much ease as she could squeeze into her greeting. She stayed where she was as he came over to her. They stood face-to-face. He was only slightly taller than Eve, and his face was as red as his beard.

He didn't say a word, simply glancing first at Eve, then at her truck sitting in his driveway, over in the direction of his house, and then again to the woman standing in front of him, the woman with a big grin still stuck on her face.

"Can I help you?" he asked, the tone of his voice offering no hospitality, kindness, or pleasantries.

She stuck out her hand. "I'm Evangeline Divine," she said, thinking honesty was best and wondering if he would remember her from his many trips to the monastery, wondering if she looked different out of her habit and in street clothes.

He didn't answer, and she couldn't tell if he knew her identity or not. She couldn't remember the last time she had seen him, and then she recalled the press conference from just the day before. She had met his eyes then. Had he noticed her there?

"It seems that I'm lost," she said, changing her mind and thinking too much honesty might not be the best way to go with this conversation. He showed no signs of recognition, and she hoped he didn't remember her face, hoped he didn't recall her from the monastery, either from the early days when she lived there or from the media event just the day before.

"Is the campground farther down?" She pointed to her left, the direction of the entrance where she had been earlier.

He didn't answer.

"I turned down this driveway because I couldn't see a house and I thought maybe this was the way to the camping sites, but now that I've gotten here, it's clear that I'm not at the right place." She grinned and held up both of her hands, trying to give the image of somebody clueless.

"It's a couple of hundred yards to the west." He never took his eyes off of Eve, never smiled, never showed anything other than suspicion and distrust. He appeared exactly the way he had appeared every time she'd seen him at the monastery, mad and aloof.

"That's what I thought once I got out of

my truck and looked around."

She waited, but there was no response.

"This is a nice place you have out here."

The man kept a close eye on her, and she knew how unlikely her story sounded. Who doesn't know the difference between a cabin, a private residence, and a national forest campground?

"I got out to ask somebody, well, ask you, I guess, where the campground is."

He didn't respond, and they could both hear the dog barking from inside.

"Wow, that sounds like quite a guard dog you've got in there." She pointed with her thumb to the house behind her. "Bet you don't have many intruders or thieves around your place."

"Campground's closed," he announced. He turned aside from Eve and peered into the front seat of the truck. She hoped there was nothing inside to give her away, hoped the revolver hadn't slid out from under the seat.

"Yes, I know," she said. "I was just scouting a few places for this summer. You see, I used to camp a lot at Holy Ghost and some at Jack's Creek. I've never been out to Panchuela, so I thought I'd drive out here and get a peek before I make reservations."

He did not reply. The line of his mouth

294

had thinned and hardened even more.

"Is the gate open at the campground? Might I be able to walk around and take a look?" She hoped she was sounding believable by this time in the conversation.

He shook his head and glanced again at her vehicle.

"You backed in from the road?"

Eve felt her face flush. She cleared her throat and thought for a second, knowing she didn't have a quick answer for that. She glanced behind her.

"I just drove behind your house and then turned around."

She could only hope there was enough room behind the cabin to make that excuse plausible. "I had just turned around and was leaving when I heard your truck coming, and that's when I got out so that I could let you know who I was, let you know I wasn't some crazy person nosing around."

The Captain would kill me right about now! The thought of her father standing there and listening to this conversation made her shake her head. She was running out of believable lies, and she wondered if she might need that gun he'd planted for her after all. And then she wondered how on earth she'd be able to get to it if she did find herself in a confrontation with John Barr.

"I guess you got your answer then," he responded and started walking away from her. "This ain't the campground."

Eve took in a breath, hardly believing her good fortune. "No, it isn't. And I'm sorry for being on your property."

"Just make sure you get off of it."

And when she turned around to thank him for the information, he had already entered through his front door.

As quickly as she could, Eve jumped in the truck and sped away.

FORTY

Sister Eve intended to drive to the Tererro Café and use the phone to let the Captain or Daniel know about her discovery at John Barr's cabin. In the closet, she had seen and touched a cape hanging on the door, a blue cape that had been ripped at the bottom. She had seen it and she had recognized it, matching it to the piece of material she had taken from the victim's hand. That little piece of blue fabric clutched in the fingers of the dead professor had come from that cape.

She threw on her seat belt and drove as fast as she could up the dirt road and back over to the state highway. She didn't stop at the intersection, didn't even look to see if another car was coming from Jack's Creek or Cowles, the only two places north of where she drove; she just made the turn and kept going. She hurried in the direction from which she had originally come, knowing that it was less than ten miles to Tererro, hoping he wouldn't try to follow her.

"Come on, come on . . . ," she said to herself as she pressed on the gas pedal and gripped the steering wheel, trying not to think about John Barr finding her phone near the window or about how close she had come to being caught inside his house. She drove, saying a prayer of thanks that she had gotten out of the residence before the owner had driven up, realizing how lucky she had been and how close she had come.

She tried to drive as carefully but as fast as she could and get to the village diner. She recalled the pay phone in the entrance and knew the Captain would be waiting for her call. She glanced up from the road ahead and to the rearview mirror. She felt a bit of relief when she did not see any vehicle following.

Eve drove quickly, thinking about what she had seen and about what she had not seen. She felt confused and a little disappointed. Barr had been assigned to the room beside the victim. And yes, the cape was in his closet. Yes, it had clearly been in the room when Kelly was poisoned.

But who had been wearing it? Barr? And why? Why would Barr kill Kelly? It made no sense. He had no motive unless he was crazier than she thought, more dangerous than the members of the community thought.

Maybe it was something else. Maybe Barr was protecting Anthony. Maybe the police were right and Anthony did kill his sister and Barr saw what happened and helped him escape, drove the monk away from the monastery, took him somewhere to hide, and then stashed away this evidence.

But Eve found no evidence in the cabin that John Barr had entertained company. There had been nothing at all proving that someone else had been staying with him. Anthony was not there, and there was nothing to show he had ever been there. No extra towels in the bathroom, no second bed made; there were two cups and saucers, but from what she had seen in Barr's house, he had spent the previous night alone.

Still, she remembered having seen Barr's truck leave the monastery on the night of the murder even if she hadn't seen that Anthony was with him. She hadn't really seen the monk in the truck with Barr that night, and yet Anthony riding out with the strange man made sense. It seemed to her that it would have been the best way for Anthony to escape. But where had the two men gone? Where had Barr taken him?

Did Anthony give the man this cape? Did he kill his sister dressed as the Blue Nun and then make his getaway with John?

Eve drove, avoiding the potholes and keeping her speed steady, trying to make sense of what it meant that John Barr had the blue cape, the cape that someone who had been in the room with Kelly Middlesworth at the time of her death had worn. Eve assumed when she found the fragment of cloth that the victim had reached out, probably from where she had fallen, and taken hold of the hem of the garment, grabbed it, and pulled, tearing away a piece.

Was John Barr the killer? Was he with Anthony? Did he come to the monastery to commit murder? Did he have the writings of Sister Maria? Or did Anthony give him the cape and go into hiding? All those books, articles, was this an obsession that could lead to the murder of one of those scholars?

And then, suddenly, there was another thought, another question that caused her to grip the wheel and press the gas even harder: *Did John Barr kill Anthony too?* She bit her bottom lip and tried to shake away thoughts of a second murder. She prayed a prayer for her friend, prayed a prayer that he was safe and away from this man he had befriended. She prayed to the Virgin Mary and even to Sister Maria that the holy women would watch over the young monk and keep him out of harm's way.

When she rounded the corner into the village of Tererro, arriving at the driveway for the café and the post office, she pulled into the shared parking area, realizing immediately that something was askew. There was not a vehicle in sight and not a soul in the vicinity. The entire area was deserted.

Eve drove to the back of the café, parked, and looked around. She turned off the engine and got out, deciding to go first to the entrance of the café and try the door. She hoped that even though there were no cars parked around the place, someone was there. She hoped that either Ralph or Jen, the waitress and the cook she remembered from breakfast, might still be somewhere on-site.

She glanced over to the post office as she made her way to the café, noticing that no one could be seen standing behind the counter. She didn't see a clerk on the side where she had gone earlier or a customer on the side where they would find their mailboxes. As she walked past she was able to make out the sign on the door indicating that the hours for Fridays were limited to only the morning. Rosemary had closed the station at noon and, according to the posted information, wouldn't return until the following Monday. The lights were out in the building and an orange Closed sign had been stuck in the window.

She got to the entrance of the café, and it was clear that the eating establishment next to the post office was also closed. The sign on the door posted the same hours as the ones for the post office for the last day of the workweek. Apparently, Eve thought, the residents of Tererro had plans to go out of town on the weekends.

Eve looked around, trying to find a driveway or house close by. She knew it wasn't that far to the monastery, less than an hour's drive, but she wanted to make a call as quickly as she could. She wanted to contact the Captain, let him know she was okay and not to call her phone again; and she wanted to call Daniel, tell him what she had found, tell him where John Barr lived and share her concern about Anthony.

She wanted to tell him to broaden the search for the missing monk. She wanted him to search harder not because she believed Anthony was a suspect, not because she was now agreeing with the police that he was involved in the murder of his sister, but because after what she had found in John Barr's cabin, she was deeply concerned for his well-being. She wanted to find Anthony and make sure he was okay.

Once she had come face-to-face with John Barr, she knew the police needed to question him about his involvement with Anthony the night of the murder. Even though it was unclear what his role was in the homicide, what she found in his closet indicated that he was somehow connected to the deceased.

Eve turned and headed to her truck, hearing the approach of a vehicle from the direction of Panchuela. She hurried to the back of the café, hoping she had pulled in far enough that her truck could not be seen from the road. She crouched behind the rear of the building and peeked around the corner.

John Barr's white truck went flying past.

FORTY-ONE

Eve jumped in the truck and started the engine. She wasn't sure where John Barr was going, but once she considered the fact that he might lead her to Anthony, she knew she had to follow him. At that particular moment, she realized, she was the only one who knew of the connection between the older man and the missing monk. She didn't want to lose this lead; she didn't want to lose the opportunity to find Brother Anthony.

Of course, she thought as she pulled out of the driveway, she had intended to make a phone call and let others in on what was happening. She had tried to find a phone and make a call letting the police and her father know what was going on just a few miles north of the monastery. However, after encountering John Barr and then seeing him speed away, she knew her first priority was to find the young monk. And after everything she had come across at the cabin, she was growing more and more certain that the man from Pecos Canyon knew where Anthony was.

She pulled onto the state highway and headed south, following the white truck that had just blown past the Tererro post office and café. She topped off at sixty miles an hour but still couldn't see him anywhere ahead. She knew the road she was on, Highway 63, was the only main road to travel, so she was confident that if Barr was heading to any town that had a name, Glorieta or Pecos, he would stay on that paved passageway.

She drove on, slowing down as she made the curves, wondering where the man was going, wondering if he might stop at the monastery, which she thought was a good possibility. Perhaps he did recognize her back at his cabin and he was angry that she had been there. Perhaps he was planning to go to the monastery, throw her cell phone on Father Oliver's desk, and let him know what she had done. Maybe he was going to speak to the detectives and lodge a complaint against her for breaking and entering.

However, as she followed, something told her that he had no intention of going back to the scene of the crime. Something told

305

her that he had found her phone, knew she was on to him, and was going to Brother Anthony, ultimately leading her to the missing monk.

Eve regretted losing her phone, imagining the Captain criticizing her for such a stupid mistake and Daniel's protests for putting herself in such danger. She also regretted the loss since it appeared she would be unable to place a call as long as she was in pursuit of Barr. She pushed the gas and sped up, looking quickly down every driveway she passed to make sure the man hadn't turned onto another path and was heading to someplace she hadn't considered.

She glanced down at her watch, assessing the time she had been away and what was happening at the community. It was an hour after lunch and a few more than that before vespers for those still in residence and retreat at the monastery. Eve traveled on and suddenly thought about the daily activities at her old community, how everyone who lived there had a role to play and afternoon tasks and duties to complete.

She drove along the twists and turns of Highway 63, getting closer and closer to the monastery, and knew that Father Oliver would be in his office at that hour, likely still dealing with the media and the archdiocese, perhaps even the police. Eve saw the abbot in her mind's eye, his head in his hands as he rested his elbows on his desk. He anguished, she knew, over the whereabouts of Anthony as well as the accusations the young monk would be facing when he returned. He anguished over the death of the visiting professor and the theft of the holy writings as well.

She guessed that the vice superior would have likely fasted and prayed throughout the two nights since the body of Kelly Middlesworth was found in her guest room and that he continued to lament over what was unfolding in his community with this homicide and what had occurred regarding the nuns.

As she came near the gates of the monastery, Eve spotted the white truck just ahead of her. John Barr was less than a mile ahead. Eve pressed on the gas pedal and sped past the community and through the little village of Pecos. Barr had not stopped at the monastery. He was not lodging a complaint with Father Oliver, and she was not going to be able to stop and tell anyone what was going on; she was not going to be able to call the Captain or speak to one of the detectives. She was on her own, following Barr wherever he was leading her.

He was still traveling south, and as they drove Eve wasn't sure if he would pick up Highway 25 and go in the direction of the state capital of Santa Fe or north to Rowe and Las Vegas, maybe even Colorado. She followed, uncertain of where he was going but trying to stay far enough behind him that Barr wouldn't know he had a tail.

As she drove past the monastery gates, she tried to see if police cars were still in the lot or if she could spot one of the detectives walking the grounds. She was driving fast and was able to get only a glimpse, but she saw nothing that drew her attention to the community buildings. There was no black-and-white police car, no Daniel standing near the front gates, no news van, no Texas professors that she could see, and no Detective Lujan. And again, as she thought of the man partnered with her father's old friend, she felt a slight flutter in her chest and a sense of confusion about what she was feeling.

Sister Eve shook her head, recalling her embarrassment when the Captain told Daniel that he believed she had a crush on the police officer. And she recalled the vehement denial she had made. She had changed the subject as quickly as she could, diverting the attention away from the subject of her "crush" and back to the issue at hand, namely, the murder that Daniel had come to investigate.

"I do not have a crush," she said out loud, as if she were having a conversation with the Captain. "I am following a crazy man," she added and pressed her foot on the gas, creeping a little closer to the white truck as it exited the state highway and headed south on the interstate.

FORTY-TWO

Barr hurried past all four of the exits off Interstate 25 leading into the city of Santa Fe, merging in and out of the lanes. He never slowed, never showed any signs of going to the state capital. As he moved past St. Francis Street, the Rail Runner Express station, and the relief route going around the city, Eve knew they were getting closer to Highway 14. She knew it was an unlikely possibility, but she was a bit hopeful that perhaps Barr would head in the direction of her hometown of Madrid. If he did, she was certain that she could stop by and pick up the Captain. She knew every side road and shortcut around the Cerrillos Hills and was sure that she could swing by the house, get her father, and still not lose Barr.

However, as they drove past the exit near La Cienega, past the turnoff to the Santa Fe Downs horse track, and across the highway to the state penitentiary, it didn't appear to Eve that he was going to Madrid. He maintained a southern direction, staying on the interstate while she remained close, trying not to capture his unwanted attention by keeping a safe distance between them.

Where are you going, John Barr? she wondered, following him as they both kept to the speed limit of seventy-five miles per hour, traveling toward Albuquerque, never slowing or stopping.

They headed up La Bajada, the incline south of Santa Fe that was often the reason for a closure of the interstate because of frequent ice and snow in the area during the winter months, and past the Cochiti Pueblo. He hurried beyond the village of Budaghers and the Pueblo of San Felipe before finally taking the exit at Bernalillo.

Eve followed, driving past the service station where he stopped. She watched in her rearview mirror as he pulled up next to a pump. She drove to the next intersection and did a quick U-turn, deciding to stop at a coffee shop across the street from the station where Barr had stopped. She pulled in, backed into a parking spot, and then quickly jumped out to ask to use a phone, but the coffee shop was no longer in business and there was no one else around. She got back in the truck.

She watched as he filled his tank and then went into the small store. A few minutes later he came out with two paper bags that Eve assumed contained food or drinks, perhaps supplies for what appeared to be a longer trip. She glanced down at her own gas gauge and was hopeful that the three-quarters of a tank would get her to wherever he was going. She also looked over at her supplies down on the floorboard and up on the passenger's seat, remembering all that the Captain had left in the truck when he took her motorcycle. There were granola bars and fruit, a couple of sandwiches, and several small bags of chips.

"I guess you know best again," she said out loud, glad for the extra food and hoping her father wasn't too worried about her and hadn't sent out a posse to try to find her. She suddenly thought of what else had been placed in the truck, the revolver beneath her seat, and wondered if that would also be something she would eventually be glad that he had left her.

Eve was hopeful that would not happen. She hoped she would never have to display it. One thing was sure about this quick decision she had made to follow Barr: she didn't want to use a gun.

She directed her attention back to what was happening in front of her and noticed that the white truck was sitting at the entrance to the gas station. When Eve realized that he was facing in her direction, getting a clear shot of her across the street, she ducked down, hoping that he hadn't recognized the truck and that he hadn't seen her sitting in the driver's seat. When she sat up he was gone, having pulled out from the driveway across the road, merging into the far right lane and turning onto the interstate once again, still heading south.

Eve waited a few seconds and then pulled out to follow him. She turned on her signal and took the ramp outside the bustling town of Bernalillo, moving in the direction of Albuquerque. They drove for ten or fifteen minutes before arriving in Duke City.

Traffic remained light in the biggest city in New Mexico as they traveled through town a few hours before rush hour. The lanes grew from two to four as they made their way to the Big I, the intersection of Highway 25, which they were traveling heading north to south, and Highway 40, which ran east to west, coast-to-coast.

She dropped back a bit as they sped past the downtown exits, past the hospitals and hotels, the airport and the university. They made their way past the routes to the south valley. Barr was apparently making no stops, and Eve began to wonder if he was fleeing the state, trying to get to the border of Mexico and leave the country altogether.

That doesn't make any sense, she thought as the speed limit returned to seventy-five miles per hour and the landscape changed from a highly developed city to a more rural area. She noticed the exit to the Isleta Pueblo and remembered that this was the place where Anthony had discovered the holy writings of Sister Maria. This was the place where everything began. This was the starting location of unfolding events that eventually led to theft and murder. She wondered if the people in the pueblo knew what had happened at the Pecos monastery and if they knew their holy writings had been taken.

She recalled the recent visit of the Isleta priest and several men from the pueblo, how adamant they were to find Anthony. It was clear that some of the people in Isleta knew what had happened, but she didn't know if everyone had been told. She didn't know if they were all searching for the young monk who was working on the restoration of the church.

She watched as the white truck slowed at

the exit for the casino and the campground, the exit that would lead to the plaza of the pueblo where the mission church had been for hundreds of years. She recalled as she dropped back to observe Barr's movements that the Isleta church was named for Anthony of Padua and was built in 1629 on the north edge of the main plaza and then later rebuilt after it was decimated during the Pueblo Revolt. Eve also recalled that it was Isleta where the Jumano Indians traveled, guided by Sister Maria, in search of a priest to come back to their village and baptize them. It only made sense to her that the writings would be there, since the Jumano Indians were no longer a recognized tribe. They had dispersed sometime following their Christianization, and as far as Eve knew, there were no Native Americans who identified with this group.

She wondered if Barr had not only the blue cape but also the writings and was returning them to Isleta, perhaps in response to a request made by Anthony. Or, she thought, maybe Anthony was somewhere on the pueblo, hiding out at Isleta, waiting for the supplies Barr had just purchased.

Nothing was making much sense to Eve; nothing was clear. She still didn't know if

Barr was a protector of Anthony, who was, in fact, a fugitive running from murder charges, or if Barr was the only perpetrator and the murderer of two siblings.

She watched as the white truck sped up, not taking the exit to Isleta but still traveling south. She drove on in hopes that her questions would soon be answered.

Forty-Three

The two trucks had traveled well south of Albuquerque before Eve finally understood their destination. Traffic was sparse on that Friday. Few travelers were on the interstate with them heading in either direction. There were a few trucks, a motor home or camper now and then, several sedans and sport-utility vehicles, but the farther south they got, the fewer cars and trucks they encountered.

Even with the sparcity of vehicles traveling near them, Eve had managed to keep a safe distance from Barr, still able to keep the truck ahead of her in sight, but far enough behind it that she was confident Barr hadn't seen her. She kept up with him, glad that the Captain had left her the truck, knowing that the trip she was taking would have been less comfortable if she were driving her motorcycle.

The sun was setting, the pink and red

colors trailing across the western sky, as the minutes ticked to hours and she realized she had been traveling from Tererro for most of the day. She had already eaten a granola bar and drunk half a bottle of water and was munching on an apple when Barr finally slowed, turning on his blinker to head in a different direction.

Eve watched as he took the exit just out of Belen that led to State Highway 47, which she knew connected with Highway 60 a few miles from the Abo Pass. She had not traveled to this section of New Mexico all that often, but she knew where she was and she had an idea of where he was going. When he turned east on the narrow highway, moving in the direction of the little town of Mountainair beyond the Manzano Mountains, Eve remembered the map she had seen in his house and knew for certain the strange man's destination.

Although there had been no specific site established as the place of Sister Maria's bilocation from her convent in Agreda, Spain, there were a number of educated guesses. Eve knew that most religion scholars who studied the nun and author of *The Mystical City of God* agreed that the Lady in Blue appeared to the tribe of the Jumano Indians and to the Tejas tribe somewhere east of Isleta. According to the journals and historical collections from the Franciscan movement during the time of her travels, it was said that the Indians, because of her guidance, had traveled to the pueblo along the Rio Grande River seeking a priest to come to them and offer them baptism.

It was further believed, based on the diaries of those missionaries sent to them, that she had visited the Indians somewhere in a place that took the travelers out of Isleta through the Mescalero Apache lands, across the Manzano Mountain range, and along the banks of a river. This river, which Eve knew was no longer known, was described as a channel whose waters were said to be filled with pink pearls. This was the place of a great baptism of many Indians, most of whom described the nun's visits to them as being made by a young woman dressed in a blue cape who led them to the pueblo church.

Father Benavides, superior of the Franciscan missions of New Mexico at the time when Sister Maria was said to be transported to the southwestern people, left the mission and visited the nun after going back to Mexico City and returning to Spain. He had met the Indians who claimed that the young sister had come to them, believing that she had spoken to them and taught them. And having heard from the priest in Spain, who gave further insight into the nun's travels and the possible arrival of another tribe of Indians to his mission, he intended to meet Sister Maria. Father Benavides also intended to interview this young woman who was said to have appeared to these tribes more than five hundred times.

The priest wanted to learn more about her events of bilocation and authenticate the experiences. He wanted to see for himself if this nun had been given the gift of teleportation and if these incidents had truly happened or if it had been merely some community vision given to the native peoples, attributed of course to God but without involving the mystical and well-connected Spanish nun.

After speaking on several occasions with Sister Maria, Father Benavides was said to have been convinced that indeed she had visited the area numerous times, calling attention to details of the landscape and the people there, details that only someone who had visited the location and seen the people would be able to name. He wrote later that she spoke of being present at the baptisms held in this river of pink pearls, able to give complete descriptions of the priest officiating at the blessed sacraments as well as those receiving the sacred rite.

It was also said that he was convinced of her devotion to the native people as she spoke to him of her great love for them and of her deepest desire for them to know of her faith, to become baptized and join her in her religious tradition. She believed that God had given her the gifts of love and devotion, which then led to the gift of bilocation so that she could make sure the tribes had been given instruction about the Christian faith.

The stories of the young nun's bilocation brought much fame to Sister Maria, and with the fame, Eve recalled reading, came also great suspicion. She became a target of the Holy Office of the Inquisition, created to downplay the rise of mysticism within those in the church. Many believed that the reports of mystical experiences harmed the work and mission of the faith, and those with this belief considered those who claimed to have a developed and significant mystical inner light as a threat.

So much had been made in Spain and in the New World of the young nun's gifts and actions that, like many others accused of being "alumbrados," she was quickly scrutinized. Sister Maria eventually came face-to-face with interviewers in 1635, and again in 1649, the Lady in Blue was investigated by those involved in the Spanish Inquisition.

She was questioned extensively about her visions and mystical experience, but she continued to maintain her innocence and devotion to God. After the interrogations, reports revealed that Sister Maria was never formally charged with any crime against the church. While so many religious leaders and laywomen and laymen were found guilty and suffered grave consequences, Maria remained a nun in good standing with the Catholic Church.

Whether it was because of her authenticated story of bilocation made by the well-respected Father Benavides on her behalf or because of her personal relationship with King Philip IV, having served for years as his spiritual guide and confidante, the young nun was eventually exonerated, never having been forced to stand trial.

In a letter that Sister Maria penned to the Franciscan missionaries in the New World, she told of the desert places she had visited. Eve remembered reading about the letter in a journal article discussing the strange incidents that had occurred in the southwestern states. Eve had kept the article for years because of the many facts and details it included that she had not read before.

In her letter Maria wrote that she had been in the kingdom of Quivira and with the Jumano Indians, which were the last ones to whom she had been transported. She had gone to a place the Franciscan missionaries had not traveled and visited a people they had not encountered.

Eve waited as the truck took the exit, understanding where they were ultimately heading. John Barr was traveling south from Mountainair into the West Mesa and along the Liberty Valley down to the Gran Quivira at the Salinas Pueblo Missions National Monument. He was going to the pueblo where Sister Maria was believed to have appeared to the Indians sometime in the early 1600s.

FORTY-FOUR

Eve waited as John Barr turned down the
dirt road heading south away from the Gran
Quivira at the Salinas Pueblo Missions
National Monument. She stopped at the
intersection and followed the white truck
with her eyes only as Barr headed south,
kicking up clouds of dust behind him. She
knew there wasn't much beyond the monument. A few trails led to the Pinatosa
Canyon, and a path took travelers to a small
camping and picnic site, but from what Eve
remembered of her visits to the national
monument, there was not much beyond the
restored pueblo.

At one time, Eve recalled, several villages
had been settled in the area, ranching com-
munities, a few pueblo houses, but most
were deserted in the 1920s and 1930s during seasons of drought. The next village
south on the road Barr was taking was
Claunch, and Eve knew from a visit there

some time ago that it was mostly a ghost town, abandoned years before. She didn't know exactly where he was going, but she realized she was not able to follow him undetected any farther. There were not enough vehicles on the road to keep her truck hidden, and with night approaching, Eve realized her surveillance was likely coming to an end.

She drove up the highway a bit, made a U-turn, and pulled off the road into the national monument parking lot. It appeared to be closed, probably still too early in the year, she thought, assuming it didn't open again until later in the spring. There was only one other automobile that she could see, a green truck, with a license plate identifying it as an official vehicle of the National Park Service. A ranger's ride, she figured, but she did not see anyone around and guessed that it was left there at the national monument grounds when not in use.

She was a bit chilled since the sun had set and the desert air had grown colder. She kept the engine running and turned on the heat and waited, not knowing where Barr was going or why he had driven to the monument and then gone farther south. She could only guess that he would eventually return to the road he had been traveling and head back to the main road or to the interstate.

Of course she wanted to keep following him, wanted to maintain a good visual on the man, but she also knew she didn't want to be alone and confront him again. She had been frightened enough the first time. She simply wanted to see where he was going and see if he might lead her to the hiding place of Brother Anthony.

She thought about her phone again, wishing she had it, wishing she could contact the Captain since she knew he was likely very concerned. She looked at her watch, realizing it had been more than six hours since they had talked. She guessed that he had already phoned Daniel and was sure that at that very moment, both of them were trying to locate her. She realized they would never suspect she was sitting along a desolate road in the desert almost three hours away from where they were, following a madman without any real proof that he would, in fact, lead her to Brother Anthony.

She sat back in her seat and thought about what she knew about the area Barr had driven into. She recalled reading in history books that the pueblo at Gran Quivira had been built in a commanding position on a mesa and was originally named Cueloze by its inhabitants. The first Spanish visitors were said to have arrived in the area in 1598 and called the native village Pueblo de los Jumanos, which she knew translated as the "village of the striped ones," and those striped ones, the Jumanos, were one of the tribes that Sister Maria visited.

She knew that Gran Quivira was one of the places the Spaniards had visited during their explorations for their home country, searching for the fabled gold, believing earlier reports they had heard about the seven cities of the New World. Francisco Vasquez de Coronado and Juan de Onate, both passionate Spanish explorers, had been to the pueblo, trying to locate the great treasure recounted to them in stories told by earlier surveyors.

The area where she had parked and was waiting was believed to have been settled in the ninth century by Indians known as pit-house dwellers. Three hundred years later, a larger village of Indians settled there, building adobe houses aboveground and using the distinctive pottery style that was often found in the area, Chupadero black and white. By the 1600s, when Sister Maria was said to appear to the Indians, this village, this place where Barr had led Eve, was the largest settlement of Indians in the southwestern United States, with more than fifteen hundred people living there.

Eve looked around and thought about a village that might have existed such a long time ago. She thought about the people and their mud houses, their sharpened skills of hunting and farming, their religion intimately tied to the cycles of nature, and their struggle for survival in a place with so little water. She thought about the unwanted arrival of the Spaniards and their priests, the fights and battles with the newcomers and their ongoing skirmishes with other tribes, recalling that the pueblo where she was waiting, along with several others in the area, was abandoned not long after the appearances of Sister Maria because of heavy Apache attacks.

"Where are you, John Barr?" she asked out loud, wondering where he had gone, what he was doing, and whether she should follow. She had leaned back her head and closed her eyes, deciding to rest for just a second, when she heard a knock on the window of the passenger-side door. She sat straight up as her eyes flew open and instinctively grabbed the wheel.

"We're closed," a voice from outside called out.

Eve could barely make out an image of a woman standing on the other side of the truck. She was making the gesture of rolling down the window. Eve hesitated and then leaned over to reach the lever and manually lower the window. A woman with a wide-brimmed ranger's hat looked in.

"You can't park here," she said, glancing around the inside of Eve's truck. "There's no camping in the parking lot."

Eve nodded. "I wasn't camping," she replied, and then wished she hadn't made that response, thinking that perhaps she should have just taken the instruction and driven away.

"No?" the woman answered, still looking around. She pulled out a flashlight and shined it in Eve's face. "Then what are you doing here?"

"I just stopped for a little bit to rest," she lied. "I didn't know you were closed." She put up a hand to shield her eyes. "I got information online and thought I'd drive down here for the afternoon."

The ranger paused and lowered the light. "You from Albuquerque?"

Eve shook her head. "Madrid."

The ranger studied her. "You got some identification?"

Eve reached in her back pocket for her

329

driver's license but then couldn't resist a dig. "You need to see my ID just for coming to the site and parking in your lot?"

The woman walked around the front of the truck and within seconds was standing beside Eve on the driver's side. She gestured rolling down the window again and Eve complied, rolling down the other window and handing her license to the uniformed ranger. The woman was close enough that Eve could read her name tag.

Park Ranger Rita Rachkowski was taking a good look at Eve's information.

"Well, Ms. Divine, I am allowed to ask for the identification of someone trespassing on federal property." She handed Eve back her license.

"It's *Divine*," Eve responded, correcting the pronunciation. "And I didn't know I was trespassing. I just stopped in a parking lot to rest for a few minutes."

"Uh-huh," Ranger Rita replied. "Well, the monument is closed. We don't open for six weeks. You'd have known that if you were researching us online."

Eve knew she had her there. "Okay, I'll just head back home, Ranger Rachkowski." She pulled her seat belt back on and started to roll up the window and then she had a thought. "Do you have a phone I can borrow?"

"It's *Ra-CHK-owski,*" the ranger said, making her own correction. "And no. There's no signal out here. I only use my scanner. You can go back to the closest town, Mountainair. There's a pay phone there."

Eve shook her head. That was going to take her too far away from Barr.

"Here," and the ranger pulled a brochure out of her back pocket and handed it to Eve. "For next time," she added and smiled. "Have a good evening," she said and stepped back.

Eve took the brochure and placed it on the seat beside her. She cranked the engine and slowly pulled away.

FORTY-FIVE

"Well, this certainly changes things," Eve mumbled as she sat at the end of the driveway of the Salinas monument. Of course she wasn't going home to Madrid or even returning to Pecos. She had come way too far to turn around and head back without any new information. At that point in the evening, the only direction she knew to take was the direction she had seen the man from Tererro take only a few minutes earlier.

She left the parking lot and drove down the unpaved road, heading south, following John Barr's lead and moving in the direction of Claunch. As she pulled away she glanced in her rearview mirror and could see Ranger Rita watching.

"Sorry there, Ms. Ra-*Chkow-ski,*" she said, turning her attention to the road before her.

Stars were starting to flicker in the night

sky and Eve flipped on her lights. Darkness had fallen upon the desert, and she was having a difficult time driving on the dirt road. There were lots of rough patches and potholes, narrow twists and turns, and Eve dropped her speed so that she could avoid the worst of the ruts and dips. She steadied the vehicle as much as possible to keep her father's truck from veering off the road.

Once again, she felt grateful that she was not on her Harley and that the Captain had left his truck in the parking lot at the monastery. She patted the steering wheel as a gesture of her gratitude and her faith in the old Ford workhorse that had been her father's reliable mode of transportation for years, and she said a prayer of thanksgiving as she drove farther into the desert, feeling safe and comfortable behind the wheel.

She tried to see the time on her watch, but unwilling to stop or slow down, she was unable to make out the face and its reading in the dark. Eve wasn't counting the miles she had driven from the Salinas National Monument, but with the slow speed and the descending darkness, even though she hadn't been on the road that long, it seemed as if she had been driving for an hour. She leaned forward and gripped the steering wheel with both hands, tapping on the brake from time to time as she sped ahead.

"Dear Captain," she said out loud, wondering what her father must be thinking at that moment, the day now past and no word from her. "You must be beside yourself," she added, wishing she had not lost her phone, wishing she had been able to call before leaving the Pecos Canyon to follow Barr.

She knew he had no way of knowing where she was. She was sure he hadn't put a GPS on the vehicle; he hadn't installed a tracking device. And she also recalled once again that she had not even really explained where she was going when she told him she was leaving the monastery. She had the best of intentions, wanting to keep him out of the loop, make it easier for him to be in conversation with Daniel or the other detectives, but now she questioned that objective. She was alone in the desert and he had no idea where to start a search. She had been careless, she knew, but she maintained the hope that she would find John Barr, find Brother Anthony, and before much more time had passed, be able to let the Captain finally know that she was safe.

She drove along, trying to remember how many miles she had to go to reach the ghost town at the end of State Road 55. She knew she was traveling through ranching country and that there were very few residences in the area, even though there were a number of gates with locks at the ends of paths curving and twisting away from the road. She recalled that the grazing land she was traversing used to be fields of pinto beans, and she remembered a trip as a child with her family to this very area, her father's history lessons of the Indians and the Spaniards, the farmers and the ranchers, the way families had come and gone from the desert. She wished again that she could let him know where she was and that she was fine, but she knew that was not possible and shook away the thoughts of his worry and concern.

"Mr. John Barr," Eve said out loud, thinking about the man she had encountered earlier. She was unsure if he had recognized her as a nun from the monastery in Pecos, and she also didn't know if he had found her phone in his room and if that was the reason he had sped out of Tererro and headed to the southern plains of New Mexico.

She thought about the archbishop and learning of his search for the missing monk. She wondered if they had a better lead than she did or if someone from that office was following the same man on the same road. She wondered if, in fact, she might end up face-to-face with another representative of the diocese. With this possibility in mind, Eve recalled seeing the archbishop at the monastery, his apparent displeasure that she might still be working the front desk, the way he immediately dismissed her to speak to Daniel. She wondered what he had told Father Oliver, what new complaint was being lodged against the monastery or the nuns or the abbot's leadership. She thought about the man who had only rarely attended a service in the community, rarely made an appearance, but who wielded such power over all of the monks and the nuns who lived there.

"Some things never change," she said out loud, thinking about Sister Maria and the suspicion placed on her by the leaders of the Catholic Church during the time of the questioning of her miracle of bilocation. Eve recalled once again the reports of the inquisition of the Spanish nun and how she had barely escaped the consequences that other mystics in the 1600s had faced.

Without actually casting herself in the same light as the Lady in Blue, Eve drove deeper and deeper into the desert, and for the first time began to consider the similarities between the nuns facing inquisitions at the hands of the church officials and her own story as a Benedictine sister being banned from the community she had called home for more than two decades.

She felt the disappointment rise within her, and for a moment the depth of it, as well as the articulation of the oppression of women within the church, surprised her. Sister Eve realized that she had not allowed herself to experience the full realm of her frustration and resentment regarding the circumstances that had unfolded at the monastery. She thought about the other sisters who had already left New Mexico. She had been out of touch with all of them. It was almost as if they had chosen not to speak to one another, somehow knowing that if they talked, if they shared their sorrow, it might lead them to actions that would be detrimental to their continued lives as nuns.

Eve wondered about the Lady in Blue, wondered if she was ever angry at the treatment she received at the hands of those questioning her. She thought about the contemporary critics of the Spanish nun, the articles and reports that claimed she could not have performed the miracles attributed to her, that she had erred in her thinking of Mary's revelations, that she was a charlatan or a false prophet. And finally a question came to Eve's mind that she had never allowed herself to ask.

She stopped the truck in the middle of the road, slamming on the brakes, feeling the weight of such a thought. *Has there really ever been a place for women in the church?*

Eve dropped her head onto the steering wheel, the tears stinging in her eyes. She had never put words to this emotion, never allowed herself to doubt her faith, her call, her devotion, a devotion not to an institution, she knew, but still a faith and call and devotion that were supervised by leaders in that institution, by men.

She shook her head and, keeping her foot on the brake, sat back against the driver's seat. This revelation, she thought, was both unexpected and dangerous, and as she tried to find some resolution, some prayerful way to hold it in her mind and heart, Eve closed her eyes, never noticing the lights of the vehicle coming from a path through an open gate, speeding in her direction.

FORTY-SIX

"WAIT . . ." There was no time for Eve to say anything else as she felt her head slam against the driver's-side window and then whip back to the headrest while she was immediately thrown to the side by the direct impact of the truck T-boning her from the passenger's side. Her foot slipped off the brake and the truck continued to move ahead. Shocked and confused, she was unable to stop it as it veered across the road and down the bank to her left. She felt the road beneath her, the rough terrain and the hit coming from the front this time, her forehead smashing against the steering column. There was a huge bump as the truck traveled across the bank and crashed into a fence post, where it finally came to a stop.

Eve thought she heard a sound like steam building and rising somewhere ahead of her, but she felt paralyzed, having great difficulty opening her eyes or waking up. She moaned and attempted to lift her arms, her hands, tried to feel around her to touch something that would help her understand where she was and what had happened. Everything was off and confusing, and she felt foggy, unclear, and mystified about the sequence of events.

She was in the truck, she thought, in her father's truck. She was driving somewhere, it seemed to her, driving somewhere in the desert.

The questions kept pounding in her brain. *Am I alone? Was I with the Captain? Where is he? Was I following someone?*

The answers felt like they were so close, that she could almost name the place and the reason she was there, but still, her brain was rattled and nothing was making sense to her at all.

She was finally able to lift her right hand and reach up, and when she did she touched her forehead and the left side of her face that ached, feeling a liquid that was wet and sticky. Her left shoulder throbbed and her neck and hip hurt. She had been in a wreck, she thought; she was injured from a wreck, but she still wasn't able to name where she was and she couldn't remember where she had been traveling when it happened.

She tried opening her eyes but there was only darkness around her, save for a beam of light shining ahead, cast from her own headlights, but revealing nothing that helped her place where she was. Just dirt and brush, a large trough, for water she supposed, rocks and small bushes. The desert, she thought, out on a ranch or field, but she still could make out no landmarks or familiar sights that might help her gain her bearings. She felt drunk and disoriented, lost, and in excruciating pain. The sound of the steam stopped and she heard nothing but the night wind.

Suddenly, just as she was about to lose consciousness, she felt the door open beside her, and a large, strong arm reached around her, unbuckling her seat belt and tossing it to the side, and then she felt another arm slide beneath her. The arms began yanking and pulling her out of the truck. The treatment felt harsh and severe, and she tried fighting because she could hardly stand the discomfort in her upper body and left hip. But the arms were too strong, and she could not fight or assist or think clearly about what was happening. She experienced only the sensation of being jerked and pulled, the horrible ache in her head and shoulder, her feet coming out of the truck and then her left ankle hitting the ground hard, the pain sharp and alarming, causing her to cry out.

She tried to pull away, tried to tell her rescuer to stop, to slow down just a minute and let her catch her breath. She wanted him to quit pulling her, quit yanking and manhandling her. She wanted him to stop and just let her have a little relief from the ache in her ankle, the discomfort in her head and shoulder, the agony from her left hip, as well as the distress she was feeling in so many places in her body. But the person holding her did not stop. He — or could it be she? — continued to pull and yank and then finally dragged her up the bank and then down a dirt road.

She tried desperately to open her eyes, tried to see who was pulling her along, but she felt so groggy and disoriented, so horribly in pain that she was unable to look up and behind to get a clear picture of who had her in their grasp. She fought as much as she could, struggled to turn around and see the person, but they were much stronger, forcing her arms down, her shoulders pinned, one of which felt completely dislocated, permitting her no movement at all. She could do nothing but submit.

Unable to fight back, Eve quit resisting

and tried to imagine that it was Daniel taking her to safety, giving thought to the possibility that perhaps the Captain had been able to find her after all. She wanted to believe that she wasn't far from home and that he had found her. She tried to imagine that she was out of danger as her father had called his old partner and together they had discovered her on a road somewhere.

She imagined they were getting her out of the truck and away from some accident she had been in. She tried to believe this was a rescue by a loved one. She was being dragged for her protection, being pulled as far away from her truck and impending danger as was necessary. She would soon be let down on the ground, she imagined, in a safe area, on a soft place where her injuries could be tended, the pain relieved, and where she could finally be given an explanation of what had happened.

"Thank you," she tried to say as she was being dragged along the road, but she couldn't quite shape the words, her tongue and lips struggling to form her expression of gratitude.

Soon, she told herself, *soon the pain will stop and I can rest.*

But the strong arms holding her did not let her go, and the sliding of her body across

the gravel and dirt didn't quickly come to
an end. She blacked out, her body relaxing
and then, in what seemed to be only seconds, emerging to consciousness again. It
felt like she was in a dream, more of a
nightmare really, unable to wake up and unable to end the terrible pain she was feeling.

Finally, just as she thought she was blacking out again, the yanking and pulling
stopped, and she felt the arms behind her
release her upper body, her head then dropping hard on the ground beneath her. She
felt herself groan again. She tried to listen,
hoping someone would speak to her, but
she heard only sounds, doors opening, a
person breathing hard. *Was it the man who
rescued her?* she wondered.

There were things being moved around
near where she lay, objects tossed, a kind of
shuffling. She opened her eyes and looked
up, but she could see only the night sky
above her, black velvet studded with pin-
points of light, stars and planets filling up
the horizon. It was beautiful and familiar,
and while she lay on the ground in pain, it
was also deeply comforting. This was the
sky she knew, the sky she had been born
under, the sky where she had fallen in love
with God, the sky of her mother and father,

344

and the sky under which she knew she would die. This place with its black sky and its cool spring wind, this was her home. She closed her eyes again.

She did not struggle or resist this time as the warm body knelt beside her and the strong arms came under her. She leaned back into whatever or whoever was lifting her. She felt the words of a prayer on her lips and began reciting the familiar way she had always talked to God. She mumbled first the prayer that Jesus taught his disciples to pray and then began the one she loved the most; she prayed to the Virgin Mother, the feminine presence of God, the one adored by all the sisters and saints.

"Hail Mary, full of grace," Eve said softly as she was picked up, carried, and then placed in what felt to be the back of a truck. "The Lord is with thee. Blessed art thou amongst women."

And even though Sister Eve was in undisclosed hands, she felt a divine protection.

FORTY-SEVEN

When Eve awoke, her throat and mouth felt dry, and all she could see was a narrow stream of light coming through a crack in the ceiling of the building where she lay. Sunlight, she thought, but there was no evidence to prove the light's original source. She thought the ceiling looked like it had been made with boards, and as she slowly turned to her side, it appeared as if the walls were made from the same lumber.

She had no idea how long she had been there. She had no idea of how much time had passed. She stared above her at the narrow opening and thought about where she might be. As she tried to focus her vision, Eve realized that she could open only one eye. She breathed as normally as she was able, and even though she wanted to see what was wrong with her, see if she could get up and find water or try to call for help, she wasn't sure which body part to attempt to move first. For a moment, other than the horrible dryness in her throat and mouth, there was no real physical discomfort, but that moment was fleeting. In less than a few seconds, everything hurt.

She was able to assess that she was lying on her back, her arms and hands resting across her belly. She tried to lift her head but was immediately stopped by the stabbing pain on her left side and the nausea that suddenly took over her body. After staying awake for a few minutes, trying to keep from blacking out again, she decided to remain in the same position but to attempt to take an inventory of her injuries. She wanted to know what had happened to her body.

She started with her feet, her hiking boots and the thick socks still on, trying to move them a bit, first wiggling her toes and then sliding her heels up and back. There was some success in her movements, and from what she could tell, at least from her lower extremities, there was only minimal damage. She felt only a slight ache in her right ankle.

She moved her attention elsewhere, scanning upward, thinking that her legs seemed fine. Her hips and back, however, felt terribly uncomfortable. Again, it was the left side that hurt the most. She didn't think her pelvis had been fractured, but it had certainly suffered a blow. She could hardly move from side to side, her left hip was so painful. She stopped moving and surveyed her belly and chest, again feeling that there had been no real damage to that area of her body. However, as soon as she tried to lift her arms, the pain in her left shoulder immediately pushed the breath from her body. She groaned.

It was dislocated or broken, she wasn't sure which; she knew only that the pain was sharp and radiated down her arm and up and across the back of her neck. The left side of her face was also injured. She rested her left arm across her chest and raised her right hand to explore. She immediately felt both the swelling and a sticky substance that had matted in her hair and dripped down her shirt, expecting that there was more than likely a cut or gash beneath the swelling and that blood had been shed. As far as she could tell, however, the area was not still bleeding; the blood had clotted sometime after the injury occurred.

She slid her fingers across her left eye, taking great care as she touched, but she was still unprepared for the pain that followed. She stopped and rested her right hand on her cheek. She winced in agony but tried to keep a steady and regular breath.

As best as Eve could tell, she had suffered the impact of whatever had happened on the left side of her body. She wasn't clear if she had been hit on that side or pushed hard against that side, but it was certain from the pain that the left side of her face, shoulder, head, and hip had received the brunt of whatever had taken place.

She brought her arm back down to her side, closed her right eye, and tried to remember what had happened. It took a few minutes, everything fuzzy at first, but suddenly the images and her recall became clear. She remembered that she had been driving on the road from the Salinas National Monument south toward the ghost town of Claunch. She had been following John Barr all the way from the Pecos Canyon because she had seen the blue cloak in his house. She assumed that he would lead her to Brother Anthony, and she had not told anyone where she was going.

While driving down the dirt road after leaving Salinas, she had been thinking about Sister Maria and the archbishop, and for some reason she could not name, she had been crying, she thought. She was weeping about something — she didn't quite remember what, but she was still able to feel some unnamed sadness — when she was hit by another vehicle coming from the right side, the impact causing her body to crash into the door and window on the driver's side.

From there, the details felt a bit murkier. She was unclear about the other vehicle, the other driver who had hit her, and she wasn't sure how she got from her truck to wherever it was that she now lay. What did seem clear was that she was not receiving help in this place where she was. There were no bandages on her injuries, no water at her side, no blanket or pillow, no medications to ease the pain. No one was with her. She had been taken from the accident and placed in this building that let in only a sliver of light.

As Eve assessed the situation she was in, she realized that the hit on her truck had been intended to harm her. And even though she had survived the crash, it was evident to her that she remained in danger. She had to get up. She knew she had to find a way to get out of the place she had been stashed because it seemed apparent that whoever had hit her and brought her there would at some point come back.

Eve was so thirsty, and after the brief awakening and assessment of her injuries, once again so sleepy. And yet she understood the gravity of her situation. She understood that she couldn't fall back to sleep. She had to try to stay awake, try to get up and figure out a way to get assistance.

"Help!" She tried calling out but could tell that her voice was too low to be heard. "Help me!" she called out again, the sounds of her own cries causing her to become more and more distressed.

She stopped shouting and tried to concentrate on where she might be. She recalled the dirt road she had traveled from the national monument, how long and desolate it had seemed to her at the time. She remembered the empty landscape, the pastures devoid of cattle or horses. She remembered how lonesome the plains had looked to her from the inside of her father's truck as she drove along trying to find John Barr, and she knew that if her kidnapper had taken her anywhere near where he had crashed into her on the road, there was likely no one in or around the vicinity.

Eve knew how isolated it was beyond the ruins of the Gran Quivira. She knew how practically all of the buildings in the area had been abandoned, how few residents made a home anywhere near the place. There was no water source south of Mountainair, no river or stream, and that had been the reason many scholars gave for the desolation, the reason that the fields and the towns remained uninhabited.

This was the dry and dust-caked desert, settled by Indians, conquered by the Spanish, and farmed by those thinking they could weather the storms and overcome the odds. But in the end, nobody stayed, everybody left, and as Eve considered where she had been brought and abandoned, she felt the despair of those who had come and eventually gone.

"Help me," she called out again and slowly slid her right arm out to her side to feel around her. She was surprised when her fingers touched the edge of a cloth, and when they did, she reached as far as she could, grabbed a handful, and pulled. Perhaps, she thought as she yanked, it was a blanket or sack or something that she could use for a pillow or a bandage. She pulled as hard as she could, but the garment seemed to be stuck on or attached to something, and as she grasped and tugged harder, she immediately knew what she had found.

She was lying next to someone else.

Sister Eve let go of the cloth and screamed, shocked to discover the body, but then as her nerves settled, curiosity took over. She carefully lifted herself up, trying to touch the body beside her, but just as she raised her head and leaned over, the room began to spin and Eve fell back, unconscious once again.

FORTY-EIGHT

There was a blueness all around her, soft and disarming, growing in intensity, a blur of color suddenly coming more and more into focus. So very light at first, a blue of water, an edge of the horizon, but then deeper and darker, a winter sky blueness, suddenly filling the space all around her, filling the room, filling her heart, a blueness that spoke to Eve of endless rest.

Eve felt the changes beginning within her. Small changes, not unlike the blueness, began to manifest into something transformative. She felt the pain ease away from her bit by bit. The discomfort from her injuries simply evaporated from her, part by part, bottom to top, just like the assessment she had done on herself earlier.

Feet and legs, hips and back, chest and shoulders, neck and face and head. Soon nothing ached or hurt. Her face and head were not bloody. Her eye was not swollen shut. Her shoulder and arm, the side that felt so broken, so damaged, the hip and ankle, all of the wounds had been healed.

She then felt some part of herself sit up, felt something from within her body, her spirit, her inner being, pulling slowly out of what still lay on the floor, something pulling slowly out and away, leaving the shell that she had lived in all of her life, now resting on the floor beneath, the wounds still present upon it, the blood, the swelling, the bruising, all of it still remaining there.

She felt a twinge of sorrow to leave it, this body of hers, and for a brief moment she wanted to kneel down to bless it, touch it, but in the blueness that filled the room, she was so content, so deeply happy to be out of the broken vessel that had been her body, she did not want to hover too close. No longer held within it or bound completely by it, she was not thirsty or afraid or sad or confused; she felt nothing of the things that had only seconds earlier overwhelmed her. She had been released from what had been, and there was only the blueness that moved around her and even through her, lifting her up and beyond herself.

She felt light and unattached and free, and Eve then knew a deep and abiding love, a piercing love that she recognized, had felt before, albeit fleetingly and never lasting. This love, however, this presence of such an all-consuming emotion, remained. This time the love did not leave her but rather enveloped her. And while previously in her life there had been only glimpses during such an experience, this time Eve was completely and fully immersed in this love.

Heaven, she thought as she saw her body lying beneath her. *This must be heaven, the blue of the sky, the leaving of my body; this must be what is happening. I am dying. I am dead.* But she remained somewhat confused when she realized there were no angels or spiritual beings leading her to another place. All she knew was this embodiment of love holding her in the vast and divine blueness.

Without direction or guidance, a part of Eve seemed to know what to do, an instinct telling her how to lean into the lightness, relax into the beauty of what carried her, what held her, and because of this deep wisdom within her, she did not question or doubt or worry about the suddenness and unexpectedness of what had come upon her. It was as if the very essence of her nature, the very basic element of how she was defined, knew where she was going, what was overcoming her, and what was being required of her, which Eve suddenly understood was nothing. Nothing was being asked or expected or pulled from her. For the very first time that she could recall, the simple creation of herself, showing up in her original form, was all there was for her to do.

She closed her eyes and a loosening of ties began, ties anchoring her to her body, to the earth beneath her. She felt ropes and ribbons fall from her, colored strings and thick yarns; and with each untying, she moved higher and higher into the blueness, into that perfect event of love. It was like shedding old skins, coming out of a cocoon, spinning and spinning out of chains and cords and strips of cloth. And with each letting go, she breathed into a higher state of awareness.

When the undoing was finished, she knew she was not completely unbound. There were still one or two, maybe more, but not many ties that wrapped around her as she moved away from her body, away from the building where she had been, away from the earth, all of it now below her. She was not completely unloosed, but the ties she still felt around and coming from within her were not cumbersome or burdensome. It was almost as if she felt glad that they were there even as she yearned for the complete release, the whole of letting go.

"Evangeline." The voice that spoke, the first one calling her, was so familiar, from so long ago, that immediately Eve began to cry. Just from the sound of her name, just from the way it felt to hear it spoken by that voice again.

"Evangeline, I have loved you so long."

Eve couldn't help herself, the tears held for so many years, this moment prayed for and wanted so desperately. She could hardly call out, but the word stayed on her lips as she melted into the oneness she first remembered.

"Mama," she said and was immediately engulfed in what seemed like the warmest and oldest embrace she had ever known. Her mother had come to her.

"I miss you," Eve heard herself say. "I miss you so much."

"I am always with you," she heard the reply. "Always."

And the love and the embrace held her, sustained her, filled her, until suddenly there was another presence with them, another presence that held them both, Eve and the spirit of her deceased mother.

Eve recognized it as the same presence that had been with her when she first pulled away from her body, the presence of the blueness. A cape, a cloud, it seemed so hard to name what it was, but the blueness came through her again, bathing her in warmth and peace.

"You are safe," another voice spoke out, a voice other than her mother's.

Eve wanted to shout the words, sing the words, laugh the words, "I know." She felt them so deeply. "I know, I know, I know."

"Not here," the voice replied.

And Eve was stunned by the revelation.

"You are safe there," the voice added.

"But I don't want to be there," Eve said, hearing how she sounded, so young and so fierce. "I want to be here, with you, here."

"You will be safe there," the voice said. "But you must go back because there are still bindings that are not ready to be loosed. There is still work to be done."

Before she could even respond, before she could ask for more time, Eve was already starting to feel the blueness lifting from her, away from her. She could feel the memory of her mother's embrace, the feeling of such a thing, but not the embrace itself any longer.

She felt herself being called back, quietly, easily, but still back to what lay beneath her, back to the earth, back to the old shed, back to the hard wooden floor, back to her broken body. It was slow and not painful, not disturbing, just a simple return, a baby placed back into the crib after being in her mother's arms. It was gentle and done with great compassion and love.

"He needs you," the voice called out, sounding farther and farther away. "You must go back for him."

And suddenly, she fully realized the agony and brokenness of her body.

Eve screamed out in pain.

FORTY-NINE

When Eve first heard the moans, she thought they had to be coming from her own mouth, a response to her own pain. Once conscious again, she had heard herself scream, and she imagined that the groans were what followed, a consequence to feeling once more her injuries. However, as she turned her head and felt beside her again, touching the body near her that she had discovered earlier, she understood that the other person in the room where she had been abandoned was alive and making the noises.

She tried to roll over onto her right side, the side that had not felt the full impact of the car wreck and that was facing the other person. She tried lifting first her left shoulder and then her left hip, but the pain was unbearable. She tried again, gritting her teeth and closing her eyes and concentrating as hard as she could to turn her body and move through the agony.

Slowly, she pulled and turned until she was on her right side, and as she fell on her hip, she felt ahead of her with her right hand and realized she was indeed facing a leg, a man's leg, she thought, shoeless but still wearing socks. She moved her fingers up the leg until she felt what seemed like a gown or a long skirt, the cloth she had yanked earlier, and Eve understood she was feeling the simple cotton tunic of a monk.

She pushed with her right leg, sliding herself up to the man's face.

"Anthony," she said, touching her friend's neck, feeling for a pulse. "Anthony, it's Eve," she said again, no longer aware of her own pain. She felt along his face, his chin, his cheeks, his closed eyes.

Slowly, she pulled herself up so that she was sitting next to the young man. There was still little light in the room, so she was unable to see the face of her friend, but she leaned in close enough to feel him breathing even if he would not respond to her calls.

"Anthony." She pulled his head and shoulders onto her lap, patted him on the cheek and across his forehead. "Anthony, you need to wake up."

He moaned, winced, and moved a little, pulling himself away from her lap and back onto the floor.

Eve leaned over him and, with her good arm, tried to pull him up. "Anthony, we need to get out of here. You need to wake up."

He responded only by pulling away and groaning again.

Eve stopped. She couldn't tell what had happened to the monk. She couldn't see any injuries on him, no blood around his body, no apparent wounds that she could feel, but it was so dark in the room she was not able to get a clear look at the man, not able to do a decent assessment of his injuries.

He was hurt or sick, that much she could tell, but whether he was not responding clearly and not able to stay awake because of a head injury or because he was hurt elsewhere on his body or if he had ingested something or been drugged, she couldn't tell.

"Anthony," she tried again, calling out his name and shaking him by the shoulders. "Anthony, you've got to wake up. You've been here long enough. Wake up! We have to get out of here."

There was no reply and Eve's concern was only growing.

"I . . . I'm sick," he said softly.

Eve moved closer to him, leaning down to hear. "Anthony, what happened? How did you get here?"

"He . . . he . . ."

Eve couldn't make out any words. He was mumbling.

"Was it John Barr?" she asked, remembering how she had followed the man out of Terrero.

"Did he poison you, Anthony?" Suddenly she thought that the man might have poisoned both the siblings and that not only had he T-boned her and brought her to this building somewhere near the road to Claunch, but that he must have brought Anthony here after killing Kelly and taking him away from the monastery. She remembered the blue cloak in his closet.

"Answer me, Anthony. Did John Barr poison you? Did he give you something?"

"Kelly . . ." He moaned the name of his sister, and Eve thought he was crying.

"I know, Anthony, I know. Kelly's dead, but you and I aren't. That's why we have to get out of here."

The monk moved a bit. His hands reached out. "Eve," he said, sounding a bit more alert, a bit more like himself.

"Yes, Anthony, it's me. It's Eve."

She felt him pull away from her. "Where

are we?" he asked.

Eve held her left arm across her chest and sat up. "I don't know," she answered. "It's some building or cabin, shed, I don't know."

"In Pecos?" he asked, looking around.

"No," she replied. "John Barr brought you out here. We're near Mountainair."

"I . . . I feel so . . ." And he dropped back down again.

"Anthony, you have to wake up. We need to get out of here." She shook him. "Anthony!" She pushed and pulled on his tunic, trying to get his attention, but he had become nonresponsive once again.

Eve knew she would have to get out to find medical attention for both of them, that Anthony wasn't going to be able to help her. She also knew that if John Barr had brought them to that shed and left them there, he was more than likely coming back. What he intended to do at that point, she had no idea.

"Did he leave you anything?" she asked the monk, not really expecting an answer. "Is there any water? A phone?"

Eve slid her legs beneath her, rocked forward, and landed on her knees. She felt a sharp pain in her hip and stopped, taking a few breaths. She pushed up, getting her right foot, her ankle still tender and sore, squared beneath her, and by bracing herself with her right hand, she was able to rise to a standing position. Immediately she felt the room spin and she reached out with her right hand, touching the wall behind her. She steadied herself and waited. Getting accustomed once again to the dim light in the space, Eve took a good look around.

It was an old cabin, not unlike the one she had been in earlier, the one where John Barr lived out beyond the little village of Pecos. It was made from rough lumber, old, hand-hewn, and held together with some kind of sap or glue, which she could feel along the wall behind her. There was no window, only the tiny bit of light she had noticed before, a bit of sunlight coming from an opening above. With it, however, she could see there was a door at the other end.

Leaning against the wall and then stepping over Anthony, Eve slowly moved over to it. Her ankle hurt, probably sprained, she thought, and she limped to a position right in front of the door. She searched for a handle but felt none. She pushed, but it wouldn't budge.

She pushed again. "Come on, come on."

Nothing.

Eve closed her eyes and tried to think of

how to exit, tried to imagine what would work, how she might open the door. "Sister Maria . . . ," she whispered and pushed again, harder this time. It did not open, but it did move slightly, giving Eve enough of a reason to push again.

With that final shove the door flew open. She dropped to the ground. Light flooded the room.

FIFTY

"Help!" Eve called out as she fell forward when the door flew open, catching herself just before she spilled out onto the ground. She grabbed the door with her right hand and was somehow able to remain upright. She felt the pain surge across her left shoulder when she pulled, but this time it was manageable; she didn't feel as if she was going to pass out again. She wobbled, but once she got her bearings, she was able to look around as she squinted against what appeared to be the late-afternoon sun.

Only able to open one eye, she searched from side to side, trying to locate herself, trying to figure out where she and Anthony had been kidnapped and left, but nothing was familiar. The barren landscape, the cloudless blue sky, the hardscrabble plains could be anyplace in New Mexico, she thought.

Within a few minutes, however, she recalled where she had been when she was rammed by the other vehicle and made the assumption that she must be somewhere close to the Salinas National Monument. She guessed that John Barr had crashed into her while she was driving down the dirt road to Claunch, dragged her from her vehicle, and driven her someplace close by, to this one-room cabin he'd built on property he owned or leased.

"Help!" she called out again, wishing there was someone in the vicinity who might hear her. "Help me!"

There was only silence.

She turned back to the shed and limped in. As she stood at the entry, she looked for water or food, any supplies that might have been left by Barr in the cabin. Much to her surprise, in a far corner just beyond where she had lain, there were several bottles of water, a couple of towels, even what appeared to be snacks of some kind. If she had only turned to the other side when she woke up, she realized, she would have seen them, and learning this made her wonder about Barr's true intentions. These necessary supplies had obviously been left for her or for Anthony, but it still didn't make any sense.

"Is this from you?" she asked out loud,

remembering the dream and the words of instruction that she was to take care of someone, the someone she assumed to be Brother Anthony. "Is this some divine gift?"

Taking the weight off her right ankle, she hopped over to the stash and gently leaned down and picked up a bottle of water. She drank too quickly, almost choking, and pulled the bottle away from her lips to catch her breath. When she felt settled, she took another long sip and then quickly moved over to the other person in the cabin.

"Anthony, here's some water. Can you hear me?" She slowly knelt beside him, panting through the pain, and placed the bottle to his lips. "Anthony, wake up. Here's some water." Eve took the bottle from his mouth and poured a little on his face, hoping the shock of it would push him out of his sleep.

It seemed to work as she watched him groan and even slap at Eve's hands. He reached up and wiped the water away but would not open his eyes.

Feeling more confident about the outcome, Eve splashed some more on his face. "Anthony, you have to wake up!"

This time he didn't move.

She took another long swallow from the

bottle of water; her thirst felt unquench-able.

Suddenly Anthony began to rouse again. "Who . . ." He glanced around, blinking and squinting. "Where . . ." He did not finish the questions he clearly wanted to ask.

"It's Eve," she said, hoping he had not lost his cognitive abilities and recalling that he had recognized her previously. "It's Eve," she repeated, trying to get a good look at her friend.

"Eve . . ." Anthony shook his head, put a hand up to his forehead, feeling the spilled water. "What's . . ." He raised up, taking in his surroundings.

"It's water; here, take a few swallows," she said and handed him the bottle, which he took and then sat up a little more.

"Wait, take it slow," she said, taking the bottle away from him after he started to guzzle it. "Just a few sips, not too much, you might choke."

He nodded and she handed the bottle to him again, which he took and drank only a little.

"I'm so thirsty," he said.

"Yeah, I know, me too," Eve replied, watching him carefully as he took another sip.

She waited before asking the questions.

There were so many forming in her mind, so many things she didn't know or under-stand, but she waited, trying to give him a little more time before she started the interview. She managed to get into a sitting position next to him and leaned against the wall behind her.

Anthony turned to her and stared. "What happened to you?" He examined her face, the puffed and swollen eye, the caked blood in her hair.

"I was hit," she answered and could quickly see he didn't understand. "My truck, I was crashed into." She paused. "Last night or maybe a couple of nights ago, I don't know. I've lost track of time," she said, glancing down at her left wrist, re-alizing that her watch was broken, the glass shattered.

"What are you doing here?" he wanted to know. "Where are we?" He looked around the cabin.

"You don't know?" she asked.

He shook his head and then winced, the movement apparently causing his head to hurt. He reached up, grabbing his forehead, and suddenly leaned away from Eve and vomited the water he had only just drunk and then collapsed once again.

"Anthony!" She shook him, but he appeared to be out of it once more. She felt his chest and, with the rise and fall, could tell that he was still breathing.

Not wanting to feel the pain in her hip and ankle again by standing, Eve slid back over to the supplies that had been left in the corner. She grabbed a granola bar, tore open the package, and began to eat. She was ravenous. She opened another bottle of water and drank almost all of the contents.

"What am I going to do?" She asked the question out loud, hoping the voice would speak to her again, hoping the pain might stop, hoping she would figure out how to call for help.

She finished the granola bar and turned her attention back to Anthony. There was no way, she knew, that she could carry him out of the cabin. There was no way that she could support him even if she could get him to wake up enough to walk out.

Eve understood that if she was going to get help, she was going to have to go without her friend. She would push the supplies closer to him and leave the water near enough that he could reach it if he woke up, but she was going to have to leave him there.

She folded the towel and slid back over and placed it beneath Anthony's head. She put the water and granola bars at his right hand, just at the fingertips. She pulled down his tunic, which had gathered at his waist, and placed the blanket that had been underneath him across his legs.

She sat beside him and said a prayer for him and then slid back to where she was able to lean against the wall and push herself up from the floor. She stumbled a bit, kept her left arm close to her chest, trying not to move her shoulder, and limped to the door. She stepped out and closed the door.

Eve placed her hand on the door, closed her eyes, asked once more for the protection of angels for her friend, and then turned in what she hoped would be a right direction.

FIFTY-ONE

What if I walk for miles and find no one? What if I follow a path and run right into John Barr? What if I fall and can't go any farther?

The doubts and questions were endless for Eve as she stood outside the cabin. She remained at the edge of the building, waiting, trying to decide what she should do. The pain was excruciating. She could hardly walk, hardly see, and she didn't want to leave Anthony, fearful he might die while she was gone and also, although she didn't want to admit it, fearful that she might die once she walked away. And yet Eve knew that to wait in the cabin, just to stay there and do nothing, was the poorest choice she could make.

She knew John Barr would be coming back; it only made sense that he had left them there but intended to return. He didn't lock the door, so he must have thought she was too injured and Anthony too drugged to escape. Or maybe he simply knew there was nowhere to go, and in such a desolate, isolated area, no one else would come to them.

She didn't know where the man might have gone. She imagined that if he planned to kill them both where he had abandoned them in the cabin, perhaps he'd left to retrieve an appropriate murder weapon. She also wondered if he had gone back to the scene of the accident to move her truck, tow her vehicle away so there would be no sign that she had traveled in that direction. Perhaps he was attending to covering any evidence of her whereabouts, and once those details had been taken care of, he would return to finish what he had started.

Eve glanced back at the cabin where she knew Anthony lay, still passed out on the floor. She had no idea what had happened to him, but she knew he wasn't himself. He had been drugged or poisoned or was otherwise sick, and Eve didn't know how long he had been in that state or how much longer he could stay that way. She assumed that John Barr had done that to him, that he had given him something harmful and left him in the cabin where she eventually found him. Surely the man she had followed from Pecos had done all of this.

And yet, she thought, *if he had planned to kill Anthony, why is he still alive? Wouldn't he already be dead and not just sick?*

She thought about the almond smell she had immediately noticed from Kelly when she found her on the floor of her guest room and how she had not detected the same smell while in the cabin with Anthony. Still, she knew that didn't really mean anything. It had been many hours since Kelly had been poisoned and killed; if Anthony had been given the same tea at or near the same time, he would surely also be dead. Even if he had survived that ingestion, Eve did not think there would be a lingering odor days after drinking the poison. There were so many questions about what had happened to Anthony and his sister and to herself, and all of them had to do with the man she had followed from Pecos.

She couldn't understand what John Barr would have gained from killing three people, especially the one person he seemed to consider a friend. She knew he cared about Brother Anthony, and she knew Anthony cared for him. They were friends, the young monk had told her on more than one occasion. It didn't make sense that he would hurt him so deliberately.

She knew there had been the theft of

Sister Maria's papers, but she had also seen how John Barr lived and understood that he did not appear to be someone who would be motivated by greed. Eve stopped. She was not getting anywhere with these kinds of thoughts. She shook away the questions and the fear of Barr. She knew it was useless to try to understand a crazy man's motives. She knew it was up to her to get herself and Anthony the medical attention they both needed. And she took in a deep breath, resolving herself to do what had to be done, do what she had been instructed to do, "take care of him," and she knew that the only way to do that was to leave him to find help.

Eve took in another deep breath and limped around the side of the cabin. She paused and glanced around. All she could see near her and in the distance was the barren brown earth and the blue of the sky. She look again to her left and noticed a stick leaning against the side of the cabin, and she limped over and grabbed it. It surprised her that it was just the right height, a most useful crutch to help her begin her journey. She took a few steps, leaning on it, and then stopped and once again offered a word of thanks for the divine gifts she was finding.

"Sister Maria, Mother Mary, Mama,

whoever it is watching out for me, I thank you," she said. "And now if you'd just give me a sign of which direction to go, I'd greatly appreciate it."

As she moved away from the cabin, she looked around again, still able to see with only her right eye, and something caught her attention just on the edge of her vision, just to the right, the east, she thought, since the sun was lowering on the opposite side of the horizon. A tiny smudge of blue showed itself emerging from the brown earth. Not knowing what it was and recognizing it as an unusual splash of color in the otherwise drab desert, Eve hobbled over to it. When she got closer to it, she could see that it was a small clump of blue flowers, a clump of flowers that were somewhat atypical for the southwestern land in late winter.

She leaned down to pluck one of the blooms, and as she held it in her fingers, she could see that it was the delicate petals of a bluebonnet, the state flower of Texas.

"Wait a minute," Eve said, standing erect. She immediately understood the meaning of the flower. She needed no divine explanation about the azure blooms. She knew that the bluebonnets were said to be the sign that the Blue Nun had visited the Jumano Indians in eastern New Mexico and in its neighboring state of Texas. She recalled learning of the legend when she listened to a Franciscan friar speak about the Spanish nun's gifts of bilocation. It was her way, the speaker had reported, to remind the native people that she had been there, that she had been present with them.

Eve realized that she was being given another sign, another means of assistance, because as she peered ahead from where she stood, she could see the small clumps of flowers marking a way east, denoting a path that she knew she should follow. Just like the pebbles and the tiny pieces of bread that Hansel used to help him and his sister, Gretel, find their way home in the fairy tale, the wildflowers, Eve understood, were marking the path she should take.

She leaned on the walking stick, following the small clusters of bluebonnets, moving farther and farther away from the cabin and Brother Anthony.

She soon grew thirsty and wished she hadn't drank the entire bottle of water when she found it. Perhaps she should have taken the other one instead of leaving it for Anthony. She limped along, following the bluebonnets, glancing up from time to time to see if there was a sign of anyone on the horizon.

The sun was fading, and Eve was becoming more tired when she noticed there were no more blue flowers to follow. It was as if they had just stopped. Eve peered ahead, and for some reason she could not explain, she knew where she was. The path, the open gate, the road that led to the national monument where she remembered meeting the park ranger; she knew she was at the right place. It was exactly the spot where she had been hit by another vehicle. She limped over to where she knew the wreck had occurred and noticed that it appeared to have been cleaned up; her father's truck was gone, but shards of glass were strewn on the ground. She was certain that she knew where she was. She turned to face a northerly direction, where she could see the outline of the Sandia Mountains miles ahead, and continued to walk.

She had gone less than half a mile when she saw the clouds of dust moving toward her. She stopped, swallowed hard, and prayed another prayer.

FIFTY-TWO

Eve was at a loss. She was completely unsure of who the driver behind the wheel of the approaching vehicle might be. If she remained standing in the middle of the road and waved the driver down and it was John Barr, that could be disastrous. But if she tried to hide, counting on it being John Barr, she might easily miss the only opportunity she had to get a ride to the park ranger's station or borrow a phone.

She glanced around the immediate area where she stood and realized, however, that even if she chose the second option, she would not likely find a hiding place. There was not a piñon pine tree or juniper bush anywhere close. She figured that she could climb through the barbed-wire fence that marked off the ranches and move as quickly away from the road as she could, thinking that if it were John Barr, he wouldn't be able to chase her in his truck since there was no open gate that she could see. He could certainly outrun her, though; she knew that. And she also knew that one shot from a rifle would make it to her even more quickly than a man running after her.

She remembered her ankle. She was in no position to run a footrace. Her entire foot was swollen, and even though she wanted desperately to take off her hiking boot, she knew that if she removed it, she would not be able to put it back on. The swelling would expand and the shoe would no longer fit. The pain and discomfort, however, were growing more and more intense.

She wasn't sure how many miles she had to go to return to the intersection of Highway 55, a more likely place to get a ride or some help, or to Salinas, but feeling the way she did, she wasn't sure she could go another three or four miles. She knew her only choice was to hope for the best, to stand by the road and gain the attention of whoever the driver might be. She made the sign of the cross on her chest, bowed, and waited. When she looked up, the vehicle was close enough to recognize, the dust pouring out behind it, the driver traveling way too fast on such a rough desert road. Eve started to cry.

It was a new BMW M3 sedan, Yas Marina

Blue Metallic, TwinPower Turbo inline six-cylinder engine, delivering 431 horsepower and managing up to 406 foot-pounds of torque. It had a carbon fiber reinforced plastic construction and M carbon ceramic brakes. It had a state-of-the-art navigation system, Bluetooth mobile office, surround-sound system, and satellite radio. It was everything an automobile connoisseur could ask for. A person could use it for luxury drives to faraway destinations or for in-town business. Doctors drove it. Lawyers drove it. Successful CEOs drove it. And so did one police officer from the Santa Fe Police Department, and she knew this because she had been with him when he picked it out from the lot in Albuquerque.

Detective Daniel Hively was driving right toward her.

Eve dropped down onto the side of the road, the walking stick falling from her hand and rolling away, and she just kept crying. Even when the car braked in front of her, skidding and fishtailing past her a couple of hundred feet, all four doors opening, Eve could not stop sobbing.

"Evangeline, Holy Mother, Evangeline . . ." It was the Captain who was calling and who was having the hardest time exiting Daniel's new car. "Holy Mother . . .

would somebody please help me out of this ridiculous car?"

Eve's weeping then turned to laughter as she watched her father pushing and pulling out of the passenger's side. One of the men from the backseat who was walking in her direction turned around and walked back to assist.

"What on earth?" It was Daniel kneeling beside her. "You look terrible. You look like you've been in a train wreck." He placed his finger beneath her chin and turned her face so that he could see her injuries better. He pulled down the collar of her shirt and made a terrible face. He placed himself right in front of her and stared into her right eye. "Can you see me?"

She cried and laughed and nodded, unable to form the words to answer.

"What on earth?" The Captain had finally made his way next to her, asking the same question as Daniel had asked. "Mother . . ." He leaned in. "Who did this to you?" he asked. "Who beat you like this?" And then he stood up and looked around. "Where's my truck?"

Eve tried to catch her breath and was soon given a bottle of water by one of the car's passengers, the detective from Taos, Lujan. She took a few sips.

She could overhear a call on a scanner being made by the other detective somewhere out of sight. He was asking for an ambulance, giving directions to their location. She heard him describe her condition, and even though she wanted to say that she had been this way for some time, that she had managed for hours, maybe days, he said it was an emergency and she let the assessment stand.

"What day is it?" she asked the men standing in front of her. "How long have I been gone?"

"It's Sunday," her father answered. "You left the monastery early Friday morning. Not a peep from you since then." He shook his head. "You worried me to death, you know that?" He rubbed his chin. "And where the heck is my truck?"

Detective Lujan took off his jacket and gently placed it around her shoulders. "Give me your coat," he said to Officer Bootskievely, and the other officer, finished with his call, took off his police windbreaker and handed it to him. Lujan placed it on her lap. "Take a few more sips of water," he said, handing her the bottle. "But not too much."

She did as she was instructed and started to feel a little better.

"Can you tell us what happened?" he asked, kneeling on the other side of her from Daniel.

"I was T-boned, just up the road," she said and gestured with her chin. "I don't know when," she added. "I was hit on the passenger's side and I guess when the impact happened, I slammed into the door and window." She glanced down. "I think I've dislocated my shoulder and my hip is pretty shot."

"Anything else?" He was checking her for broken bones, touching various parts of her body. When he reached her right ankle, she gasped. He rolled up her pants leg to get a better view and shook his head. "Looks broken," he said.

He turned to his partner. "Where's the unit coming from?"

"Socorro," came the answer. "Should be here in thirty or forty minutes," he added. "Unless they got somebody driving like Mr. Indy 500 here." He threw out his thumb in Daniel's direction, getting a smile from Eve.

"How did you know where I was?" Eve finally thought to ask. "How did you know to come out here?"

"Found your cell signal in Terrero. So we started there," Daniel answered.

"Then a park ranger from up here at the

monument called me this morning," the Captain added. "She said you were out at the site night before last, and she waited a few hours but never saw you come back that way. She got concerned, she said, and the next day followed the dirt road she had seen you take. Saw signs of a wreck, she thought, but no cars. So she looked you up in Madrid, remembering your name and residence, found me, and well, that was that."

"Have you been here all this time?" Daniel asked.

"I was taken down to some cabin." She pointed behind her. "I woke up and . . ." Suddenly she remembered her friend. "Anthony's there," she said. "Anthony was in the cabin I was taken to and he's sick. He's been poisoned or drugged. You have to go down there to get him."

Daniel turned to the other detectives and headed for the car. "You stay here," he said to the Captain, who nodded in response.

"It's Barr, right?" the Captain asked Eve. "He's the one behind all of this? We found some pretty weird stuff in his house when we found your cell phone, and he seemed very strange when we talked to him this morning. He's the killer, isn't he?"

Eve was about to answer when they all noticed another vehicle flying down the road toward them. It was a white truck, one they all seemed to recognize. She heard Detective Bootskievely shout out, "It's him!" and all three of the officers drew their weapons on the approaching vehicle. The Captain quickly jumped in front of her, blocking her vision.

She moved to see around him, and although Eve knew the truck was Barr's, she noticed something else that was very surprising. She grabbed ahold of her father's coat, pulling herself up from the ground, and started to yell, "Don't shoot! Wait!"

FIFTY-THREE

Somehow Eve was able to get up from her resting place on the side of the road and push her way in front of the Captain. She was standing almost in the middle of the road when Barr slammed on his brakes. He skidded to a stop just a few feet from her.

Daniel and the other detectives were screaming at her to get out of the way as they stood behind the BMW with their guns pointed at the driver in the white truck. Eve reached out with her right hand, touching the hood of the truck and leaning on it, guiding herself as quickly as she could until she stopped right at the driver's-side door.

"It's not him," she yelled. "It's not Barr."

It was clearly Barr's truck, and he was certainly recognizable through the windshield. Misunderstanding Eve's revelation, all of the men appeared confused, especially John Barr, who still had his foot on the brake and had raised both hands up above the steering wheel.

"Evangeline, get out of the way," the Captain shouted. "You're going to get yourself killed." He had moved closer to her and was holding out his hand, trying to get her to step away from the vehicle.

She stood her ground and shook her head. "No, he didn't do this. He didn't do any of this."

Daniel, with his revolver still raised, walked slowly over to Eve and her father. He stood just at the front of the vehicle. "Move out of the way, Eve," he said, gesturing for her to step aside.

She blew out a breath and hobbled over to stand by the Captain. "It wasn't him," she said again to Daniel as he kept his gun pointed at the man behind the wheel.

"Just get out of the truck nice and slow," he instructed Barr, apparently not paying Eve any attention.

The Captain took her by the arm and assisted her as they walked behind Daniel. She stopped and turned around, still trying to get the officers to listen to her.

John Barr put the truck in park, turned off the engine, and opened the driver's door.

"Slowly," Daniel said. "Just step out and turn around and put your hands where I can see them."

The man stepped out of the car, obeying all of Daniel's instructions. He got a good look at Eve before he turned around.

"Now, put your hands above your head." Daniel walked over to Barr, pulling out his handcuffs. When he got to him, he cuffed him and turned him around. "What are you doing out here?" he asked.

"He brought Anthony here," Eve answered for him.

Daniel turned and gave her a look that clearly told her to stay out of this conversation.

The Captain steered her toward Daniel's car.

"Answer me, Barr, what are you doing out here?"

"I came to check on the two of them," Barr replied. "She's right, I did bring Anthony here because he was sick and I knew you were searching for him. I thought I could get him better and give him some time to make a plan. I figured you'd find him if he was at my house, so I brought him here."

"What kind of plan?" Detective Bootski-evely had joined Daniel. "Are the two of you in this together?"

Eve shook her head as Barr remained silent.

Detective Lujan had moved to the other side of Barr's vehicle and appeared to be examining the contents of the rear of the truck. Eve watched him as he walked back to the passenger's side and peered through the window. "Do you mind if I take a look inside?" he asked the driver.

"Go ahead," Barr replied.

The detective opened the door and appeared to go through things he found on the seat. He held up a plastic bag. "First-aid equipment," he said to his colleagues. He opened the bag. "Bandages, tape, ibuprofen, wraps, antibiotic ointment, clean towels." He pulled out what appeared to be an inhaler. He held it up. "Who're the poppers for?" he asked Barr.

Barr turned away without responding.

"It's for Anthony," Eve answered. "He's trying to get the poison out of Anthony. It's the antidote for cyanide — amyl nitrite, right? He needs it because he was poisoned too, and that means somebody needs to get to him soon."

"How do you know all this stuff?" Officer Bootskievely asked.

She shrugged. "Agatha Christie, Michael Connelly? I don't know. I read a lot of mysteries."

Daniel glanced over to Lujan without

making a comment on Eve's reply.

"I'll check it out," the younger officer said, seeming to understand the look he had been given. "You want me to drive your car?"

Daniel shook his head. "No, you and Boots take Barr with you, drive his truck with him nice and secure between you both so that he can tell you where he has him stashed. I'll stay here and wait for the ambulance."

"Take the handcuffs off, Daniel." Eve was trying to get closer to the truck, but her father had a firm grip on her.

"You need to sit down," Captain Jackson said to his daughter. "Let me put you in Daniel's backseat. You're starting to look flushed."

"Well, that's because I am flushed! I'm trying to tell you John Barr isn't a threat. He didn't do anything except try and help Anthony. He's innocent! And I'm flushed because I'm angry that no one is listening to me!"

The Captain had taken Eve by her right arm and was trying to pull her to the other car parked on the road.

"Okay, tell us why you're so sure he's not guilty. Why should we take off the handcuffs?" Daniel had turned and started walking toward Eve.

Bootskievely remained next to Barr. "Tell us, Sister, what you know that we don't know."

The Captain let Eve go and she limped over to Daniel, who had taken a position between the two vehicles.

"Look at the truck," she said, stumbling over to him. "Look at the front of his truck."

All three of the police officers and the Captain turned their attention to Barr's vehicle. Barr watched Eve closely.

"He wasn't the one who hit me," she said, finally able to get out what she had been trying to tell the men. She felt a little wobbly, but she wasn't about to stop talking. "He's the only one who drives this truck, and he didn't hit me." She faced Barr. "You didn't hit me. You found me and took me to the cabin to take care of me, just like you're doing with Anthony. And you left to try and find the antidote. You left us water and food. You did your best. You aren't the killer; you're the hero."

Barr glanced away. "It took too long. I took too long."

"She's right about him," the Captain pointed out. "There's been no damage to his vehicle. It's true. He can't be the one who hit Evangeline. But I still don't have the answer to my question, 'Where the heck

395

is my truck?' "

Eve opened her mouth to say something else but suddenly stopped. Everything went black, and she collapsed to the ground.

FIFTY-FOUR

"I'll take care of him. I'll take care of him."
Eve woke herself up with the promise she
was making and quickly discovered the
Captain sitting by her side. She glanced
around, trying to figure out where she was,
still only one eye opening. Nothing was
familiar to her. She was in a bed, tethered
to IV lines.

"You're in the hospital," Jackson told her,
sitting up a bit in his chair to get closer to
her. "Albuquerque," he added. "You've had
surgery."

"What?" She tried to make sense of what
he was saying. Everything was blurry.

"Surgery, two of them, in fact." He stood
up and leaned over the side of the bed.
"They reset your shoulder, which is why
your arm is bandaged to your body; they
repaired your ankle, which is why your leg
is hanging from a pole down there. You've
got a bunch of stitches in your head, a

bruised pelvis, concussion, damaged ear-drum, black eye." He shook his head. "Well, that's all I can remember. There's some more stuff too."

She tried to sit up but didn't get very far before she fell back in the bed. She felt queasy and still very confused. "What day is it? How long have I been in here?"

"Now, you see, that's exactly what I asked you after my surgery and you got all snippety. You remember that? Seems like you said, 'Well, it's three days since the operation, four days you've been in the hospital.' You remember that? You see now why I asked the question?" He was holding the side bars of the bed. She knew he was close to her, but he seemed very far away. "It's confusing being a patient, isn't it?"

Eve closed her eye. It was as if she were being assaulted by sounds. Everything hurt.

"You want some more drugs?" he asked. And before she could answer, she watched as he pressed a button on a machine near her. "It's sleepy time at the push of a button! Works like a charm."

It wasn't long before she was feeling groggy again. Jackson took his seat. Eve tried to focus on him as well as the others in the room. She was certain he wasn't the only one there, but she was unable to call out a name or put words to her questions. She blinked a few times and fell back to sleep.

When she awoke the next time, the room was dark. She had no idea of the hour. She glanced around. Someone was sitting in the chair next to her. A woman, she thought. She felt comforted by the presence of the visitor and fell back to sleep again.

"Ms. Divine." Someone was calling out her name, calling it out and mispronouncing it. She wanted desperately to correct them, but she was unable to respond. She felt her right eye flutter as she tried to keep it open. There was light coming in the window, and a woman was standing over her. Another one stood behind her.

"Evangeline, my name is Deedee. I'm your nurse today. How are you feeling? Can you wake up just a few minutes so we can talk?"

"Deedee . . . nurse . . . I . . . I . . ."

"Yes, I know, you're still very wobbly, but it's time for you to rouse a little more than we've seen. It's been awhile. Your dad's been here every day and night. We finally made him go home."

Eve tried to make herself wake up. The woman talking to her or over her was pulling sheets and checking various places on her body, moving her, shaking her. It was all very uncomfortable.

"Frankly, he needed a shower," Deedee said, and Eve was unsure of what she was saying.

"The Captain?" Eve asked, trying to put the clues together. Her mouth felt so dry, and it hurt to swallow.

"The very one. He's got a temper, doesn't he? He was bossing everybody around, asking for a written explanation for every procedure we were doing, yelling if he thought we didn't come in fast enough to check on you. He's quite the protector. You should be glad you have him with you."

Eve wanted to sleep. She just wanted to forget everything and go back to sleep.

"Dr. Moulson should be in to check on the surgery sites. He's just down the hall. You'll like him. He's British."

There were more things that Deedee was saying, but Eve couldn't quite grasp the words or the meaning. She was still feeling very unsettled. She closed her eyes and fell back to sleep.

"Eve, are you awake?"

Eve opened her eyes, both of them this time. She glanced around, trying once more to get her bearings. She knew she was in a hospital. She knew she had broken bones

400

and had come through surgeries. A woman stood near the window, but it wasn't her voice speaking to her. She knew her father had been with her, but it wasn't him either. This was another man standing near her.

"I've got the sister duty tonight," the voice added. "Jackson is back in Madrid. He just left a couple of hours ago. Frankly, I almost had to handcuff him and drag him out of here. He needed to get some rest."

Daniel. Eve recognized the voice and smiled. She tried to nod, but she felt a sharp jabbing pain in her head when she moved it. She flinched.

"Yeah, you really shouldn't try to move too much. The concussion was a pretty bad one. In fact, everybody's been coming in to look at your injuries. You're quite the star around here. They call you the Bionic Nun. Apparently the doctors and nurses can't believe you walked away from the wreck. They say with the impact you suffered that did this kind of damage, you shouldn't have been able to get up and walk. It's a miracle, actually."

Eve could hardly make out what her friend was saying. "Anthony?" She was able to say her friend's name.

"Brother Anthony is fine. He's here too, but he's in much better shape than you. He tried to kill himself. He wasn't poisoned like his sister. It wasn't cyanide in his system; it was too many sleeping pills. He's going to be okay.

"Your sister came for a couple of days . . . ," he continued, but then his voice trailed off.

Eve started to drop back off to sleep. She noticed a smile from the woman standing behind Daniel.

"Hi."

Eve glanced around. Days had run into nights and back into days again. She wasn't sure about anything, but she was starting to feel more clearheaded. She tried to focus on the person sitting next to her.

"You've been through quite a lot," he said. "You're out of the intensive care unit, though."

The voice, the face . . . the identity of the person talking to her wasn't quite coming to her.

"You've been having some pretty crazy dreams," he said.

It was a man. She was able to tell that much.

"I think you've had an angel watching over you. She's been here the entire time," he added. "You talk about her a lot." The voice was so smooth, so comforting. "Well, when you're not talking about the murder and who did it, that is."

A police officer, she thought. And she was about to ask who did it, but then realized who it was.

"The boyfriend," she said, watching him smile.

Fifty-Five

"It was Peter Pierce," she said, feeling so much better than she had in days. She was even able to sit up a bit without the sense that she was going to pass out. She cleared her throat.

Earl Lujan was sitting beside her. He was wearing a UNM sweatshirt and a pair of jeans, looking more casual than she had remembered ever seeing him. He was smiling. "You want some water?" He stood next to her.

Eve nodded and he handed her a cup of water.

He watched as she drank it all. She handed the cup back to him, and he poured more from the pitcher on the stand beside the bed. He gave her the cup.

"Peter Pierce," she said again. "Did you get him?"

"How did you know that?" he wanted to know.

She hesitated. "Well, it's usually the boy-friend."

"In the Connelly mysteries," he added, recalling the author she had mentioned when they were waiting for the ambulance.

She smiled. "He didn't really love her."

"And how did you know that?"

"When I met him with his wife, she said he had a thing for the coeds, a history with them. Apparently he had a problem with monogamy. I doubt he really even planned to marry Kelly, just told her that to keep her affections."

Lujan didn't respond.

"And he had debts, which I didn't check out, but I'm guessing you did."

"There is a clear motive," Lujan replied. "He owed some folks a large sum of money."

"And it wasn't a long amount of time, but it was enough time to frame Anthony. It's not hard to find a monk's room at a monastery. You just ask anybody." She sat up a bit more in bed. "So he set him up, hid some things in his room, cash. He heard about the fight with her brother from Kelly and used it to his advantage. And I guess he just got lucky with the tea."

"We figure he was there at the monastery before anybody knew it and saw Anthony put the tea out there."

"See! I knew he wasn't telling the truth about his arrival. I knew he got there in time to do the murder and set up Anthony."

She faced the detective. "So, what about him? What do you have?"

Lujan sat back down. "Well, there's some good news and bad news about him."

Eve took a sip and waited.

"We definitely got him with a hit-and-run charge. Found him at a hotel near the airport right after we got you to the hospital. We went over license plates of guests at the monastery, looking for evidence of an accident. Found out he was gone and had returned his rental car, which the agency reported had a fair amount of damage done to it. He had great coverage, but he also had a record of the transaction. We tracked him down. He confessed to hitting a truck, but he claims he didn't think anybody was in it at the time, said it was parked on the side of the road and he just smashed into it because it was dark and he didn't see it."

Eve started to speak.

The detective nodded. "I know, it's a lie. He says he was visiting the monument, drove out to see the place where the bilocation occurred."

Eve rolled her eyes.

"You know, there's been something bugging me since we arrested him," Earl said.

Eve waited for his explanation.

"Why did he wreck you? What did he think you knew? You were after Barr, so why did he chase you all the way down there and try to kill you?"

There was a pause as she considered both the question and her answer.

"He thought I had something," she confessed, remembering their one encounter, the trap she had set.

"What did he think you had?"

"A page," she answered.

"A page from what?"

"I let him use his own imagination about that."

She felt his eyes on her and knew he was waiting for more.

"When we met, I had this suspicion he wasn't telling the truth about his relationship with Kelly or about the time of his arrival at the monastery, so I just thought I'd put something out there. I wanted him to think I knew more than I did, had something he wanted; I wasn't sure at the time." She blew out a breath, rested the back of her hand across her forehead, winced, and returned it to her side. "I told him Kelly had given me something. I wanted to see his reaction. I guess it wasn't the smartest move to make."

Detective Lujan shook his head but didn't make a comment about the wisdom of her actions. "How do you think he knew where you were?"

"I guess he followed me when I was following Barr. We went right by the monastery; maybe he saw me then. Or maybe he was watching all along. He must have searched my room back at Pecos, and when he couldn't find anything, he came for me to see if I had it with me." She hesitated, recalling the crash. "I guess he took the bait."

"I'd say he took the bait, all right."

"He's in jail, though?"

"Metropolitan Detention Center, indeed he is. And we got a high bail set because he's a flight risk."

Eve took another sip of water. "So what's the bad news?"

Lujan shook his head. "We can't really charge him with the murder of the professor yet."

"You couldn't get him to confess?" She handed him the cup.

"No, and it wasn't for lack of trying. He lawyered up right away, and we couldn't talk to him about anything other than the hit-and-run."

"No cyanide in his briefcase?" She was starting to feel a bit tired again.

"That would have been helpful, but no."

"No ancient writings worth millions in his suitcase?"

He smiled and shook his head, but something on his face told Eve there was more to that part of the story.

"What?"

He reached into the front pocket of his jeans and pulled out what appeared to be a receipt.

"What's that?" she wanted to know.

He opened it and read it to her. "Pecos Post Office, dated three days after the murder. Sales receipt for a Priority Mail three-day delivery with extra insurance and a tracking number, scheduled to arrive in Austin, Texas, with the zip code the same as the one listed for his residence."

"Three days? Why three days, and what day marks today?"

"Well, funny you should ask. Three days is actually today, the day Dr. Pierce was scheduled to fly out from Pecos to Austin, the day he was planning to arrive back home."

"And pick up his mail," she added.

"And pick up his mail," he confirmed.

She felt a bit confused. "But why was he

staying three more days?" she asked, thinking that if he was the killer, he would want to get away from the murder scene as quickly as he could.

"That part is a little unclear to us, but we do know his calendar had a few meetings scheduled for the last couple of days."

"Let me guess, dealers in religious artifacts."

Lujan nodded. "Sketchy dealers," he noted. "None of whom are willing to confirm any such meetings."

Eve rested her head back on the pillow. "Well, that makes sense." She took in a deep breath; it felt good to be alert and alive. "So, I assume you have someone at his house waiting for the mailman." She looked over at the officer.

"And a warrant to open any package from Pecos, New Mexico, arriving sometime today."

"Thereby granting you the evidence you need to add a few charges to one jail inmate, Dr. Peter Pierce."

"That's our hope."

Eve smiled and closed her eyes.

There was a pause.

"You want to take a nap, go back to sleep?" He stood up as if preparing to leave.

She glanced over at him and shook her

head. "No, just thinking about everything," she answered.

He sat back down. "Can I ask you a question?"

She nodded.

"What made you go to John Barr's house?"

She shrugged. "Just a hunch. I saw his truck leaving the monastery the night of the murder. He and Brother Anthony are friends; I figured Anthony left and Barr gave him a ride, maybe took him to his cabin in Tererro."

"Makes sense," Lujan commented.

"When I got to his place, there was no evidence that Anthony had been there, but I did find some strange things."

"Like what?" the officer asked, leaning forward, his elbows on his knees.

Eve remembered the blue cloak, the one she had found that matched the piece of cloth clutched in the victim's hand. "Uh-oh, I have another confession," she said.

Lujan leaned against the back of the chair. "Besides setting traps for dangerous murderers?"

She nodded.

"Okay, let's hear it."

"I found something in Kelly Middlesworth's hand the night of the murder."

He waited.

"It was a piece of blue material, and I took it."

She cleared her throat and started to finish.

Lujan interrupted. "And when you got to Barr's place, you found a cape, a blue one, torn at the bottom, and I'm guessing it was a perfect match to the piece in the victim's hand."

She was surprised that he knew about the discovery.

"We did a thorough investigation of Barr and a very thorough search of his cabin. The cape was an interesting find. It looked a lot like the one the Jumanos recorded as being the cloak of Sister Maria, but we didn't know when or where it had been torn or why he had it."

Eve turned to Lujan, giving him a surprised look.

"What? You think I didn't do my research?"

Eve shrugged, suddenly feeling her injured shoulder for the first time. She winced.

"You okay?" he asked, noticing her pained expression.

She nodded.

"Anthony said the cape was in his room after he found his sister. He thought it was a sign of his sin, and after he found it —"

"He decided to take his own life." This time she interrupted him.

"Apparently he had some sleeping medications that had been prescribed for him a couple of months ago. He hadn't taken any of them until that night, and he took them all."

Eve felt a sadness overcome her. She hated the thought of her friend being in such despair.

"After the police arrived at the monastery, Barr got worried and went to find his friend, expecting that he would be upset about his sister's passing and knowing a bit about the evidence that was starting to stack up against Anthony. He was in the room next door to Kelly, heard some things." He drew in a breath and continued. "By the time he found him, Anthony had taken the drugs and was unconscious. Barr found a suicide note and the cape, and he thought his friend was guilty of murder, thought he had taken the cyanide poison he had given the victim and needed help."

"So he snuck him out of there," she surmised. "Weren't you curious about the person in the room next to Kelly? Didn't his disappearance raise some concern?"

The detective cleared his throat. "A very

definite mistake on our part. If you recall, right after the murder there was a bit of overlap between the investigations of the sheriff's department and the city police, so we just missed him. We thought the deputies had questioned him and released him with the other guests. They thought the same thing. When we did finally get to him, a few hours after we arrived, a few hours during which he had driven Anthony to his cabin and then driven back, he was sitting in the dining room, packed and ready to go home. He had no more motive than any of the other guests, and we got his contact information, but he wasn't really on our radar."

"So, he did take Anthony to his house?"

"Just for that first night, and then once we got all his information, once he got back and answered our questions, he drove him to Mountainair."

"Where he hoped to revive him as well as keep him hidden." Eve was putting the pieces of the story together. "But why did he go back to his cabin if he thought Anthony was dying?"

"He was gathering some of his own things, thought he was going to have to leave the country with Anthony. He had been trying to find the antidote to cyanide, and once he thought the monk was stable, he went home to take care of things, find a place for his dog, close up the place. He also planned to destroy the cape that he had taken from Anthony's room. He thought he might not return."

"I guess I scared him even more," Eve responded.

"Probably more when he came upon the wreck. He said that when he found you, you had been hit by another vehicle, and even though he knew he should take you to the hospital, he was worried that you knew he had Anthony and would bring the police to him."

Eve nodded, understanding that if she had not been hit by Pierce, that's exactly what she would have done.

"So Barr is actually the good guy."

Lujan shrugged. "I suppose if you think someone harboring a fugitive is a good guy, then yes."

"But Anthony wasn't a fugitive."

"But Barr didn't know that."

Eve considered all of this information. It was almost too much to take in. She was starting to feel tired from so much talk.

Lujan stood to leave. "I've overstayed. You need some rest."

Eve was about to contradict him, ask him

to stay a little longer so that she could ask more questions, when his cell phone started to ring. She sat up a bit, hoping it was a call from Texas.

FIFTY-SIX

"Well, look who's up and finally in the land of the living!" The Captain walked in just as Lujan took the call.

The detective stepped out of the room and Eve strained to overhear the conversation. She wanted to know if the call was from Austin. She wanted to know if they had the evidence they needed to prove Pierce was the killer.

"What?" her father asked, turning to watch as Lujan moved out into the hallway and closed the door. "You still thinking about coming over to the dark side?"

She shook her head, not understanding.

"The dark side, disavowing yourself as a nun and settling down with a tall, dark, handsome police detective," he explained.

She rolled her eyes. "No."

"Okay then, why are you so interested in his conversation?" He took the seat next to her bed.

"He was waiting to hear from the police in Austin. He tracked a package that Peter Pierce sent from Pecos. We're hoping that it might be the writings that were stolen from the murder victim."

"Well, of course it is," the Captain responded. "That's a slam dunk, for sure."

"How can you be so certain?"

"Because he's guilty. Everybody could tell that when he was arrested for hitting my truck. I don't guess you know, but Barr took us to it. There's nothing to be done." He shook his head. "Had it towed to the graveyard. Man, I loved that old truck, bought it with my first paycheck as a police officer."

"And me," she said. "He hit me."

"Yeah, and you." He reached for the cup of water she had been drinking and took a big gulp. "But the truck is totaled."

This raised her eyebrows. "You're more concerned about your truck than you are your daughter?"

He finished the water and placed the cup back on the bedside table. He scratched his head without an answer.

She again glanced at the door, hoping Lujan would come back in with some news. "You're a terrible actor," she noted as she turned back to her father. "You can pretend like you don't care, that you haven't been fussing at the nurses, screaming at the doctors, staying here every night, holding my hand. But I know the truth. You aren't fooling anybody. You've been at my side since I got in here. You've been acting like a nervous hen watching over her little chick."

He waved away her protest. "You got to stay on these people or they'll overcharge you, make you pay a hundred dollars for an aspirin."

Eve grinned. "Right," she said, sounding as if she didn't believe him.

There was a pause.

"You okay?" she asked.

He reached through the rails of the hospital bed and took her hand. "You actually had me worried there," he said, squeezed, and then pulled away his hand. "I'm glad you're back."

"Back?" she asked, surprised. "Where did you think I had gone?"

"You were crazy those first couple of nights, talking about bluebonnets and angels and your mother."

Jackson got up from the chair and went to the door. He opened it and she could see the detective still talking on his phone. He closed it again and took his seat. "Why were you going on about bluebonnet flowers?"

Eve remembered the visions, the dream of

heaven, the ties that kept her from leaving the earth, her mother's sweet embrace, the presence of the Lady in Blue. "The bluebonnets were blooming in the field from Barr's little cabin near Mountainair all the way to the road where the wreck happened."

When she looked over at the Captain, he was shaking his head. "There weren't any bluebonnets in that field. It's not even spring yet, and besides, those flowers don't grow way out there. It's too close to the salt lakes. Nothing grows out there."

Eve was surprised. "How did you find the cabin then?"

"Barr took the detectives, remember?"

Eve closed her eyes, thinking about her father's comment. She recalled Daniel telling the officers to go with Barr to find Anthony. "You didn't see any blue flowers?"

"No blue flowers, no white flowers, no yellow flowers. Nothing but tumbleweeds."

The news was startling to Eve, and she began to think that maybe she was overmedicated and making everything up. She thought about leaving the cabin and remembered the vibrant blue wildflowers that led her to the road. She knew they had been there and began to realize she had experienced an amazing miracle. She had been with the Blue Nun.

Suddenly she remembered her instructions, "Take care of him," and for the first time considered that the "him" she was told to attend to wasn't Anthony but the Captain, her father, the one she had been caring for since his amputation and rehabilitation.

She opened her eyes and looked at him. "Thank you," she said softly.

As he sat back down next to her, he gave a quick nod, acknowledging her words of appreciation and the truth of what he had done for her. He cleared his throat, and Eve thought for a moment there were tears in his eyes.

"So, you've got about three months of rehab," he informed her. "It ain't for sissies," he added.

"I remember," she replied. "And I think I'm up for the challenge."

"You can stay somewhere here in Albuquerque in a facility if you want."

She nodded. She hadn't actually considered what lay beyond her hospitalization. She hadn't thought about being in a nursing home for a period of time.

"Or you can come home and I'll watch you do your exercises. I'm pretty good at giving orders."

She nodded. "Yes, that much I know. I'll see what the doctor advises and figure out what's best for both of us. It might be better for me and you if I'm fully healthy before returning to a normal routine."

"That doctor isn't even American," the Captain responded. "Talks all high and mighty. There's a reason we broke away from them and started our own country."

"And what is that?" Eve asked, uncertain of why she was taking the bait for a certain rant.

"Well, sports, for one thing. Sports and better food."

Eve waited. She knew he had more to say on the subject.

"Baseball and football," he explained. "They got some ladies' game they call cricket, and they play soccer, running up and down the field without even tackling."

Eve shook her head. "I'll ask him anyway," she said, talking about the doctor. "I don't really care what kind of sports he likes; I just want to know his recommendations for my getting better."

"Probably doesn't even know what the Super Bowl is."

"Probably doesn't," Eve agreed. "But I don't really care."

"They eat a lot of potatoes," he added.

"I think that's actually Ireland, but again, I don't really care."

The Captain cleared his throat again, making a loud noise.

"Where's Daniel today?"

"Still gathering evidence against the murderer," he answered. "The professor claims he has an alibi, has some receipt he says proves that he was still on an airplane at the time of the murder."

"It's a receipt that shows he bought a ticket for a late flight, but that doesn't mean he didn't buy two tickets and then take an earlier one. That's easy to check out." She recalled seeing the receipt from the airlines that he showed her when they met at the monastery.

"And that's exactly what Daniel's doing," the Captain explained. "He's at the Albuquerque airport now."

Eve nodded. "I suspect they're going to find out he's lying." She was staring at the door to her room, hoping the detective would come back in and give the news about the phone call he had taken.

"I suspect the same thing," Jackson agreed, watching her.

"What?" she asked when she noticed him peering at her.

He shook his head. "Nothing."

"Look, I do not have a crush on the detective," she said, objecting to what she knew he was implying.

He held up a hand. "I didn't say a word."

Eve was about to explain once again why she was curious about the detective's whereabouts when he opened the door and entered the room.

"Sorry," he said, sensing the tension between the two and starting to back out, apparently thinking he had walked in on a private conversation.

"NO!" Eve shouted. Realizing the volume of her protest, she lowered her voice. "Was that Austin?"

He nodded as he placed his phone in his pocket and stood at the door, both hands on his hips. "It arrived about half an hour ago, and according to the officer who opened the package, there are about twenty pages of some writings that he couldn't read but verified they look very old and very authentic."

Eve held up her hand and received the high five from the Captain she was waiting for.

FIFTY-SEVEN

Eve held on to Anthony's arm as the two walked back to the community from Monastery Lake. He carried the empty urn with his other hand. They were returning from having dispersed Kelly's ashes on the trail the two siblings had hiked together on many occasions. He explained to Eve that she had told him once it was the most beautiful place she had ever visited, and the friends agreed that it seemed appropriate for her remains to be scattered there.

"I'll be able to visit her every day," he said, taking small steps so that Eve wouldn't have to walk too fast.

"That's nice for you," she replied.

It had been a couple of months since the murder and a couple of months since both of them had been released from the hospital, Anthony back to the monastery, Eve to Madrid, her father's home. Since the accident the archbishop had given her more time to decide which convent she wanted to join, more time to decide what she was going to do.

"I miss this place," she said as they ambled along, both of them slowed by their sorrow.

"It's wrong what they did to you and the other sisters, Evangeline. I never told you, but the brothers wrote a petition and sent it to Rome. Some of us even considered leaving too. We all thought it was wrong. All of us have been deeply bothered by this decision."

Eve nodded. She had heard about their responses; she knew about the petition.

"We were a family," he added.

"So we were," she replied. "But sometimes families don't stay together; sometimes they have to leave the nest and make new families." She was thinking about the time she left her parents to take her vows. It had been an exciting time but a sad one too.

She leaned into him as they took the small steps.

"The bench is just up there. Do you want to stop and rest?" he asked, the concern evident in his voice.

Eve nodded, feeling like she could use a break. The recovery from the surgeries was harder and taking longer than she'd expected. She was still limping a bit, and her shoulder often ached.

They walked the short distance in silence and both sat down on the long wooden bench. It had been built and placed on the trail years before when several members of the community were aging and having a more difficult time walking the path from the lake to the monastery.

"Pierce has been sent to the prison in Santa Fe," Anthony noted.

"I hadn't heard his final sentencing," Eve responded. "I guess I thought they'd put him in a Texas facility since that's where he's from."

"He doesn't have anybody to visit him in Texas, so I suppose he didn't make any special requests."

"Does he have anybody to visit him in New Mexico?" She turned to get a good look at the monk. She had a feeling she understood why he was telling her this news.

"I will never completely get over the grief of losing my sister." He paused. "I believe that I can be released from some of the pain of Kelly's death, but that release will come only through forgiveness," he explained. "I am working on letting go of my anger, and I'm quite sure that visiting her killer is the only way I will be fully able to offer forgiveness to Dr. Pierce and to myself."

Eve nodded. She hated the thought of her friend's sorrow and pain, but she, too, agreed that bearing anger and resentment did not lead to healing. She and her father had discussed this topic already when he argued with her about her plans to one day make her own visit to see Pierce. She had tried to get him to understand that she had to offer the gift of forgiveness to the man who had hit her and then left her to die. She had tried to explain that a visit to see the prisoner was necessary for her to find healing.

"That's good news for me too," she said to Anthony.

He smiled, understanding that she would be visiting the man as well.

"Does that mean you aren't moving to one of the other convents? Does that mean you're staying here?"

Eve looked out over the recently plowed field beyond the walking path. The monastery leased the land to farmers. Hay had been planted and harvested in that field for as long as the monastery had been in existence. That was one of the other reasons she had loved and now missed the monastery. It was a working farm. It was how she had always envisioned her life in a religious community.

"I wish I knew the answer to that, my brother." She shook her head. "I have prayed and sought guidance. I have lit candles and asked for intercessory prayers." She reached over and took the monk by the hand, knowing that he had been praying for her as well. "I even asked Sister Maria to give me another sign, something clear for me to follow, blue flowers in a field or something similar, but there's been nothing. I think it comes down to what I feel in my own heart, what is right for me, and I still don't really know what that is."

"Sister Cathy went to Roswell," he said, uncertain if Eve knew the whereabouts of the other nuns who had left Pecos.

"The Poor Clares," Eve responded. "I know." She blew out a long breath. "She invited me to visit, spend some time with her, but I don't think I could take that kind of cloistering," she added. "I need to be out in the world a little more. And they like to get up to pray at one o'clock in the morning or something ridiculous like that."

Anthony laughed. "I think she had to change her name and she's actually considered a novice again."

"Sister Paul, if you can believe that," Eve replied, having heard the news of her sister. She shook her head. "I have to say this denial of the feminine as a part of our religious tradition has become very difficult for me. That's part of the reason I'm having trouble making the decision to stay a nun."

"It's never been easy for women in the church, that's for sure," Anthony agreed. "Maria and the Inquisition, Joan of Arc burned at the stake, the refusal to allow them to become priests. I have to say I'm really surprised women stay in the religious life."

"Kind of like the Native Americans," Eve said. "I've always wondered why they remained Catholic after the Spaniards were so cruel to them.

"Did you know it was the Jumanos who were said to have ambushed a party of Spaniards near Gran Quivira and that the retaliation included the killing of nine hundred people and the taking of almost four hundred more as prisoners, more than likely sold into slavery?" While recovering from her injuries, she had been reading more of the history of the Pueblo Indians in the area.

"And yet, after Sister Maria visited them they wanted to be baptized as Catholics. And all of the Pueblos are still Catholic." Eve leaned forward, elbows on her knees. "It's amazing to me."

A crow flew above their heads and perched on a limb of a tree close by. They both watched the bird in silence.

"Do you like solving mysteries, finding missing persons? Do you like working for your father?" Anthony wanted to know.

Eve thought about the question. "I do, actually."

The monk nodded. "You're good at it," he said.

Eve smiled. "Thank you, Anthony."

"You know that you don't have to be a nun, wear the habit, live in community, take all the vows to be devoted to our Lord."

"I know," she agreed.

"And sometimes nuns and priests and monks choose a different path later in their lives. It doesn't mean they broke their vows or left the order, as people usually describe it. It could mean that, I guess, but it could also mean that their paths moved them in different directions. It could mean they received guidance leading them into new areas of service."

She nodded. "Yes, that's true."

Anthony bumped into Eve, a familial show of affection. "And you'll always be my big sister, whether you're wearing a long black robe, chanting and praying, or a leather jacket and cowboy boots, catching killers."

Eve put her arm around the young monk. "And you will always be my little brother," she said, giving him a hug. "Always."

FIFTY-EIGHT

The church was full at St. Anthony's in Isleta and the service was long, with several priests offering remarks and the archbishop delivering the sermon. Eve made the trip by herself after the Captain decided not to join her. She drove her motorcycle down to the pueblo from Madrid, enjoying the summer breeze and the opportunity to be back in the saddle of her old Harley.

She sat near the back with a couple of the women from the pueblo that she knew from other worship services they had been in together, and she was able to pick out Anthony near the front with the other monks from Pecos. He seemed at peace, even though she knew he still felt great shame for what he had taken from the church. They had been in contact with each other frequently since the murder, and she knew he was working at the pueblo mission many hours, trying to make up for what he had done.

Eve glanced around the sanctuary, noticing the fresh paint and the many renovations Anthony had made. The service was the blessing of the papers written by Sister Maria that had been returned to the pueblo. There had been a lot of speculation about where the writings would land, but in the end, they had been returned to where they had first been discovered. Eve suspected that the archbishop had not been pleased by the final decision made by the pope himself, but in true submissiveness he was offering his blessing and a rather long-winded exposition on the importance of the nun's writings and the importance of the pueblo mission churches to the Catholic Church at large.

Eve was surprised to have received a phone call in recent days from the diocese telling her that the archbishop had actually selected her to be on a special committee chosen to read and translate the writings of Sister Maria. She was greatly honored when she received the call, and she thought about it quite a lot, but after a few days she chose to refuse the opportunity. She'd had her own experience with the Blue Nun, and she decided that experience was enough for her. She did not need to continue to read or study the experiences of others.

When the service was finally over, Eve was heading out the door to the parking lot when a familiar voice called out from behind her. "Sister Evangeline."

She turned to find Detective Earl Lujan coming in her direction. He was wearing traditional Native American clothes, brightly colored sashes, a kilt, and moccasins. He was carrying a stick adorned with feathers that Eve knew was a prayer stick used during religious ceremonies as well as during other events in the pueblos. She had noticed the group of Pueblo representatives sitting together near the monks from Pecos but had not recognized him.

"Hello," she said, realizing that they had not seen each other since the Pierce trial. "You look different," she said. "Nice," she added and then felt embarrassed at having made the compliment.

"Thanks," he responded. "You're not staying for the feast?"

Eve turned to the parking lot to locate her bike, knowing she had not expected the service to last so long. She had told the Captain she wouldn't be gone for more than three or four hours. "I really don't know many people, and I need to get back to Madrid."

"You know your brothers from the monastery," he said.

"Yeah, I do know them." She took a breath, realizing she needed to explain to the detective what had happened in Pecos, the departure of the sisters, and about her recent decision regarding her vows.

"You know me," he added, interrupting her explanation.

She blushed.

"I do," she said. "Look, I need to clear something up."

"You're a nun and you're not sure you want to stay a nun. You have a motorcycle, which apparently they let you keep at the monastery and take with you since you've been away."

She was surprised and didn't know how to respond.

"And you're very good at solving mysteries and yet you feel guilty for not loving the religious life." He shrugged. "It's a quandary, really." And he smiled. "My people feel that all the time. Are we Catholic or are we traditional? Do we have Mass or do we have a feast?"

He turned and watched the people walking out of the church. Eve followed his line of sight. There were priests and monks and laymen and those in Native wear and those in contemporary clothes. Hispanic, white, and Native, all coming out together, heading over to the picnic tables near the parking lot.

He turned back. "But here's the thing. There's no quandary today. No struggle or inquisition. Today is about putting something back where it belonged, returning something to its people. Today there is Mass and there is a feast. So you attended Mass, and now you'll attend the feast. Come and celebrate. Come and enjoy today."

She waffled. "I told my father I'd be home before dark," she explained.

"I'll make sure you're on the road before dark," he answered.

She hesitated. He was not making this easy for her.

"They have red enchiladas, green chile stew; they have sopapillas."

"Sopapillas?" she said, grinning. "Well, why didn't you start with that? Of course I'm staying if they have sopapillas." And as she headed in his direction, she caught a glimpse of something blue just beyond where he stood. It was there for just a second and then disappeared.

"Did you see that?" she asked.

He glanced behind him in the direction she was looking. "What?" he asked.

She turned to the detective, realizing the burst of color was gone, and shook her head, her heart light. "Nothing," she answered. "Just thought I saw something."

He smiled. "I hope it was something good."

"Very good," she replied. "It was something very good."

And they walked back to the church together.

SOURCES CITED

Lance Chilton, Katherine Chilton, Polly E. Arango, James Dudley, Nancy Neary, and Patricia Stelzner, *New Mexico: A New Guide to the Colorful State* (Albuquerque: University of New Mexico Press, 1984).

Jay W. Sharp, "The Blue Nun — Maria Jesus de Agreda: Mystical Missionary to the Indians," in *Texas Unexplained: Strange Tales and Mysteries from the Lone Star State* (Austin: University of Texas Press, 1999).

DISCUSSION QUESTIONS

1. What do you know about the Blue Nun? Had you ever heard of her?
2. What happened at the monastery that created even more confusion for Eve in her discernment process about whether to remain a nun? Do you think she should keep her vows or go in the direction of her father's work?
3. How might the news of this newly discovered correspondence lead to the beatification of Sister Maria?
4. What are some of the qualities of saints? Had you ever heard of bilocation as a spiritual gift?
5. What do you think was the relationship between Vice Superior Oliver and Eve? Do they respect and care for each other? Is he a good leader at the monastery?
6. Why was the blue cape significant in this story?
7. Will Detective Lujan and Eve end up as a

couple? Does he really understand her struggle? What do you think she feels for him?

8. How has working as a private detective with Captain Jackson changed Eve? Does she see the world differently?

9. Do you think Captain Jackson has a preference as to what Eve decides about keeping her vows or working with him?

10. What are the aspects of being a nun that Eve loves and misses? What are the aspects that trouble her? What do you think she will choose to do?

ACKNOWLEDGMENTS

God is good. All the time. That's what they used to say every Sunday at First Congregational United Church of Christ in Asheboro, North Carolina, when I served as their pastor, and it has come to be a mantra for me. I am grateful for the goodness and faithfulness of God every day of my life.

I am indebted to the wonderful team at HarperCollins Christian Publishing, especially my new editor, Becky Monds; Karli Jackson; and the excellent copy editor, Deborah Wiseman. You women rock! Thank you also to all those who help market and publicize the book. Your work means so much! Sally, as always, I could not do it without you.

Friends and family, thank you for your continued support and love. I am blessed to have such caring and encouraging people in my life.

ABOUT THE AUTHOR

Lynne Hinton is the *New York Times* best-selling author of *Friendship Cake* and *The Art of Arranging Flowers,* along with sixteen other books. She holds a Master of Divinity degree from Pacific School of Religion in Berkeley, California. She has served as hospice chaplain, church pastor, and retreat leader. Lynne is a regular columnist with *The Charlotte Observer.* A native of North Carolina, she lives with her husband and dog in Albuquerque, New Mexico.

Visit Lynne's website at
www.lynnehinton.com
Facebook: Lynne-Hinton-Books